THE CLOCKMAKER
OR THE SAYINGS AND DOINGS OF SAMUEL SLICK

"Only a remarkable development" says I

NONSUCH CLASSICS

THE CLOCKMAKER

OR THE SAYINGS AND DOINGS OF SAMUEL SLICK

Thomas Chandler Haliburton

Volume Three

Nunquam aliud natura, aliud sapientia dicit.—Juv.

Folk say that natur' is one thing, and wisdom another, but it's plaguy odd they look so much alike, an speak the very identical same language, ain't it?—S. S.

NONSUCH

First published 1843
Copyright © in this edition 2005
Nonsuch Publishing Ltd

Nonsuch Publishing Limited
The Mill, Brimscombe Port, Stroud, Gloucestershire, GL5 2QG
www.nonsuch-publishing.com

Distributed in Canada by Vanwell Publishing

British Library Cataloguing in Publication Data.
A catalogue record for this book is available from the British Library.

ISBN 1-84588-050-1

Typesetting and origination by Nonsuch Publishing Limited
Printed in Great Britain by Oaklands Book Services Limited

CONTENTS

I

THE DUKE OF KENT'S LODGE

THE communication by steam between Nova Scotia and England will form a new era in colonial history. It will draw close the bonds of affection between the two countries, afford a new and extended field for English capital, and develop the resources of that valuable but neglected province. Mr. Slick, with his usual vanity, claims the honour of suggesting it, as well as the merit of having, by argument and ridicule, reasoned and shamed the Government into its adoption. His remarks upon the cruelty of employing the unsafe and unfortunate gun-brigs that constituted the line of Falmouth packets, until they severally foundered and disappeared with their gallant crews, are too personal and too severe to be recorded in this place, and the credit he claims for having attracted the attention, and directed the indignation of the public to this disgraceful sacrifice of human life, is so extravagant, that one would suppose this obvious and palpable error had escaped the observation of all the world but himself, and was altogether a new discovery. But, whatever praise he may deserve for his calculations and suggestions, or whatever blame is to be attached to the Admiralty for their obstinate adherence to the memorable "coffin-ships," I prefer looking forward to dwelling on a painful retrospect, and indulging in pleasing anticipations of the future, to commenting on the errors of the past.

This route, by its connexion with that of New York, will afford an agreeable tour, commencing at Halifax, passing through the colonies, and terminating at the Hudson. It will offer a delightful substitute for that of the Rhine, and the beaten tracts on the Continent. As soon as it was announced that Government had decided upon adopting Mr. Slick's designs, I wrote to him informing him of the fact, and of my intention to proceed to St. John, the State of Maine, New England, and New York, and requested him to meet me as soon as possible, and accompany me on this journey, as I proposed taking passage at the latter place in a steamer for Great Britain. I left Halifax on the 10th of May last, and embarked on

board of the Great Western in July. It was the third, and will probably be
the last tour on this continent performed in company with this eccentric
individual. During the journey there were few incidents of sufficient
novelty to interest the reader, but his conversation partook of the same
originality, the same knowledge of human nature, and the same humour
as formerly; and whenever he developed any new traits of character or
peculiarity of feeling, not exhibited in our previous travels, I carefully
noted them as before, and have now the pleasure of giving them to the
public. As a whole they form a very tolerable portrait of an erratic Yankee
trader, which, whatever may be the merit of the execution, has, at the least,
the advantage, and deserves the praise, of fidelity.

The morning I left Halifax was one of those brilliant ones that in this
climate distinguish this season of the year; and as I ascended the citadel hill,
and paused to look for the last time upon the noble and secure harbour,
the sloping fields and wooded hills of Dartmouth, and the tranquil waters
and graceful course of the North West Arm, which, embosomed in wood,
insinuates itself around the peninsula, and embraces the town, I thought
with pleasure that the time had now arrived when this exquisite scenery
would not only be accessible to European travellers, but form one of the
termini of the great American tour. Hitherto it has been known only to
the officers of the army and navy, the former of whom are but too apt to
have their first pleasurable impressions effaced by a sense of exile, which a
long unvaried round of garrison duty in a distant land so naturally induces;
and the latter to regard good shelter and safe anchorage as the greatest
natural beauties of a harbour.

After leaving Halifax the road to Windsor winds for ten miles round
the margin of Bedford Basin, which is connected with the harbour by a
narrow passage at the dockyard. It is an extensive and magnificent sheet of
water, the shores of which are deeply indented with numerous coves, and
well-sheltered inlets of great beauty.

At a distance of seven miles from the town is a ruined lodge, built by
his Royal Highness the late Duke of Kent, when commander-in-chief
of the forces in this colony, once his favourite summer residence, and
the scene of his munificent hospitalities. It is impossible to visit this spot
without the most melancholy feelings. The tottering fences, the prostrate
gates, the ruined grottos, the long and winding avenues, cut out of the
forest, overgrown by rank grass and occasional shrubs, and the silence

and desolation that pervade everything around, all bespeak a rapid and premature decay, recall to mind the untimely fate of its noble and lamented owner, and tell of fleeting pleasures, and the transitory nature of all earthly things. I stopped at a small inn in the neighbourhood for the purpose of strolling over it for the last time ere I left the country, and for the indulgence of those moralising musings which at times harmonize with our nerves, and awaken what may be called the pleasurable sensations of melancholy.

A modern wooden ruin is of itself the least interesting, and at the same time the most depressing, object imaginable. The massive structures of antiquity that are everywhere to be met with in Europe, exhibit the remains of great strength, and, though injured and defaced by the slow and almost imperceptible agency of time, promise to continue thus mutilated for ages to come. They awaken the images of departed generations, and are sanctified by legend and by tale. But a wooden ruin shows rank and rapid decay, concentrates its interest on one family, or one man, and resembles a mangled corpse, rather than the monument that covers it. It has no historical importance, no ancestral record. It awakens not the imagination. The poet finds no inspiration in it, and the antiquary no interest. It speaks only of death and decay, of recent calamity, and vegetable decomposition. The very air about it is close, dank, and unwholesome. It has no grace, no strength, no beauty, but looks deformed, gross, and repulsive. Even the faded colour of a painted wooden house, the tarnished gilding of its decorations, the corroded iron of its fastenings, and its crumbling materials, all indicate recent use and temporary habitation. It is but a short time since this mansion was tenanted by its royal master, and in that brief space how great has been the devastation of the elements! A few years more, and all trace of it will have disappeared for ever. Its very site will soon become a matter of doubt. The forest is fast reclaiming its own, and the lawns and ornamented gardens, annually sown with seeds scattered by the winds from the surrounding woods, are relapsing into a state of nature, and exhibiting in detached patches a young growth of such trees as are common to the country.

As I approached the house I noticed that the windows were broken out, or shut up with rough boards to exclude the rain and snow; the doors supported by wooden props instead of hinges, which hung loosely on the panels; and that long, luxuriant clover grew in the eaves, which had been originally designed to conduct the water from the roof, but becoming choked with dust and decayed leaves, had afforded sufficient food for the nourishment of coarse grasses. The portico, like the house, had been formed of wood, and the flat surface of its top imbibing and retaining moisture, presented a mass of vegetable matter, from which had sprung up a young and vigorous birch-tree, whose strength and freshness seemed to mock the helpless weakness that nourished it.[1] I had no desire to enter the apartments; and indeed the aged ranger, whose occupation was to watch over its decay, and to prevent its premature destruction by the plunder of its fixtures and more durable materials, informed me that the floors were unsafe. Altogether the scene was one of a most depressing kind.

A small brook, which had by a skilful hand been led over several precipitous descents, performed its feats alone and unobserved, and seemed to murmur out its complaints, as it hurried over its rocky channel to mingle with the sea; while the wind, sighing through the umbrageous wood, appeared to assume a louder and more melancholy wail, as it swept through the long vacant passages and deserted saloons, and escaped in plaintive tones from the broken casements. The offices, as well as the ornamental buildings, had shared the same fate as the house. The roofs of all had fallen in, and mouldered into dust; the doors, sashes, and floors had disappeared; and the walls only, which were in part built of stone, remained to attest their existence and use. The grounds exhibited similar effects of neglect, in a climate where the living wood grows so rapidly, and the dead decays so soon, as in Nova Scotia. An arbour, which had been constructed of lattice-work, for the support of a flowering vine, had fallen, and was covered with vegetation; while its roof alone remained, supported aloft by limbs of trees that, growing up near it, had become entangled in its net-work. A Chinese temple, once a favourite retreat of its owner, as if in conscious pride of its preference, had offered a more successful resistance to the weather, and appeared in tolerable preservation; while one small surviving bell, of the numerous ones that once ornamented it, gave out its solitary and melancholy tinkling as it waved in the wind. How sad was its mimic knell over pleasures that were fled for ever!

The contemplation of this deserted house is not without its beneficial effect on the mind; for it inculcates humility to the rich, and resignation to the poor. However elevated man may be, there is much in his condition that reminds him of the infirmities of his nature, and reconciles him to the decrees of Providence. "May it please your Majesty," said Euclid to his royal pupil, "there is no regal road to science. You must travel in the same path with others, if you would attain the same end." These forsaken grounds teach us in similar terms this consolatory truth, that there is no exclusive way to happiness reserved even for those of the most exalted rank. The smiles of fortune are capricious, and sunshine and shade are unequally distributed; but though the surface of life is thus diversified, the end is uniform to all, and invariably terminates in the grave.

> "Pallida mors æquo pulsat pede pauperum tabernas
> Regumque turres."

Ruins, like death, of which they are at once the emblem and the evidence, are apt to lose their effect from their frequency. The mind becomes accustomed to them, and the moral is lost. The picturesque alone remains predominant, and criticism supplies the place of reflection. But this is the only ruin of any extent in Nova Scotia, and the only spot either associated with royalty, or set apart and consecrated to solitude and decay. The stranger pauses at a sight so unusual, and inquires the cause, he learns with surprise that this place was devoted exclusively to pleasure, that care and sorrow never entered here; and that the voice of mirth and music was alone heard within its gates. It was the temporary abode of a prince,—of one, too, had he lived, that would have inherited the first and fairest empire in the world. All that man can give or rank enjoy awaited him; but an overruling and inscrutable Providence decreed, at the very time when his succession seemed most certain, that the sceptre should pass into the hands of another. This intelligence interests and excites his feelings. He enters, and hears at every step the voice of nature proclaiming the doom that awaits alike the prince and the peasant. The desolation he sees appals him. The swallow nestles in the empty chamber, and the sheep find a noon shelter in the banqueting-room, while the ill-omened bat rejoices in the dampness of the mouldering ruins. Everything recalls a recollection of the dead; every spot has its record of the past; every path its footstep; every tree its legend; and even the universal silence that reigns here has an awful eloquence that overpowers the heart. Death is written everywhere. Sad and dejected, he turns and seeks some little relic, some small memorial of his deceased prince, and a solitary, neglected garden-flower, struggling for existence among the rank grasses, presents a fitting type of the brief existence and transitory nature of all around him. As he gathers it, he pays the silent but touching tribute of a votive tear to the memory of him who has departed, and leaves the place with a mind softened and subdued, but improved and purified, by what he has seen.

The affectionate remembrance we retain of its lamented owner may have added to my regret, and increased the interest I felt in this lonely and peculiar ruin. In the Duke of Kent the Nova Scotians lost a kind patron and a generous friend. The loyalty of the people, which, when all America was revolting, remained firm and unshaken, and the numerous proofs he received of their attachment to their king and to himself, made an impression upon his mind that was neither effaced or weakened by time or distance. Should these pages happily meet the eye of a Colonial Minister, who has other objects in view than the security of place and the interests of a party, may they remind him of a duty that has never been performed but by the illustrious individual, whose former residence among us gave rise to these reflections. This work is designed for the cottage, and not for the palace; and the author has not the presumption even to hope that it can ever be honoured by the perusal of his sovereign. Had he any ground for anticipating such a distinction for it, he would avail himself of this opportunity of mentioning that in addition to the dutiful affection the Nova Scotians have always borne to their monarch, they feel a more lively interest in, and a more devoted attachment to, the present occupant of the throne from the circumstance of the long and close connection that subsisted between them and her illustrious parent. He was their patron, benefactor, and friend. To be a Nova Scotian was itself a sufficient passport to his notice, and to possess merit a sufficient guarantee for his favour. Her Majesty reigns therefore in this little province in the hearts of her subjects, a dominion of love inherited from her father. Great as their loss was in being thus deprived of their only protector, her faithful people of Nova Scotia still cling to the hope that Providence has vouchsafed to raise up one more powerful and equally kind in her Majesty, who, following this paternal example, will be graciously pleased to extend to them a patronage that courtiers cannot, and statesmen will not give. While therefore as proteges of her royal house, they claim the right to honour and to serve the sovereign of the empire as "*their own Queen*," they flatter themselves her Majesty, for a similar reason, will condescend to regard them as "*the Queen's own*."

1. This was the case when I was there in 1828; since then porch and tree have both disappeared.

II

PLAYING A CARD

I HAD lingered so long about these grounds, that the day was too far spent to think of reaching Windsor before night, and I therefore determined upon wiling away the afternoon in examining, by the aid of a diving-bell, the hulls of several ships of a French fleet, which at an early period of the history of this country took shelter in Bedford Basin, and was sunk by the few survivors of the crews to prevent their falling into the hands of the English. The small-pox, at that time so fatal a scourge to the human race, appearing among them soon after their arrival, nearly depopulated the fleet, destroyed the neighbouring village, and swept off one third of the whole tribe of Nova Scotia Indians. So dreadful a mortality has never been witnessed on this continent; and the number of strangers thus suddenly smote with death at this place, exceeded by several thousands the amount of the population of the country in which they were interred. Of one of the most powerful armaments ever fitted out by France, a few hundred of persons only survived to return to their native land to tell the sad tale of their misfortunes. The ships are still distinctly visible in calm weather, and the rising ground in the neighbourhood where the Duke d'Anville and his mighty host were buried is again clothed with wood, and not to be distinguished from the surrounding forest, except by the inequality of the surface, caused by numerous trenches cut into it to receive the dead. The whole scene is one of surpassing beauty, and deep and melancholy interest. The ruined Lodge, the sunken fleet, the fatal encampment, and the lonely and desolate cemetery of those unfortunate strangers, form a more striking and painful assemblage of objects than is to be found in any other part of British America.

On my return to the inn I had the good fortune to meet Mr. Slick, who was on his way to Halifax, for the purpose of arranging the details of our journey. In the course of the evening I succeeded in obtaining his consent, not merely to attend me to New York, but to accompany me to England. He was in great spirits at the idea of transferring the scene and subjects of our conversation to the other side of the water, where, he said, he could indulge in greater freedom of remark than he could here, having always been afraid of wounding the feelings of his own countrymen, and alienating the affections of his old friends the colonists, for whom he professed great regard.

On the following morning, when the little light travelling-waggon was driven round from the coach-yard, I was delighted to see that the Clockmaker had brought his favourite horse, "Old Clay," with him. Come, step in, squire, said he, as he held the reins; "Old Clay" is a-pawing and a-chawing like mad; he wants to show you the way to Windsor, and he is jist the boy that *can* do it. Hold up your head, my old *gi*-raffe, said he, and make the folks a bow, it's the last time you will ever see them in all *your* born days: and now off with you as if you was in rael wide-awake airnest, and turn out your toes pretty. Never stop for them idle critturs that stand starin' in the road there, as if they never seed a horse afore, but go right over them like wink, my old snort, for you'll be to Conneticut afore they can wake up the crowner and summon a jury, *I* know. There's no occasion to hurry tho' at that rate, or you'll set my axle a-fire. There, that will do now, jist fourteen miles an hour. I don't calculate to drive faster on a journey, squire, for it sweats him, and then you have to dry him arterwards afore you water him, so there is nothing gained by it. Ain't he a horrid handsome horse, a most endurin' quickster, a rael salt, that's all? He is the prettiest piece of flesh and bone ever bound up in horse hide. What an eye he has—you might hang your hat on it. And then his nostrils! Lord, they open like the mouth of a speakin' trumpet. He can pick up miles on *his* feet, and throw 'em behind him faster than a steam doctor a-racin' off with another man's wife.

There now, squire, ain't that magnificient? you can hear him, but can't see him; he goes like a bullet out of a rifle, when its dander is up. Ain't he a whole team that, and a horse to spare? Absquotilate it in style, you old skunk, from a squirrel's jump to the eend of the chapter, and show the gentlemen what you *can* do. Anybody could see he ain't a Blue-nose, can't they? for, cuss 'em, they don't know how to begin to go. Trot, walk, or gallop is all the same to him, like talkin', drinkin', or fighten to a human. Lord, I have a great mind to take him to England, jist for the fun of the thing, for I don't know myself what he *can* do. When he has done his best, there is always a mile an hour more in him to spare: there is, upon my soul.

But it takes a man to mount *him*. Only lookin' at him goin' makes your head turn round like grindin' coffee:—what would ridin' him do? And now, squire, here goes for Slickville, Onion county, state of Conneticut, United States of America. Here's for home.

The very mention of Slickville awakened in my mind a desire to see its venerable and excellent pastor, Mr. Hopewell, so often quoted and so affectionately remembered by Mr. Slick. Every saying of his that I had heard, and every part of his conduct, in private or public life, recorded in the previous volumes, had been marked by such a benevolent and Christian feeling, and by such sound sense and good judgment, that I was fully prepared to honour and to love him. Indeed one of the best traits in the Clockmaker's character was the great affection he always expressed for his old friend and preceptor, whose opinions and maxims he had carefully treasured, as rules of conduct that were infallible. With natural shrewdness, Mr. Slick, like most men of his class, was eminently gifted; but the knowledge of men and things which he derived from his learned and exemplary friend made him a wiser man, and more of a philosopher, than is usually found in his station of life.

It made him "*a great card;*" a saying of his with which I was furnished in the following whimsical conversation. In the course of our morning's drive, I happened to ask him if he interfered much in politics when he was at home at Slickville. No, said he, not now. I was once an assembly man, but since then I ginn up politicks. There is nothin' so well taken care of as your rights and privileges, squire. There are always plenty of chaps volunteerin' to do that, out of pure regard for you, ready to lay down their lives to fight your cause, or their fortins, if they had any, either. No; I have given that up. Clockmakin' is a better trade by half. Dear, dear, I shall never forget the day I was elected; I felt two inches taller, and about a little the biggest man in all Slickville. I knew so much was expected of me I couldn't sleep a-tryin' to make speeches; and when I was in the shop I spiled half my work by not havin' my mind on it. Save your country, says one; save it from ruin; cut down salaries.—I intend to, says I. Watch the officials, says another; they are the biggest rogues we have. It don't convene with liberty that public sarvants should be the masters of the public.—I quite concur with you, says I. Reduce lawyers' fees, says some; they are a-eatin' up of the country like locusts.—Jist so, said I. A bounty on wheat, says the farmer, for your life. Would you tax the mechanic to inrich the agriculturist? says the manufacturer. Make a law agin' thistles, says one; a regulator about temperance, says another: we have a right to drink if we please, says a third. Don't legislate too much, says a fourth—it 's the curse of the state; and so on without eend. I was fairly bothered, for no two thought alike, and there was no pleasin' nobody. Then every man that voted for me wanted some favour or another, and there was no bottom to the obligation. I was most squashed to death with the weight of my cares, they was so heavy.

At last the great day came, and the governor, and senate, and representa*tives* all walked in procession, and the artillery fired, and the band of the caravan of wild beasts was hired to play for us, and we organized in due form, and the Governor's message was read. I must say that day was the happiest one of my life. I felt full of dignity and honour, and was filled with visions of glory to come. Well, says I to myself, the great game is now to be played in rael airnest, and no mistake: *what card shall I play?* The presidential chair and the highest posts is open to me in common with other citizens. What is to prevent me a-comin' in *by honours*, or, if I have good luck, *by the odd trick*. What shall I l*ead off* with? I laid awake all night considerin' of it, a rollin' and a-tossin' over, like cramp in the stomack, not knowin' what to do: at last I got an idea. *Extension of suffrage*, says I, *is the card I'll play*. That will take the masses, and masses is power, for majorities rules. At that time, squire, we had the forty shilling freehold qualification, and it extended no farther; so I went for universal suffrage; for, thinks I, if I can carry that, I can go for governor first, on the strength of the new votes, and president arterwards; and it *did* seem plausible enough, too, that's a fact. To all appearance it was the best *card in the pack*.

So out I jumps from bed, a-walkin' up and down the room in my shirt tail, a-workin' away at my speech like anything, and dreadful hard work it was, too; for it is easier to forge iron any time than a speech, especially if you ain't broughten up to the business. I had to go over it and over it ever so often, for every now and then I'd stick fast, get bothered, and forget where I was, and have to begin agin; but when day was e'en about breakin', I was just drawin' to a close, and had nearly scored and rough-hew'd it out, when all of a sudden I run agin' the bed-post in the dark, and nearly knocked my brains out. Well, next night I worked at it agin, only I left the candle burnin', so as not to be a-stumblin' up agin' things that way, and the third night I got it all finished off complete; but I got a shockin' cold in my head, a-walkin' about naked so, and felt as weak as a child for want of sleep. I was awful puzzled to fix on what to do on account of that plaguy cold. I didn't know whether to wait till it got better, or strike while the iron was hot and hissin', for I warnt sure sum o' the speech wouldn't leake out, or the whole get flat, if I kept it in too long; so as soon as the house opened, I makes a plunge right into it; for what must be, must be, and it's no use a considerin'.

So I ups and says, Mr. Speaker, says I (Lord, how thick my tongue felt; it seemed to grow too thick for my mouth, like the clapper of an old horse,) let me perpound this resolution, sir, said I; all men are free and equal. No one doubts it, Mr. Slick, said an old member: no one denies that; it's a truism. I didn't somehow expect that interruption, it kinder put me out, and I never got a-goin' altogether right agin arterwards, for I lost my temper; and when a man ain't cool, he might as well hang up his fiddle, that's a fact. Have I freedom of speech, sir, said I, or have I not; or is that last rag of liberty torn from the mast of the constitution too? I stand stock still a-waitin' for your answer, sir.—Oh, sartain, said he, sartain; you may talk for ever, if you like: go on, sir; only no man doubts your position.—It's a lie, sir, said I, it 's a lie writ—. Order! order!—chair! chair! says some. Knock him down!—turn him out!—where did you larn manners? says others.—Hear me out, says I, will you? and don't be so everlastin' fast: what's the use of jumpin' afore you come to the fence. It's a lie written on the face of the constitution.—Oh, oh! says they, is that it?—Yes, says I, it is, and contradict it if you darst. We are not free; we are slaves: one half of us is tyrants,—unremorseless, onfeelin', overbearin' tyrants, and vile usurpers; and the other half slaves,—abject, miserable, degraded slaves. The first argument I advance, sir, is this—and the cold in my nose began to tickle, tickle, tickle, till I couldn't hold in no longer, and I let go a sneeze that almost broke the winders out. Oh, Lord, what a haw! haw! they sot up. The first argument is this, sir; and off went both barrels of my nose agin like thunder: it fairly raised the dust from the floor in a cloud, like a young whirlwind in the street afore rain. It made all spin agin. Why, he is a very ring-tail roarer, says the members, a regular sneezer; and they shouted and roared like anything. I thought I should a-died for shame one minit, and the next I felt so coonish I had half a mind to fly at the Speaker and knock him down. I didn't jist cleverly know what to do, but at last I went on.—Did the best blood of the land flow for forty shillings? Was Bunker Hill fought out to loosen British chains, merely to rivet American ones?

Was it for this the people died covered with gore and glory, on the bed of honour? Was it the forty shillings alone that fought the revolution or the Polls? I am for the Polls. Taxation and representation should go hand in hand, and freedom and equality likewise also. How dare you tax the Polls without their consent? Suppose they was to go for to tax you without your consent, why who would be right or who wrong then? Can two wrongs make a right? It is much of a muchness, sir,—six of one, and half a dozen of the other.

What's that feller talkin' about? says a member.—A vote to help the Poles agin' Russia, says the other: what a cussed fool he is. It put me quite out, that, and joggled me so I couldn't make another line straight. I couldn't see the Speaker no longer, for my eyes watered as if I had been a stringin' inions for a week, and I had to keep blowin' my nose the whole blessed time, for the cold in it corked it up as tight as a bottle. Who calls them fools? says I: who dares insult free citizens because they are not forty shillingers? You couldn't treat them wus if they was nasty, dirty, disposable niggers; and yet you boast your institution. Will any member answer me this? Have they blood in their veins?—and if they have, it must be free blood; and if free, it must boil. (Tickle, tickle goes my boscis agin, and I had to stop to sarch my pocket for my noserag.) The honorable gentleman, says some feller or another, for most on 'em were strangers to me, means a blood puddin', I suppose. Ah! I thought I should have gone ravin' distracted mad. I knew I was talkin' nonsense, that I had run off the tracks with all steam on, and was a-ploughin' thro' the mud in the fields like anything. Says I, I'll have *your* blood, you scoundrel, if you dare to say that agin, see if I don't, so there now. Oh dear, such shoutin', and roarin', and clappin' of hands I never heerd: my head run round like a spinnin' wheel; it was all burr, burr, burr, buzz, buzz, buzz. I bit in my breath to keep cool; I felt I was on the edge of a wharf, and only one step more was over head and ears chewallop in the water. Sam, says I to myself, be a man; be cool,—take it easy: so I sot off agin, but I was so confused I got into my other speech on agricultur' that I had larned by heart, and mixed the two together all in a ravel. Thistles, says I, is the bane of all good husbandry. Extirpate them from the land; they are usurpin' the places of grain, and all Slickville will be filled with Polls. If they have no voice in this assembly, how can you expect them to obey the laws they never made. Compel folks to cut them down in the full of the moon, and they'll all die; I have tried it myself with universal suffrage and the ballot.

Well, artillery is nothin' but a popgun to the noise the members now made,—it was an airthquake tipped with thunder and lightning. I never heerd nothing like it. I felt I was crazy; I wished I was dead a'most, or could sink through the floor into the middle of the sea, or anywhere but where I was. At last cousin Woodberry took pity on me, and came over to where I was, and said, Sam, said he, set down, that's a good feller; you don't know what you are a-doin' of; you are makin' an ass of yourself. But I didn't hear him. Confound you! said he, you look mean enough to put the sun into eclipse, and he laid hold of the skirts of my coat, and tried to pull me down; but instead of that he pulled 'em right off, and made an awful show of me. That sot me off agin, quite ravin' as bad as ever. I won't be put down, says I, Mr. Speaker; I fight for liberty and the Polls: I stand agin' the forty shillingers. Unhand me, you slave! said I; touch me not, or I'll sacrifice you on the altar of my country; and with that I ups fist and knocks Woodberry over as flat as a pancake, and bolts right out of the hall.

But I was so blinded with the cold in my head and rage together, I couldn't see no more nor a bat, and I pitched into several members in the way out, and 'most broke their necks and my own too. It was the first and the last of my speech making. I went by the name, for years arterwards, in our town of "Free-and-equal Slick". I wish I could wipe out that page of my follies from my memory, I tell you, but it's a caution to them that navigate in politicks, that's a fact.

Nothin' on this side of the water makes so big a fool of a man, squire, he continued, as goin' to the house of representatives without bein' fit for it. Them that hante jist got the right weight of ballast are upset in no time, and turned bottom upwards afore they know where they be. Them that are a little vain by natur' get so puffed up and so consaited, they become nothin' but laughin' stocks to all the world, most ridiculous fools; while them whose principles ain't well anchored in good holdin'-ground, let the rogue peep out o' their professions plainer than they are a-thinkin' on. The skin of the beast will show through, like an Irishman's elbow, though he has three coats on. But that ain't the worst of it, neether. A man is apt to become bankrupt in business, as well as in character, by it. Doin' big and talkin' big for three months in the year, and puffin' each other up till they are ready to burst with their importance, don't convene with sellin' tape by the yard, or loadin' on carts, when they return home to their business. In short, squire, a country ought to be a rich country, with larned men in it, and men o' property to represent it, or else assembly work is nothin' but high life below stairs, arter all. I could point you out legislaturs on this here continent where the speakin' is all kitchin' talk, all strut, brag, and vulgar impedence. It's enough to make a cat sick to hear fellers talk of independence who are mortgaged over head and ears in debt, or to listen to chaps jawin' about public vartue, temperance, education, and what not all day, who spend the night in a back room of a market tavern with the key turned, drinkin' hail-storm and bad rum, or playin' sixpenny loo. *If mankind only knew what fools they were, and how they helped folks themselves to fool them, there would be some hope of them, for they would have larnt the first lesson of wisdom.*

But to sum-totalize my story: the next time I went to poor old minister's arter that, says he, Sam, says he, they tell me you broke down the other day in the house of representa*tives*, and made a proper gag of yourself. I am very sorry for you, very sorry indeed; but it is no use now a-cryin' over spilt milk. What can't be cured, must be endured, I do suppose; but I do wish with all my heart and soul you had a-taken my advice and left politicks alone.—Don't mention it, minister, said I; I am ashamed to death of myself, and shall leave Slickville till it's blowed over and forgot: I can't bear to hear of it; it fairly makes me sick. *It was a great card* I had tho', if I had only *played it right*, says I, a very *great card indeed*. In fact it was more *than a card*,—it was *high, low, Jack, and the game.*—What was it, said he, that was worth all that are nonsense?—Univarsal suffrage, says I.—Sam, said he, (and I know'd I was in for a lectur', for he knit his brow, and looked in rael right down airnest,) you don't know what you are a-talkin' about. Do you know what univarsal suffrage means?—To be sure I do, says I; it's every man havin' a vote and a voice in makin' those laws that is to govern him; and it comports with reason, and stands to common sense.—Well, says he, what's all that when it's fried? why, it amounts to this, and nothin' more nor less: *Now men of property and character make laws to govern rogues and vagabonds,* but by your be*autiful scheme of univarsal suffrage, *rogues and vagabonds will make laws to govern men of property and character.* It is revarsin' the order of things: it is worse than nonsense; it is downright madness. We are fast approaching this state without your aid, Sam, I can tell you; and when we do arrive at it we shall be an object for the finger of scorn to point at from Europe. We shall then have wound up the fearful tragedy of our revolution with as precious a farce as folly and licentious ever produced.—Minister, says I, I don't know how it is, but you have such a shorthand way of puttin' things, that there is no contradictin' of you. You jist squeeze all the argument up in a ball, as easy as dough, and stop a feller's mouth with it. How the plague is it that you seem always right?—Because *I never play a card,* Sam. I never consider what is *expedient,* but what is *right;* never study what will *tickle the ears of people,* but what will *promote their welfare.* You would have been all straight, too, if you had only looked to the right and wrong of the measure; but you looked to *popularity,* and that sot you to *playin' of a card.* Now the upshot of this popular gambling, or *card playing*, is patriotism; and mark my words, Sam, mark my words, my boy, for I am an old man now, and have read the human heart well,—in ninety-nine cases out of a hundred, *patriotism is the trump card of a scoundrel.*

III

BEHIND THE SCENES

IT is not to be supposed that Mr. Slick had made such an absurd exhibition of himself in the Legislative Hall of Slickville, as he thought proper to pourtray in the anecdote related in the last chapter. He was evidently a man of too much tact and natural good sense, to have rendered himself so ridiculous; nor must we, on the other hand, attribute his making himself the hero of the tale to an absence of vanity, for few men had a greater share of it than himself. It probably arose from his desire to avoid personalities, and an amiable anxiety not to furnish a traveller with names that might hereafter appear in print to the annoyance of the real actors. Indeed, so rich did he think himself in experience and knowledge of the world, that he felt he could afford to draw at will on his own reputation. How true to nature is the graphic sketch in the last chapter, and how just the reflections to which it gave rise! I can call to mind so many instances, even in my own limited sphere of observation, to which his remarks are applicable, that I recognise at once the fidelity of the picture and the hand of a master. Upon my expressing to him an intention to record his illustration of "playing a card" as a valuable lesson in life,—Ah, sir, said he, with the air of a man who felt he had a right to boast, I have larned to "look behind the scenes." Major Bradford taught me that airly in life. It was him put that wrinkle on my horn. He was the gentleman that traded in calves and punkins for the Boston market, him that you've got down in your first series, that took me to the *Tre*mont House, the time the gall lost her runnin-riggin' in the crowd. Well, one arternoon, havin' nothin' above pitikilar to do, I goes and dresses myself up full fig, and was a-posten away as hard as I could leg it, full chisel down by the Mall in Boston to a tea and turn-out to Sy Tupper's. Sy had an only darter called Desire; she warn't a bad lookin' piece of farniture neither; folks said she would have fifty thousand dollars, and to tell you the truth I was a-thinking of spekelating there, and was a-scouterin' away as hard as I could leg it to the party. Who should I meet on the road but the Major a-pokin' along with his cocoanut down, a-studyin' over somethin'

or another quite deep, and a-workin' up the baccy in great style, for nothin'
a'most will make a man chaw like cypherin' in his head to himself.— Hullo,
Major, said I, whose dead, and what's to pay now? why what's the matter of
you? you look as if you had lost every freend you had on airth.—H'are you,
boy? said he: give us your fin, and then tell us which way you are a-sailin'
of this fine day, will you.—But jist as I was a-goin' to take hold of his hand,
he drew back the matter of a yard or so; and eyed me all over from head to
foot, as if he was a-measurin' me for a wrastlin' bout.

Says he, I'll bet you a five-dollar piece, Sam, I know where you are
a-goin' to-night.—Done, said I, it's a bargain: now, where?—A-whalin',
says he.—A what! says I.—On a whalin' voyage, said he.—Hand out your
five dollars, says I, for you missed your guess this hitch anyhow. I am
agoin' down to Sy Tupper's to tea and spend the evenin'—Exactly, said
he, goin' a-gallin', I know'd it, for you are considerably large print, and it
don't take spectacles to read you. She is rich in iles, that gall; her father
made his money a-whalin', and folks call her "Sy Tupper's spermaceti."
Bah! she smells of blubber that greasy-faced heifer; let her bide where she
be, Sam. You hante been "*behind the scenes yet*," I see, and that screetch owl
in petticoats, Mother Tupper, is an old hand. She will harpoon you yet, if
you don't mind your eye; now mark what I tell you. Come with me to the
the*atre,* and I'll show you a gall of the right sort, I know. Helen Bush comes
on in tights to-night. She is a beautiful-made crittur that, clean limbed and
as well made as if she was turned in a mould. She is worth lookin' at, that's
a fact; and you don't often get such a chance as that are.—Dear, dear, said
I, in tights! well if that don't beat all! I must say that don't seem kinder
nateral now, does it, Major?—Nateral! said he, what the devil has natur'
got to do with it? If she followed natur' she wouldn't wear nothin' at all.
Custom has given woman petticoats and men pantaloons, but it would be
jist as nateral for woman to wear the breeches and men the apron string,
and there is a plaguy sight of them do it too. Say it ain't modest and I won't
non-concur you, but don't talk about natur', for natur' has no hand in it at
all. It has neither art nor part in it, at no rate. But take my advice, my green
horn, and study natur' a bit. Folks may talk of their Latin and Greek till
they are tired, but give me natur'. But to study it right you must get "*behind
the scenes;*" so come along with me to the house.

Well, I never was to a the*atre* afore in all my life, for minister didn't
approbate them at no rate, and he wouldn't never let me go to 'em to

Slickville; so thinks I to myself, I don't care if I do go this once; it can't do me no great harm I do suppose, and a gall in tights is something new; so here goes, and I turns and walks lock-and-lock with him down to the play-house. Well, I must say it was a splendid sight, too. The house was chock full of company, all drest out to the very nines, and the lamps was as bright as day, and the musick was splendid, that's a fact, for it was the black band of the militia, (and them blacks have most elegant ears for musick too, I *tell* you), and when they struck up our blood-stirrin' national air, it made me feel all over in a twitteration as if I was on wires a'most, considerable martial.

But what gave me the gapes was the scenes. Lord, squire, when the curtain drawed up, there was Genesee Falls as nateral as life, and the beautiful four story grist-mills taken off as plain as anything, and Sam Patch jist ready to take a jump in the basin below. It was all but rael, it was so like life. The action too was equal to the scenes; it was dreadful pretty, I *do* assure you. Well, arter a while, Helen Bush came on in tights; but I can't say I liked it; it didn't seem kinder right for a gall to dress up in men's clothes that way, and I sorter thort that nothin' a'most would tempt me to let Sister Sall show shapes arter that fashion for money. But somehow or somehow-else, folks hurrawed and clapped, and cheered like any thing. It was so excitin' I hurrawed too, at last, as if I was as well pleased as any of them, for hollerin' is catchin', like barkin' among dogs, and you can't help it no how you can fix it. Well, arter legs lost their novelty, a whole lot o' dancin' galls came forward and danced *quod*-drills, gallop pards, hornpipes, and what not, the most beautiful critturs, I think, I ever laid my eyes on,—all young and bloomin', and graceful and light as spirits a'most. They seemed as if they e'en a'most belonged to another guess world from ourn, only the rosy cheeks and bare necks, and naked arms, and dear little ankles, all smacked of rael life.

What do you think of *them?* said the Major; hante they fine glass-spun heels, them critturs. I guess you don't often see such fetlocks in Slickville as them; for your galls, if I don't mis-remember, are rather beefy about the instep: what do you think of them, my boy, eh?—Think? says I, why I never seed the equal of it. Where the plague did they pick up such a lot of elegant galls? they are horrid pretty, I must say: are they foreigners or natives?—Na*tives*, said he, genu*wine* Jonatheenas, all raised in Conneticut, and silver-skinned inions every soul of them.—Would you like to be

Behind the Scenes

introduced to them?—Well, says I, I would, that's a fact, for its enough to set a feller crazy a'most, actilly ravin' distracted mad with pleasure, the sight of so many splendid little fillies, ain't it?—Well, come along with me then, said he, jist foller me, and I'll take you round there. So out we goes into the entry, and follers along into a dark passage, a pretty difficult navigation it was too, among trap-doors, and boxes, and broken steps, and what not; and arter a while we enters a great onfarnished barn of a room alongside of the stage, and there was the players, and dancers, and singers, and ever so many actin' people. Well, it was a wonderful sight, too; p'raps in all my born days I never see anything to equal it. I never was so staggered. I don't think all *my* starin' put together, would come up to the great big endurin' stare I then gave. I was onfakilised, that's a fact; I stood for the whole blessed space of five minites without movin' or speakin'. At last one of the dancin' galls came a-figerin' up to me a hornpipin', and a-singin', and dropt me a low curtshee.—Well, my old rooster, said she, the next time you see me; I hope you will know me; where did you larn manners, starin' so like all possest.—Well, I warn't much used to town galls, and it took me all aback that, and struck me up all of a heap, so I couldn't stir or speak.—Oh fie, Julia, said another, how can you! And then comin' up and tappin me on the shoulder with her fan, to wake me up like, said she,—Pray, my good feller, "Does your mother know you're out?"—The whole room burst out a-larfin' at me; but no, move or speak I couldn't, for I was spell-bound, I do believe. There I stood as stiff as a frozen nigger, and all I could say to myself was, "Heavens and airth!"

At last another gall, the best and lightest dancer of them all, and one that I rather took a leetle fancy to on the stage, she was so uncommon spry and ac-*tive*, took a flyin' lep right into the middle of the room, and lit down on one foot; and then, balancin' herself as she did on the stage with her hands, stretched the other foot away out ever so far behind her. Well, arter perchin' that way a minit or so, as a bird does on a sprig of a tree, she sprung agin, right forrard, and brought herself bolt upright on both feet jist afore me.—What will you give me, my young Coon, said she, if I show you the way?—What way, said I at last, a-scratchin' of my head and a-pluckin' up spunk enough to find my tongue.—The way out, said she, for you seem as if you sorter lost your road, when you came in here. I thought every one in the room would have gone into fits, they larfed so; they fairly screetched till they most loosend their teeth, all but her, and *she* looked as quiet as a baby.

Well done, Angelica, said the Major; what a wicked little devil you be! and he put his arm round her waist and kissed her; and then said he, waiter, half-a-dozen of iced champaigne here to pay for Mr. Slick's footin'; and if he and them galls didn't tuck in the wine in great style it's a pity, that's all. Well, a glass or two of liquor onloosed the hinges of my tongue, and sot me all right agin, and I jined in the joke and enjoyed the larf as well as the best of them; for it won't do to get cross when fellers are running of their rigs, it only makes them wus.

Arter a while we left the theatre to go home, and as we progressed down street, says the Major to me, well, Slick, says he, how did you like them little angels, the dancin' galls? you seemed as amazed as if you was jist born into the world, and looked rather struck with them, I thought, pitikilarly Angelica; a neat little article that, ain't she? There's no nonsense about her; she is as straight as a shingle in her talk, right up and down, and no pretence. I guess she has put " Sy Tupper's spermaceti" quite out, hante she?—It puts all creation out, said I; I never was so stumpt afore since I was raised from a seedlin'. Heavens and airth! only to think them nasty, tawdry, faded, yaller, jaded, painted drabs was the beautiful dancin' galls of the the*a*tre? and them old, forrerd, impudent heifers was the modest, graceful, elegant little cherubs that was on the stage an hour afore; and then to think them nasty daubs was like Genesee Falls, Lord, I could paint them pictur' scenes better myself, with a nigger wench's house-mop, I could, I snore.—Exactly, says the Major; you have been " behind the scenes" you see, Sam, and you have got a lesson not to trust to appearances altogether.—Rael life is one thing and stage representation is another. The world "behind the scenes," and what is exhibited on the boord is as different as day is from night. It tante all gold that glitters in this life, I can tell you. Jist so it is with "Sy Tupper's young spermaceti;" for I see you want to spikilate in iles there.

When you double Cape Horn, as yer in hopes for to do,
There's a-plenty of sparm whale on the coast of *Peru*.

What a life for a man, to be the wick of an ile lamp, ain't it? and have your wife snuffing you with her fingers. It's as bad as having your onquestionable ugly nose pulled.—Oh yes, take her by all means, only get, "behind the scenes" first; you have only seed her yet of an evenin', and then she was actin' rigged out for a party, a-smilin' and a-doin' sweet and pretty, and a-wearin' of her company-face, and singin' like a canary-bird. But go into "the green room," see her of a mornin', get a peep at a family scene, drop in on 'em of a sudden, onexpected like, and see the old cat and her kitten a-caterwaulin' and clapper-clawin' each other till they make the fur fly, and you will be jist as much dumfoundered as you was at the dancin' galls: you won't know her, that's a fact; you'll find that your beautiful "spermaceti" has turned out nothin' but tallow, and damn bad tallow too. Such critturs run more nor half away to waste, and give more grease than light, by a long chalk. But come, said he, s'posin' you and me settle our little account, for short reckonings make long friends, as the sayin' is. First, there is your five dollar bet; then six bottles of iced champaigne, at three dollars each, is eighteen dollars more; and then two dollars for tickets, makes a total of twenty-five dollars; do you undercumstand? Come into the iseter shop here, and plank the pewter, and I will go sheers with you for a supper of iseters. It's a considerable of a dear lesson that; but it's the best you ever got, I know. —Dear! said I, a countin' out of the money to him, I guess it is dear. If all my schoolin' in town is to cost at that rate, I guess I'll have more larnin' than capital when I get thro' my trainin'. Twenty-five dollars for bein' made a fool on, for them dancin' galls to laugh at for two hours, what a pretty go that is, ain't it? I must say, I don't thank you a bit, Major; it warn't pretty at all.—Who the devil axed you for thanks! said he; you have done better, you have paid for it, man, and boughten wit is always the best; but you *will* thank one for it some o' these days, see if you don't. It's better to be made a fool on for two hours than for life. I have known a feller silly enough to marry a dancin' gall afore now; but then he'd never been "behind the scenes," as you have; yes, it's a valuable lesson that. Your old fogey of a parson that you are always a-talkin' of, old Hop, Hope, something or other, may preach away to you till he is blind, but he can't larn you anything equal to that. It's a lesson from life, and a lesson from life is worth a hundred sarmons. In everything a'most, Sam, in this world, consider you are either deceived or liable to be deceived, and that you can't trust even the evidence of your own senses, unless you "look behind the scenes." But come, said he, preachin' is not my trade, let us walk into half a bushel of these iseters; they are rael salts, they come from Nova Scotia, and better than any we have, or the British either: and we sot to and did justice to them, at least *he* did you may depend. He walked 'em into him as a duck does a June bug. He could open, pepper, and swaller a

dozen to my one, for somehow I never could get my knife into the jinte
of one until arter half an hour's bunglin'—I hadn't got the knack.—You
don't seem to like them, said he at last, a-drawin' breath and a-swallerin' a
gill of pure whiskey; p'raps you are too patriotic to eat blue-nose's iseters,
and perfer the free citizens of our own beds?—No, said I, it tante that; I
can't open them, they are so oncommon tight about the jaws.—Hem! said
he, I forgot that. You never seed an iseter, I do suppose, or a dancin' gall
nother afore to-night. Do as I do, younker; this is the way, freeze down
solid to it, square up to it, as if you was a-goin' to have an all out-door fight
of it, and he slipped 'em out o' the shells into, his mouth as fast as a man
dealin' cards, until he fairly finished all we had. You don't drink said he,
now that's not wholesome; you ought to take enough of the neat liquor
to make 'em float light on the stomach; and he jist tipt off the balance of
the whiskey without winkin'. Ah! said he, making a wry face, that's no go;
that last iseter was not good, it's upset me a-most; call for some more, and
I'll be in agin in a minit; I must go into the air, for I feel dizzy.—Well, I
called for some more iseters and some more whiskey, and I sot and worked
away at my leisure, and waited for him to come back and pay his share of
the shot. Well, I waited and waited for ever so long, till I e'en a'most fell
asleep, and still no Major. At last I began to get tired, so I knocks on the
table with the handle of a knife for the nigger help. Snowball, says I, have
you seen anything of the Major? where on airth is he? I'm waitin' for him
to settle the bill.—Massa hab to wait den, one berry long time, sar: de last
iseter, sar, he always fix Major's flint, sar, and make him cut his stick. You
won't see him no more, sar, and he grinned from ear to ear like a chessycat.
De bill is four dollar, massa, and a quarter-dollar for Snowball.—Hem!
says I to myself, a nod is as good as a wink to a blind horse: I see it now,
I'm bilked; so I paid it, and said no more on the subject. That was another
"peep behind the scenes," that "he who incurs jinte expenses should look
to the honesty and solvency of his partners."

    I didn't grudge the money for what I larned that night, altho' it came
to a horrid sum, too—twenty-nine dollars and a quarter—for it's worth
every cent of it, that's a fact. But what did touch me to the quick was
this: he drew the wool over my eyes so about Desire Tupper that I gin up
a-going there, and then he cut in there and got the prize hisself—he did
upon my soul! All that talk about her temper was made out of whole cloth,
and got up a-purpose, along with her nick-name of "Spermaceti," to put

me out of consait of her, and it answered the purpose most beautiful. Yes, he did me most properly all the way through the chapter; but, p'raps, it will all turn out right in the long run, for I was too young then to marry, or to handle so much money, for light come is plaguy apt to turn out "light go" but, at the time, I was most peskily ryled, I tell you; and if I had a-seed him while I was so oncommon wrathy, I do believe, in my soul, I should have tanned his jacket for him, so that he would have been a caution to behold. I am a good-nater'd man, and can bear spittin' on; but hang me if I can stand and have it rubbed in that way. I didn't know what to do when I got home, whether to tell the story or not; but I knew it would leak out, and thought my own varsion of it would be the best, so I jist ups and tells father all about it, from first to last.—He is a nasty, dirty, low-lived, mean feller, says father, and a disgrace to the commission, though one comfort is, he ain't a reglar and never seed sarvice, and I dispise an officer that has never smelt powder. No man in the country but a veteran desarves the name of soldier, and them, it ain't no vanity to say, are the first troops in the univarse,—for the British have whipped all the world, and we whipped them.—Yes, he is a scoundrel, said the old man; but still the information you got is worth havin'. It is a knowledge of the world, and that is invaluable; although, from what I've seed in the wars, I am most afeerd a man of the world ain't a man of much heart in a gineral way. Still the knowin' it is worth the larnin' it. Acquire it, Sam, if you can; but you musn't pay too dear for it. Now the Major gin more for his wit than you. — Possible? said I; why, how is that? Why, says father, he bought his at the expense of his character, and the leastest morsel of character in the world is worth more nor all that is to be larnt "*behind the scenes.*"

The Black Brother

IV

THE BLACK BROTHER

YES, squire, said the Clockmaker, there is nothin' like lookin' "behind the scenes" in this world. I rather pride myself on that lesson of Major Bradford. It came airly in life, and was, as he said, the best lesson I ever had. It made me an obsarvin' man. It taught me to look into things considerable sharp. I've given you a peep behind the scenes in assembly matters, so that you can judge how far patriots and reformers show the painted face; and at the theatre what devils little angels of dancin' galls turn out sometimes; and now I'll tell you a story of "the Black Brother," to show you how cantin' fellers can carry two faces also, when they choose, for I've been "behind the scenes" there, too. I mentioned to you afore, if you recollect, that we had a split once to Slickville in our congregation, about the voluntary, and that some of the upper-crust folks went off in a huff, and joined the "Christian band" as they called themselves, or the awakeners as we call 'em. Well these folks went the whole figur', and from bein' considerable proud men, affected great humility, and called each other "Brother," and only associated with each other, and kept the rest of mankind off at arm's length, as if they were lost ones, and it would contaminate them, like, to keep company with them. It broke poor old minister's heart a'most, for they parsecuted him arterwards most dreadful; there was nothin' too bad for them a'most to say of the old church, for in a gineral way, them that secede *don't go of in peace; but go off armed for a fight, as if they expected to be chased and brought back again. Pride and temper is almost always at the bottom of schism, you will find.* Ahab Meldrum was one of these superfine overly good men, and jist about as parfect a specimen of a hypocrite as I e'en a'most ever came across in all my travels. Well, I was to Ahab's one day a settlin' some business with him, and a pretty tough job I had of it—for you might as well drag out an eyetooth, without lancin' the gum, as to drag a debt out of these whitewashed gentlemen—and who should come in but a scentoriferous blackman, his woolly head all done up in roll curls like cotton in the cardin' mills, and a large shovel-hat in his hand, and wearin' a fine frill shirt, and

dressed off to the very nines, for a nigger is as fond of finery as a peacock
is of his tail. They are for spreadin' it out and a-struttin' about in it for ever
and ever a'most. If there was a thing on airth that Ahab hated like pyson, I
do believe it was a great bull-nigger, so seein' him come in, in that free and
easy manner, he looks up at him quite stiff—for the better a man is, the
prouder he grows in a gineral way—and, without biddin' him the time o'
day, (which wouldn't a-hurt him one morsel, tho' the crittur was as black as
Comingo,) or movin' from his chair, or axin' him to sit down, says he, Well,
sir, what brought you here, what's your business? It made me laugh, for I
knew humility was the dress coat of pride, and that we was a-goin' to have a
scene, for I seed by the cut of the feller's jib that he was a preacher. O massa,
said he, I is a broder labourer in de Lord's wineyard, de onworthy (and he
made a bow at that word, as much as to say there is a peg for you to hang
a compliment on if you like), de onworthy shepherd ob de little flock of
free color'd Christians to Martin Vanburinville. I jist call'y, massa broder, to
cossult you about some business ob *"our little Christian band."*—Sit down,
sir, if you please, says Ahab, a colorin' up like anything, for he seed his own
professions was set like a fox-trap afore him, and he knew it was nuts to me,
and that I wouldn't spare him one mite or morsel. Sit down, sir.—Tankey,
sar, tankey, said Dr. Query, for that was the nickname the crittur went by;
how is all your consarns, and your leetle flock? I hope dey is all well, and
none on em jumpin' de fence, and gittin' out o' de fold, among neighbour's
sheeps: mine gib me great bodder dat way, werry great bodder indeed. Mine
all shockin' fond ob musick, and go whereber dere is de best singin but I
believe we may stump any sec for dat, and werry fond ob Greek too.—Of
Greek! said Ahab, who was dumfoundered at the turn things took; did you
say Greek?—Yes, massa, said the Doctor, of Greek; and he took an old well
worn grammar from his pocket, and openin' it, said, Broder, said he, what
you call him? pintein' to a pitikilar word.—That, said Ahab, who I seed was
a gittin' of his dander up quite fast, that is *"eureeka."*—Ah, said the Doctor;
I know him by sight, but I no recollect his name; by golly! but Greek him
werry hard, werry hard indeed. I try to larn a few words, for dey sounds well
in de pulpit, and look grand. Colored people no tinkey you know nottin,
if you no gib 'em hard words sometimes; and Broder Sly, he teach me to
say 'em. Well, Broder Meldrum, he says, at last, I is glad I "eureeka" you at
home; here is de superscription for de new meetin' house; put your fist to
dat, broder, and come down like a man, hansum.—Poor Ahab, he shrunk

from the touch as if it was hot iron, and from the subscription paper too as if it was his death-warrant. Brother, said he, and that word brother stuck in his crop so he had to cough twice afore he could get it out, and smelt so strong in his nose he had to take out his handkerchief, all scented with musk, to get clear of the fogo of it, here are two dollars.—O massa brudder, said Blackey, only two dollar! By golly! but I ginn five myself. Member, sar, he what gibs to de church, lends to de Lord. Come, brudder, mend de figure, dat's a good soul; you won't be one mossel de poorer of it in de long run, you may depend.—But Ahab was tough. Stickin' a subscription paper into a very strait-laced man, even for building a schism-shop for his own folks, is like stickin' a needle behind an ox's ear, it kills him dead on the spot. The labourer is worthy of his hire, broth—broth—he couldn't come it a second time, so he ginn it up in despair; worthy of his hire, sir.—You were wrong, very wrong, sir, to do it: the congregation should do their own work themselves.—Well, well, said Blackey, a good deal disconsarted at the failure of his application; p'raps you is right, brudder, p'raps you is right; you noes better den us poor colored folks does. I has seed a great deal of trouble lately, brudder, said Query. My congregation is the most difficultest to manage I did ever see (pitikilarly de fair sec), and has had a split in it. Dat everlastin' sinner, and crooked 'sciple of a nigger, Ben Parsons, dat is too lazy to work hisself de good-for-notten feller, he tinks he preach better nor me, de consaited fool! and he sot up for hisself, and seceded, and I lose twenty dollar a year of my livin' by him, and some o' my best singers too. Cato Cooper's three daughters, Cleopatra, Portia, and Juno, all left to foller arter de young preacher, and dey had most superfine voices, better nor most nigga wenches has, and sing as well as te*atre* women, dey did. Yes, it's lucky for massa Ben, I is a Christian man, dat uses no carnal weapon, or I'd feel his short ribs for him, and take my change out of his hide, de villain.

> De Raccoon ginn to scratch and bite,
> I hitty once wid all ma might,
> I bungy eye and spile his sight,
>   Oh, *Ise* de child to fight!

But I is a new man now wid de ungenerate heart, and only fight old Scratch, old Adam, or old sin, but not a brudder in de flesh—no naber I ain't goin' get mad no more.

> For little childer neber let
>   De angry passions rise,
> Your little hands were neber made
>   To tear each oder's eyes.

Nothin' else save him from catchin' it, for I is de boy dat could do it. Lord, I'd run him foul of a consternation, afore he know'd what was de matter of him. Temper, him werry trong, and say cuss him, bung up both he eye, and put in de dead lite; but I is a preacher now, and religion advise werry different, and say, "let him go to de debil his own way, de willain." He ain't worth powder and shot, and dat is de fack, for he is more crookeder in his ways nor a dog's hind leg, or ram's horn, the ungenerate, ungrateful beast. Den I hab great trouble to home too; I lost Miss Wenus, my wife, last week; she died of de ribilious cholic. But she died happy,—werry happy indeed, screetchin' and screamin' for joy, and made a most lovely corpse. I tink she was de most beautifulest corpse I ever did see—it was a pleasure to look at her. Broder Sly improved de occasion, and spoke four hours and a half widout stopin', werry powerful did de leetle man; we had a werry refreshin' time of it, and beautiful singin'; oh, by golly, but it was grand! Yes, I hab great trouble, and I 'most fear I will ab go to sarvice agin, for troubles rise up as de sparks do; and if I do gin up preachin' agin, if I don't pitch into Ben Parson's ribs like a tousand of bricks, it's a pity, that's all. I'll make hawk's meat oh him. Cryin' over spilt milk is no use tho,' s'pose we conclude our talk with a varse of musick; and before Ahab could recover from amazement at the freedom of his new brother, and the mortification of my witnessing the scene, he was struck speechless with vexation at Dr. Query pulling out a flute from his pocket, and putting the parts together, with a great many flourishes, and a lot of baboon cries, wettin' the threaded ends in his mouth, and forcin' them together with main strength. Now, brudder, said he, spittin' on the eends of his fingers to make 'em stop better, if you and de entire stranger dere, pointin' to me, will strike up a varse of musick, ticklin' metre, I will jine you wid de flute,—

> Adam was de fust man
>   Eve was de tudder,
> Cain was a wicked man
>   Cause he killed his brudder.

Abel wasn't name right, was he, for he warnt "able" for Cain, by no manner
of means. But it makes beautiful musick, very beautiful indeed; you have
no notion of it, no more nor a child. It is the forty elebenth varse of
Brudder Sly's new ode: and he immediately commenced playing the air.
Come, brudder, said he, begin, and I will pitch it for you.

I thought Ahab would have fainted, he was so struck up all of a heap.
He knew I would tell the story all round the town, and he was as mad
as a hatter; for nothin' makes a man boil over so quick as to have to put
the cover on and keep the steam in. He was jist ready to bust, and make
all fly agin with rage. At last, said he, a tryin' to bite in his breath,—this
gentleman, Mr. Slick, has some business of importance to transact this
mornin' with me. I am afraid I cannot now join in the exercise; but some
other time will have the pl—pleas—. I will try to do it—Oh, says I, don't
mind me, Ahab, I beg; I should like it above all things. There is nothin' I
am so fond of as psalmody in consart with the flute. Dr. Query is right: it
makes excellent superior musick; so come, says I, let's try: our accounts has
kept for three years, they'll keep for half an hour longer; don't disappoint
the gentleman.— Yes, said Blackey, by golly, but it's grand, dat is de fack.
"Adam was de fust man;" and he sot off, in a voluntary agin.—Brother,
said Ahab, for he was obliged now to bolt that word,—my friend is not in
a frame of mind: he is not a man of *experience*. Put up your instrument. Let
us take another opportunity.—Well, the poor divil felt he warn't wonted
there at all. He seed Ahab was ashamed of him, and that pride, not business,
was the stumblin'-block; so he separated the joints of his flute, put them in
his pocket, and rose to depart.

Now, squire, continued the Clockmaker, p'raps you don't know, for you
can't have seed much of the blacks, but what I'm goin' for to tell you is a
fact, I assure you. When a nigger is frightened or vexed, there is a parfume
comes from him that's enough to stifle you. If you don't believe me, ask
Lord—Lord—what the plague is his name, that was out to the West Ingees.
Well, dancin' the emancipation dance with a black heifer there, e'en a'most
killed him. It did, upon my soul, it all but pison'd him. It's awful, that's a
fact. Well, this crittur Query so filled the room with it, it most choked me.
I was glad to see him get up for to go, I tell you; but what does he do but
come round to Ahab to take leave of him. Brudder, said he, fare-de-well,
peace be wid you, my lubbin' fren'; and he held out his great ily black
paw to shake hands with him. Poor Ahab! he looked like a crittur that is

a-goin' to be put in the stocks, resigned to his fate because he couldn't help himself, but mean enough too. He prided himself on his hand, did Ahab, it was so small and so white. He used to say it was 'ristocratic, and that it would be a fortin for a single man like him to England; and he actilly slept in gloves lined with pomatum to keep the freckles off; I hope I may be shot if he didn't. He was top-gallant-sail proud of them, I tell you: so he looked at the great piece of raw nigger meat that was afore him with horror; and arter makin' all sorts of wry faces at it, as a gall does when she takes physic, he shut his eyes and dropped his hand into it. Oh, it was beautiful! It did me good to see the hypocrite worked up that way. Query, shook and wrung away at it, as a washwoman does at a wet towel for ever so long; and at last he let go his hold and went off, and Ahab drew out his hand all stained yaller, as if it had been dipped into tobacco juice. He held it out from him at arm's length as a feller does that falls into the dirt, and a bitin' in his breath, and curlin' up his nose as mad as a bear with his tail shot off, and went into the bedroom, and washed and scrubbed away at it like anything. When he was gone, I opened the winders and ventilated the room; for it smelt as bad as one of the narrer alleys in Old Town Edinboro', or a slave-ship: it was shocking nosey, I tell you. As soon as he came back, says he, Sam, that poor feller means well, but he has mistaken his calling: he has too much levity, I fear, for a minister.—I give you joy, says I, of your new "brudder" and "feller-laborer in de wineyard." It sarves you right, so it does. If you had a-stuck to your own church, you wouldn't a-had to endure what you jist went thro', I know. No bishop would ordain that man; for he would see with half an eye he had no sense, and warn't no way fit for it at all, except to make things look ridikilous: but, if anybody can go and choose preachers that please, as they do hogreeves at town meetin's, why can't niggers elect whom they please too? It's a bad rule that won't work both ways. This comes o' schism: one error always leads to another. Now don't, for goodness' sake, make such everlastin' pretences as you do, unless your practice keeps up to your professions. I hate hypocrites, and I won't spare you. Whenever folks talk of you and the Slickville schism, hang me if I don't tell 'em of *the Black Brother.*

V

THE GREAT UNKNOWN

WELL, squire, said the Clockmaker, I'm glad you are goin' to England too. I can guide you thro' Britain as well as I can thro' the States, or the Provinces, for I've been there often; I know every part of it. They are strange folks them English. On pitikilars they know more than any people; but on generals they are as ignorant as owls. Perhaps there ain't no place in the world such nonsense is talked as in parliament. They measure every one by themselves as father did about his clothes. *He always thought hisn ought to fit all his boys, and proper laughingstocks he made of us.* Yes, you have made the Yankees and the blue-noses, squire, look pretty considerable foolish in them are two books of yourn. Stand on t'other tack now, and take a rise out of the British; for fair play is a jewel, that's a fact. John Bull had been a-larfin' at us until his sides heaves like a broken-winded horse: clap the currycomb on him now, and see if his hide is thicker than ourn; for he is always a-sayin' that the Yankees are the most thin-skinned people in the world. There is a grand field in that country, you may depend, and a noble harvest for you. Walk right into 'em with your sickle, and cut and bind till you are tired; you will find employment enough, I tell *you*. We may have our weak points, and I should like to know who the plague hasn't; but John has both his weak spots and soft spots too, and I'll pint 'em out to you, so that you can give him a sly poke that will make him run foul of a consternation afore he knows it. I'll show you how to settle his coffee for him without a fish-skin, I know; so begin as soon as you can, and as much sooner as you have a mind to.

On my own part, I was no less pleased to have him with me; for few men in British America have so intimate a knowledge of the character, feelings, and prejudices of the people of the colonies as Mr. Slick, or a more clear conception of the policy that ought to be pursued towards them by the mother country. So strongly was I impressed with this conviction, that I could not help expressing to him a hope that circumstances might arise during our visit to England to bring him in contact with some of the leading members of parliament, as I felt assured he could give most valuable and useful information on a subject which, though of immense importance, was but little understood.—Lord, sir, said he, I've seen some on 'em when I was there afore (for I've been three times to England) and know it well; but they didn't want the right information, and so I bammed them: they didn't want facts to make opinions on, but facts to tally with opinions formed, like British travellers in the States, and I always stuff such folks. I had a most curious ventur' when I wast last to London.

I had been down city all day a-skullin' about, and trampoosing everywhere a'most to sell some stock in the canal that is to run through the pine barrens in the Quahog Territory, that I bought for half nothin', and wanted to put off to advantage, and returned to my lodgings awful tired, and as wet-footed as a duck. I jist drawed off my boots, got snug afore the fire, with a cigar in my mouth and my feet on the back of a chair, a-toastin' of them to the coals, when the sarvant maid opened the door and a gentleman entered a-bowin' very ginteel, and sayin', Mr. Slick, I presume.—Well, says I, I won't say I ain't; but won't you come to an anchor and be seated: you must excuse me, says I, a-gittin' up, for my feet is wet. Well, he sot down and eyed me from head to foot, as if he thought I was a little onder baked, or not altogether right farnished in the upper story.—Our humid climate, says he, at last, must be very different from the cloudless sky and pure air of Nova Scotia.—Very, says I, it rains here for everlastingly. I have only seed the sun once since I came here, and then it looked as if it had the cholera in the black stage; but my feet is what I complain of most. Now, to home I wear ingian rubbers; but they don't do on the pavements here; for they make you slide about as if you was on the ice. I had to leave them of, for I pitched into every one I met a'most, and it warn't pretty at all.—How long is it, said he, since you left Nova Scotia?—Thinks I to myself, what in natur' is this crittur after. I'll jist draw him out by doin' simple. Now *that is natur', squire*. If ever you want to read a man, do simple, and he thinks he has a soft horn to deal with; and, while he s'poses he is aplayin' you off, you are puttin' the leake into him without his seein' it. Now, if you put on the knowin' it puts him on his guard directly, and he fights as shy as a loon. Talkin' cute, looks knavish; but talkin' soft, looks sappy. Nothing will make a feller bark up a wrong tree like that: so, without answerin' to the pint, (that I might bring him to his business,) says I—for wet feet there is nothin' like toastin' them afore the fire: it draws the cold out and keeps it from flyin' to the stomack, and saves you a fit of the mulligrubs p'raps. I larnt that from the Ingians; they always sleep with their feet to the fire, and at night lays all in a circle round it like the spokes of a wheel. I never yet seed an Ingian with a cold in his nose.—How *very* good, said he, what a close observer of natur' you are, sir. I shall remember that recipe of yours; it is excellent.—As much as to say well, if you don't beat Solomon, I bean't nobody. Thinks I to myself, I dare say you will mind it, but more to laugh at than foller at any rate.

At last, says he, thinkin' it was time to come to the pint, I am desired, sir, by a distinguished friend of mine, to request the favour of you to give him an interview whenever it may be convenient to you, as he has heard much of your knowledge of the provinces, and is anxious to get all the information he can previous to the Canada question coming on for discussion. — Hem! says I to myself, I wonder whether this is fact or bam. It don't seem to hang very well together nother, but it mought be a bee for all that, as the old woman said when she looked in the hornet's nest for honey. So to prove him, says I, as to convenience, let me see—I must consider a bit,—to-morrow I go to Bristol, by Great Western Railway, and next day I make tracks for New York, so if I go at all I must go now.—Now? said he.—I seed it posed him, that he didn't expect it so soon.—Now? said he agin, and he mused a bit; and then said he, I am sorry the time is so short, sir, but if you will be so kind, my carriage is at the door, and I will drive there as soon as you are ready, for my friend would be much disappointed in not having the pleasure of seeing you.—Civil enough too, thinks I, and as I never seed a parliamentary big bug, I should like the chance, if it was only like a colony delegate, to have it to brag on arter I got home; so I goes into the chamber, puts on a clean shirt-collar, slips on a pair of dry boots, and runs the comb through my hair. Now, says I, when I comes back to the sittin'-room, let's up killock and off, for it's getting on considerably well in the arternoon, and is a'most daylight down, and if he sets me a-goin' on colony subjects I won't know when to leave off, for it takes time to spin them yarns, I tell *you*. So we showed a leg right off, trotted down stairs, and into the coach in no time, and says he to the driver "home."—"Home!" says I to myself; why who the devil can this crittur be? is he member's son, or his writin' and cipherin' clerk, or a lover of one of the galls; or who is he that he says "home," for he must live there, that's sartain. Well, I didn't like to ask him direct, for I knew I'd find it out soon, and so I let it pass. And, squire, said he, among the wrong notions the British have of us Yankees, one is about our etarnal curosity, and axing questions for ever about nothin' a'most. Now, it happens to be jist the revarse; we are not famous for *axing questions*, but for never answerin' them. Arter a while the coach stopped, and afore I could look round I was in the hall, surrounded by officers of the Life Guards, drest in most beautiful toggery, at least so I took them to be, for their uniform was splendid; I never see anything to equal it except the President's on reviewin' the troops on the 4th July day. It made me wish I had brought my militia dress, for I didn't like one of our citizens to be out-done that way, or not to do credit to our great nation when abroad.

Excuse me a moment, said my guide friend, till I announce you; and presently out comes another dressed in plain clothes, and they stood there a space a-eying' of me and a-whisperin' together.—He won't do, said the new-comer: look at his boots.—It can't be helped, said the other, he *must* see him, he sent for him himself.—Who the devil is he? said the stranger. Is he a delegate or a patriot member of assembly, or what is he, for he is the queerest lookin' devil I ever saw?—Hush! said guide, he is the celebrated "Sam Slick," the Yankee clockmaker; and, said he, they may talk about that feller's shrewdness as much as they please, but he is the d—st fool I ever saw.

Well, says I to myself, this is rather pretty too, ain't it? I guess you think flashin' in the pan scares ducks, don't you? One thing is sartain, tho' you don't often look in the glass, anyhow, or you'd know the face of a fool when you see one, which is more than you do at this present time. With that, guide said to one of the sodger officers that was a-standin' in the hall a-doin' of nothin', Show him up. So one of them, a very tall handsome man with his head all covered with powder, like a rat in a flour barrel, come up and said, your name, if you please, sir?—Well, says I, I don't know as it matters much about names, what's yourn? Thomas, sir, said he, a-bowin' and a-smilin' very perlite.—Well then, said I, friend Thomas, mine is Mr. Slick, to the backbone.—I no sooner said the word than he bawled out Mr. Slick in my ear, as loud as he could roar, till he made me start again, and then every officer on the stairs, and there was several of them there, kept repeatin' after each other "Mr. Slick," "Mr. Slick," "Mr. Slick."— Don't be in such an everlastin' almighty hurry, said I, I am a-comin' as fast as I can, and if you do that are agin I won't come at all, so there now; for I began to get my Ebenezer up, and feel rather wolfish. When I came to the foot of the stairs the officer stood back and made room for me; and, says I, after you, sir; but he hung back quite modest (seein' that an American citizen ranks with the first man livin')—so not to be outdone in manners by a mere Britisher, I took him by the arm and pushed him on.—I can't think of goin' afore you, sir, said I, but don't let's lose time in ceremony; and besides you know the navigation better than I do, for I never was here afore; and then he went on first.

As I mounted the stairs I heerd guide friend say again to the other man in plain clothes, Didn't I tell you he was a fool!—Madman, I should think, said the other.—Presently a door opened, and I was showed into a room where member, who was nothin' but a common-sized man arter all, was standin' by the fire, and three or four young gentlemen in plain clothes was a-writin' at a table, as hard as they could lay pen to paper. The officer that opened the door roared out again, "Mr. Slick!" as loud as he could, and I raily felt so dander, I do believe I should have knocked him down if he hadn't a-stept back out of reach; but member came forrard very perlite, and shook me by the hand, and said it was very kind of me to come at such short notice, and that he was very happy to have the pleasure to see me. Then he jist gave a wave of his hand, and pointed to the door, as a hunter does to his dogs, without speakin', and the people writin' got up and went out backward, keepin' their faces to him and bowin'. Arter they were gone he said, take a chair, sir, if you please: so I took one for myself and lifted one for him, sayin', it was as cheap to sit as to stand, and every bit and grain as easy too; but he said he preferred standin', and kinder sorter looked at me, as much as to say, he was too good or too proud for that; so there he stood, his elbow on the mantel-piece and his head restin' on his hand. Well, my bristles began to stand right up, like a dog's back: I didn't like the talk of the guide friend he sent for me; I didn't like the way the officers kept bawlin' out my name and snickered in the entry, and I didn't relish the way I was sot down on a chair alone, like a man to be shaved in a barber's shop. I felt as if I could chew him right up, I was so mad, and I was determined to act as ugly as him, for my coming was his seeking and not my own; and, as there was nothin' to be made out of it, and no trade spiled, I didn't see as I had any occasion to put up with his nonsense, do you? for there is nothin' I hate so much as pride, especially when any of them benighted insolent foreigners undertake to show it to a free and enlightened American. So I jist put up my feet on his fender, free and easy, to show him he couldn't darnt me by his airs and graces, and then spit right atween the polished bars of the grate on the red-hot coals till it cracked like a pistol. Well, he jumped a yard or so, as if he was shot, and if you had seen the tanyard look he gin me, it would have made you split a-larfin. Don't be frightened, Lord, said I,—for I didn't know which house he belonged to, so I thought I'd give the title, as we call every stranger citizen Kurnel,—Lord, said I, I won't hit you; I could spit thro' a keyhole and not wet the wards; but as you stand, I believe I will too, for talk atween two don't come kinder nateral, unless both sit or both stand; and now, says I, as time presses, what may your business be with me, Lord? Well, he stood back two or three feet, as if he was afeered I would touch him, and then he entered into a long parlaver about the colonies, and asked me if the people was contented with the Government. Mr. Stranger Lord, said I, they are not, and that's a fact.

He brightened up when he heerd that; he seemed as if it pleased him, as if he would raither hear that than that they were satisfied. Thinks I to myself, a nod is as good as a wink to a blind horse. I see what you be; you are an agitator, and want grievances to work on; but you got the wrong sow by the ear this time, any how.—Ah, said he, your testimony is valuable, Mr. Slick, for you are an impartial man, and have had great opportunities of knowing the condition of the people. Do you attribute this discontent to the government that has prevailed there since the American revolution, or to causes over which we have no control?—To the Government, said I, some part, and some part to other causes, but to none over which you have no control.—Precisely, said he; that is exactly my view of it. Will you allow me, said he (a-tryin' to lead me on by doin' the civil,) to offer you some refreshment, sir; I ought to apologise to you for not having offered it before. Have you lunched yet?—Thank you, Lord, said I, I have dined, and harnt no occasion for nothin'.—Then what remedies do you propose? said he: how would a union do?—Cure all evils, said I: you have hit the right nail on the head; it's exactly the right medicine.—How singular, said he; and he rubbed his hands, and walked up and down the room several times, lookin' very pleased; and I thought I heerd him say, What will the Duke say to this? You have heerd, no doubt, said he, of responsible government; pray what is your opinion of that?—It is not only a good government, said I, but no country can be either happy or contented without it. It is absolutely indispensable; you will lose the colonies without you introduce it.—Mr.

Slick, said he, I have heered much of your sagacity from others, and your conversation fully confirms the high opinion I had formed of you. I am delighted to have the pleasure of making your acquaintance. When do you leave town? (English folks always begins that way, afore they axe you to take pot luck with them.)—In the mornin', bright and airly, said I: have you any commands that way?—No, thank you, said he; but would you have any objections to my ordering up those gentlemen you saw here jist now, to hear this very gratifying confirmation of my opinions?—Not the least in the world, said I; I don't care if all London hears it. So he rang the bell, and who should answer but the self-same officer that showed me in.

Tell those gentlemen, said Lord, that I desire their presence immediately; and here, you feller, don't let me hear any more laughing out there: don't you know I never permit any one to laugh in my house; and he looked as wicked as a meat-axe at him. He said nothin', but bowed down a'most to the carpet, like a Chinese tea-marchant, and backed out wrong eend foremost. Oh! dear, dear, said I to myself, what a fool *I be*; I might have known them was sarvants if I hadn't a-been a born idiot, and that rich parliament men could afford uniform for 'em, if they liked ; but we must live and larn, and everything must have a beginning, I do suppose. While the sarvant was gone, says the entire stranger, Mr. Slick, the party I belong to is a small but very influential one. It holds the balance between the other two. It occupies the centre, and keeps the others at equal distance, whose weights retain us in our place. By this means, whichever way we incline, we turn the scale. Your information therefore is all-important. Exactly, says I, if you can only manage to keep 'em jist so, and no farther, it will work beautiful; but if they pull apart ever so little, whap you come to the ground, like a feller atween two stools, and stand a chance to break your neck, and I hope to heavens you may not hurt yourself, if you do fall. He looked as striped as a rainbow at that; but he brightened up at the close, with a look as much as to say, you Yankees put your words very far apart, very far indeed; it makes things sound odd like.

When the gentlemen came in, Lord said, Mr. Slick fully confirms my views. He admits the discontent in the colonies, much of which he attributes to Tory misgovernment: he approves of the Union, and says nothing will calm the country but responsible government.—I do, said I; and, by your leave, I will explain what I mean.—Do, said he; but pray be seated; allow me to give you a chair: and we all sot down, and he among the rest. He forgot his pride that time. How, strange it is, squire, no man is so haughty and overbearin' as a democrat or radical; and they do tell me some even of the liberal lords beat all natur' for pride, actilly the highest in the instep of any of their order. *That comes of pretence now; a man that stoops lower nor he ought in some things, is plaguy apt to straighten himself over the perpendicular in others, to make up for it again.*—Now, says Lord, I wish you to hear this man's (gentleman's, says he, a-catchin' himself as quick as wink,) this gentleman's opinion yourselves. It is very satisfactory to have such good authority in our favour.—Discontent, says I, prevails to an alarmin' extent. It exists everywhere, (I'll move to have this feller examined before a committee, said he, a-whisperin' to my guide friend; the scoundrel is quite a god-send to us,) it pervades all classes, says I.—Good heavens! said he, I wasn't prepared to hear such a fearful account; but it's very satisfactory, very satisfactory indeed. Go on, sir; I am quite delighted.—Paradise wasn't good enough for some folks, says I: how can the colonies be? Them critturs there are not satisfied with the dispensations of Providence; how can you expect them to be so with the Government. They would like to have a Government to cost nothin', to have their bread grow'd ready baked, to be paid for eatin' it, and be fed with a silver spoon. *Union*, says I, that you inquired about, is most desirable, for it would heal all differences; but not a union of the provinces, for that would only open new sources of strife, and eend in your losin' 'em body and breeches; but a *responsible Government*, says I, is indispensable. Jist thin I took a squint out of the corner of my eye, and I see he began to smell a rat, and to look all adrift; so on I went, knee deep, and a foot deeper, a-pokin' it into him like fun. Men who rebel, says I, and commit murder and arson, ought to be held *responsible* for it, or you might as well be without any law at all, unless you like Lynch law best. Wherever you see loyalty, encourage it; and disloyalty, discourage it. Whatever changes is right, make them, and then tell them, now, that's the form that's settled; if you don't like it, leave the colonies, and go where you can find things more to your mind; but if you do stay there and rebel, you will be hanged, as sure as you are born. You shall have responsibility, *but it shall be the responsibility of crime to law, and of offenders to justice.*

Heavens and airth! if you had a-only seed stranger Lord, or whatever he was, how he looked, it would have done you good. It was as grand as a play. Oh, he was as mad as a hatter, and the madder because he couldn't help himself nohow he could fix it. He actilly looked as small as the little eend of nothin' whittled down. He was so bungfungered he couldn't speak, and t'other fellers looked as if they were afeerd of their lives to speak either. They seemed, them critturs, as if they darsn't call their souls their own, he kept them in such awe. Oh dear, what a bam it is for such men to talk liberal, when they actilly don't believe that they are made of the same clay as other folks. At last things began to look rather serious for a joke; so says I, risin' up and takin' my hat, I believe I must be a-movin', Lord, says I; and if I don't sail, as I some expect, I shall be back next week; and if you want to see further into matters, jist send for me, and I will come with pleasure; or if you want to examine me before that committee, tip the scoundrel a subpener, and he'll testify through a three inch plank for you. Do you take? (It made his teeth grit that, like two mill-stones; he grinned like a fox-trap: fact, I assure you.) Yes, says I, send for me, and I'll come; for you and I, I see, agree in opinion about them colonies 'zactly. Indeed you are the only man I've met since I came here that talks a word of sense about them. Good day. And I turned and walked out, guide and his companions follerin' me.—What a d—d hoax, said guide, a-whisperin' to the other. That feller is no fool, after all; he is more rogue than dunce that. He has given him a fit of the jaundice.—Do you know the name of the nobleman? said I; for I cannot conceive from your description who it can be, for there are many proud lords, and many wrong-headed one too.—No, said the Clockmaker, I can't even give a guess, for his coach carried me home, and I was so full of the bam I played off on him, I didn't mind to look at the name of the street; and he never sent for me agin, as you may calculate. I guess one dose was enough to do his business for him. I don't know nother whether he was a senator or a representative, Indeed, I don't know any lord to England. Some on 'em I hear brag that they were quite intimate with me when I was there; but that's only their boastin' to look big. No, I don't know his name, or whether he was upper or under-crust; but when I tell the story I call him the—*Great Unknown.*

VI

SNUBBING A SNOB

ON our arrival at the inn at Windsor we were shown into a spacious apartment, in some respects answering in appearance and use to an English coffee-room. At the upper end, near the window, sat a stranger, looking at rather than reading a newspaper.

Look there now, said Mr. Slick in an undertone, jist look there now, for goodness gracious sake! Did you ever see the beat of that? That is a Britisher I know him by the everlastin' scorny air he wears—for them benighted English think no one can see in the dark but themselves. He is what they call a snob that, and a full-fed one too; for when nuts grow ripe, hogs grow fat. He is a-doin' a bit of Paris that man, to astonish the weak narves of the natives with. He has been across the Channel, you see; and he has got a French barber to make him look like a bigger fool than he was afore he left home. Look at his hair, divided like on the top of his head, combed down straight over each ear, and fallin' full and curly on the cape of his coat; his mustachios squared out at each eend like the brush of a weasel's tail, and that little tuft of hair a-hangin' from his under lip, like a turkey-cock's beard. Ain't he enough to charm the heart of a kitchen broom stick, that's all? He looks for all the world like one of them ancient heads in the old picturs at the Jews' shops to London. Then see that chalky, white, bleached hand he is passin' leisurely over his mouth to show the flash rings on his fingers; and how slow he passes his eye from the paper over the room, to meditate knowin' like, as if he could see what's what, and take it all in at a draft. That goney is half puppy, half philosopher, I expect. How I would like to walk into him! It's such fun to "Snub a Snob," ain't it? and to knock the rust off of him! Oh, dear! I suppose we shall get some rael travellers at last, that do know somethin', for the dirt always goes before the broom. Jist so it is to Florida: a horse won't live there on a new farm, so they have to use asses till the pasture gets old and good, and the feed sweet. And I suppose, now we have got steam and good inns, these asses of travellers will get a walkin' ticket, and men of sense will take their place. I must say, if he only had a good strong horse sense, I'd like to show him how to tell a wood-chuck from a skunk; but he hante, that's clear; so I'll set him off on a hand-gallop, and then *snub him*—He accordingly walked over to that end of the room, and commenced making his acquaintance.

The conversation that ensued turned on the value of the North American Colonies; and although a native and a resident of one of them myself, I am free to admit I was not aware of the unlimited extent to which they are dependant on England for their manufactures, until my attention was drawn to it by the lively and pointed sketch of Mr. Slick. His utterance was so rapid that I fear I have missed some parts of his illustration, although I committed the substance of it to paper the same afternoon. I have only to regret that some of the opponents of the Colonies were not present to hear so triumphant a vindication of these neglected and undervalued possessions.

Tabular accounts few men read, and still fewer know how to appreciate. A personal application like the present, which shows the practical working of the trade, could it only be given in his own words, and his own peculiar manner, is worth a hundred of the dull speeches, and still duller articles of the modern political economists, for it establishes beyond all doubt this important fact, that these provinces are as much dependant on England for every article of manufacture used in them, as Oxford or Cambridge is, and that a colonial market is strictly and literally a home market.

I suppose, said Mr. Slick, you didn't come by the Great Western, did you?—I did, sir.—How was rice when you left England, and cotton? Have they riz in markit? How was they quoted when you quit? Biddle made a great spec' in cotton, didn't he. I guess some of the Liverpoolers will pass out of the leetle eend of the horn afore they are done yet, won't they?

These interrogatories, and many others, were all answered with great good-humour by the stranger, who appeared much amused with the ease and freedom of the Clockmaker's manner. At last Mr. Slick put the never-failing American question, "How do you like the country?" To this Snob replied in terms of great admiration of the beauty of the scenery, and the fertility of the soil; but being of the reform school of politicians, could see nothing that did not require change, and denounced all colonies in general, and the North American ones in particular, as useless and expensive incumbrances; stated his conviction that the day was not far distant when they would demand their independence; that the sooner both parties separated the better it would be for them, and that true wisdom, as well as their mutual interest, dictated immediate separation. He concluded by asking Mr. Slick if he did not concur in that opinion?

Well, said, the Clockmaker, I will give you my opinion, free gratis for nothin', if you won't be offended.—Oh! certainly not, said Snob. I shall not only not be offended, but most happy to hear your views; the object of travelling is not to disseminate one's own opinions, but to hear those of others.—Well, then, said Mr. Slick, like begets like in a gineral way, for it's a law of natur'. Horses, do ye see, beget horses, owls beget owls, and asses beget asses—it never fails; and stupid parents seldom nor ever have wise children. Now I ain't a-goin' to say that John Bull is a cussed, stupid, thick-headed old goney, (for I don't mean no offence, stranger, but only to argue it out plain, and nothin' parsonal, and because it wouldn't be pretty talk that,) but I estimate he *is* a considerable some tho, and if Blue-nose is a leetle soft like, a leetle onderbaked or so, why it's no great wonder considerin' the stock he comes of. John Bull has got a'most a grand estate in these colonies, and a'most an excellent market, too, and don't know nothin' about either—fact, I assure you; and if it warn't they speak better English here than the British do, you would fancy yourself at home a'most, *for everything you hear, see, or touch here, is English.* Jist look at Blue-nose and see what a woppin', great, big, two-fisted crittur he is: you won't find such a made man nowhere a'most. He is more nor six foot high in his stocking feet, (and he has got 'em to put on, too, which is more nor half the British have,) as strong as a horse, and as supple as an eel. Well, when he is born, he isn't much bigger than a kitten; a squallin', squeelin', kicken, ongainly little whelp as you ever see a'most. Now, what is the first thing they do with him? Why, they wash the young screetch owl in an English bowl; wrap him up in English flannel, and fasten it with English pins; and then dress him in an English frock, with an English cap trimmed with English lace. If the crittur is sick, they give him English physic with an English spoon; and the very first word he larns to speak is "*English.*" As soon as he begins to use his trotters, and run about, he has an English hat, shirt of English linen, coat of English cloth, and shoes of English leather. Arter that they send him to school, an' he writes with an English pen, made from an English quill by an English knife, uses English ink out of an English inkstand, and paper made in your country, and ruled with an English pencil. He spells out of an English dictionary, and reads out of an English book. He has

hardly learned what Ampersand means, afore they give him a horse, such
as it is, and he puts an English bridle into his mouth, and an English saddle
on his back, and whips the nasty, spavin'd, broken-winded brute, with an
English whip; and when he stumbles, and throws him off, he swears a
bushel of horrid English oaths at him, trims the great, shaggy, hairy beast
with English scissors; combs his nasty thick mane with an English comb,
and curries his dirty hide with an English curry comb; and then ties him
up in his stall with an English halter. Then comes sportin'; and, to give the
crittur his due, he ain't a bad shot nother, seein' that he is fond of fowlin',
or troutin', or anything but work. Gunnin' is his delight; and a wild-duck,
a moose, or a carriboo, when they see him a-comin' to parsecute them,
know it's gone goose with them. But where does his gun come from?
and his powder? and his shot? and his flask? and his belt? why, clean away
from England. Even his flint comes from there, for there ain't a flintstone
in all Nova Scotia; and if there was, the crittur couldn't cut it into shape
so as to be any use. He hante the tools; and if he had, he don't know how.
That's the reason, I suppose, anyone a'most can "fix his flint for him." It's
more nateral this should be the case in gunnin' than in fishin'; but even
here the chap can't help himself. Tho' the country is covered with wood,
he imports his rod, his net, his line, his leads, and even his flies. He does,
upon my soul! altho' the forest is filled with flies big enough and strong
enough to bite thro' a boot. As soon as his beard comes, (and sometimes
afore, for I have known boys actilly shave *for* a beard,) why he goes and
gets a British glass to admire his young mug in; he lathers his chin with an
English brush and English soap, a-lookin' as big as all out doors, and mows
away at it with an English razor, sharpened on a British bone, and stropped
on a British strop; then he puts on an English collar, and ties it up with
an English stock, and I hope I may be skinned if he don't call himself an
English*man*. A chip of the old block he is too: and young Blue-nose is as
like old John as two peas, the same proud, consaited, self-sufficient, know-
nothin' crittur; a regular gag, that's a fact.

Why really, sir, said Snob, who was much and very justly offended at this
indecent language, I don't understand ———. Oh! but you will understand,
said Mr. Slick, if you only hear me out. In a giniral way, 'bout this time he
begins to feel raither pitikilar, and he pays a visit to the "tropolis," to see
the world, for a man that hante been to the capitol has see'd nothin'; so,
instead of taking a continental trip, as British boys do, he takes a coastin'

trip in his father's shollop to that are great city of great men, Halifax. He fills his first office in this life, supercargo of two or three jags of fire-wood, a dozen birch-brooms, a basket of bad eggs, a sick calf, and a measly pig; and, when he has squandered all the proceeds of the plunder a-larnin' to drink and swear like a man, he comes to tell of the wonderful sights he has see'd, and talk reform politics. But, look to his vessel, ropes, sails, blocks, anchor, bolts, copper, iron, compass, and all the fixin's—where do they come from? Why, from where every part of the vessel except the sappy, buggy, dry-rotted wood she is built with comes from—from England. Look at the old, battered watch he is rigged out with, the case half lead, half pewter, that he swapped his wood for on the wharf with a woman with a painted face and dirty stockings, who cheated him by calling him "captain," and "squire," and "your honour; where did that watch, and that old trull come from?—from England, like the rest.

The next thing the sinner looks out for is a gall, for few created critturs go a-gallin' so early as he does. He is hardly cleverly growed up and cut his mother's apron-string afore he is spliced. He never waits till he has a place to put his wife in, or anything to support her with; he trusts luck for that, catches the bird first and then makes the cage. Well, see how he goes about that; he cuts down the trees to build it with an axe of English iron, saws it with an English saw, planes it with an English plane, puts its together with English nails, driven by an English hammer, and then paints it with English paint and an English brush. The sashes has English glass, kept in by English putty; the doors are hung upon English hinges, and secured by English locks (against British thieves tho', for they forgot to reform them afore they shipped them out); the floor is covered with imported carpets, the windows with imported curtains, and the fire made in imported stoves, and fixed with imported tongs and shovels. When he gives a house-warmin' to his friends, for he is rather amorous of a frolick, the plates, knifes and forks, decanters and glasses, and everything else is English, and when the boys and galls go for to dance, hear the musick, that's all! Pretty musick it is too, afore tunes came in fashion, I guess; but hear it. English fifes, English flutes, English drums, English pianoes, and English fiddles (not to mention Scotch ones, of which mum is the word). But what's the use of talkin'. If I was to tell you what they have got that they have to send to Britain for, it would take a month; but I'll tell you what don't come: wood, water, stone and airth, is all that they can call their own, that doesn't come from England, unless it be a few thousand wooden clocks I introduced here, to let 'em know when grog time of day comes. Well, the next house Blue-nose gets into is a small one, where his nose and his toes touches the roof. You'd think he was done with England now, and that he could take nothin' out of the world with him, no more than he brought into it; but he ain't finished yet. The goney wouldn't die happy if this was the case. He don't like to be separated from English manufactures even in death, for he is so used and so attached to the Old Country, that he calls his own native land Nova Scotia, and England he calls—what do you think now? why, he *calls it* "*home;*" he does, upon my soul! No, sir, the grave don't part 'em, nor death shut his pan nother, for, as soon as he is stiff, he is dressed in an English shroud, and screwed down with English screws into his coffin, that is covered with English cloth, and has a plate on it of English ware, for the worms to read his name and age on, if they have larned to spell. The minister claps on an English gownd, reads the English sarvice out of an English book, and the grave is filled up agin with airth shovelled in with an English shovel, while every man, woman, and child that bears his name pulls out an English handkerchief, to wipe their eyes and blow their noses with, and buy as much English black cloth, crape, and what not, as would freight a vessel a'most; for, havin' larned the multiplication table airly in life, the number of his descendants would make you stare, I know. His children run the same rig round the same course, till they eend by being packed up in a snug pill-box in the same grave-yard. And yet, John Bull says, colonies are no good. Why the man is a drivelin', snivelin', divelin' idiot, an everlastin' born fool, that's a fact.

This second outbreak was more than the good-natured stranger could endure, and though amused myself at the rhodomontade style of his argument, I could not but participate in the annoyance he felt at these gross national reflections.

Really, sir, said Snob, this is too much.—I—I'll cut it short then, said Mr. Slick, again misunderstanding him; but it's true, sir, for all that. Now how is colonist *able to pay for all* this almighty swad of manufactured plunder, seein' that he has no gold nor silver; why, mainly *by his timber*, and yet them onfakilised, onderbaked goneys, the British, actilly want to tax it and reform out the trade, so as to give a preference to Baltic timber. We don't want colony timber, says they.—Don't you tho', says Blue-nose, then I hope we may be tetotally extinctified if we want your manufactures.—

What's the name of your great gun to Canada?—you mean Sir John Colbourne, said Snob.—No, replied Mr. Slick, I don't mean the "man-o' war," I mean the "marchant man." Oh! I have it, Pullet Thompson. Well, Pullet will larn somethin' to Canada about timber he never knew afore, or it ain't no matter. When you see him, stump him; friend Pullet, says you, when a log is hewed and squared can you tell the south side of it? and if he don't answer it right off the reel (and I'll go my death on it he can't) tell him to send out the Board of Trade, ay, and the Board of Works too, to Sam Slick the Clockmaker, to go to school for a spell, for he is jist the boy can teach 'em something that ain't sot down in the Reform Bill, knowin' coons as they be. Yes, sir, if ever you was to Antwarp, you'd see what it is to lose colonies. When that place belonged to Holland, and had colonial trade, five thousand marchants used to meet on 'Change; now the Exchange is left, but the marchant is gone. Look at the great docks built there at so much expense, and no shipping there. Look at one man-of-war for a navy that has a pennant as long as from to-day to the middle of next week, that can't get out for the Dutch forts, is of no use in, and if it did get out has no place to go to. Buonaparte said he wanted ships, colonies, and commerce; one fool makes many! Every delegate, patriot, and humbug, that goes from here to London, if he gets by accident to a public dinner (for folks to see he ain't black), and is asked for a toast, rises up, lookin' as wise as a donkey, and says, "Ships, colonies and commerce!" till it becomes a standin' toast. Buonaparte was a fool, and didn't know what he was a-talkin' about, for *colonies means all three*. Them that have colonies will lose the other two along with them. Yes, John Bull is a blamed blockhead, a cus—— Excuse me, said the stranger, rising and effecting his escape at last; but really, sir, your language is so offensive you must permit me to retire, and he very properly left the room.—Well, I didn't mean to offend him nother, said Mr. Slick, I vow. There was no occasion for him to hop about as mad as a parched pea that way, was there? I am sorry he kicked afore he was spurred tho', for I was only speakin' in a giniral way like. I wish he had a-heerd me out too, for I was only a-breakin' of the crust when he began to look all wrath that way. I hadn't got rightly into the subject; I only spoke of manufactures, but that is merely one item; there are many other political ones that he never heerd of, *I* know. But what can you expect of such critturs? all they can do is to grunt like a pig at corn time. The way they don't know nothin' is most beautiful, and them that make speeches to England about the colonies too. There ain't, p'raps, no one subject there is so much nonsense talked about as these provinces: it's ridiculous, it makes me larf so it actilly busts my waistcoat buttons off; it fairly gives me a stitch in the side; and I must say I do like, when I get a chance, to "*Snub a Snob.*"

VII

PATRIOTISM, OR THE TWO SHEARS'S

AS soon as the conversation related in the preceding chapter had ceased, I committed the heads of it to paper, and as I intended to proceed on the following day to New Brunswick, I retired early, in order to secure a good night's rest. In this expectation, however, I was disappointed. The bar, which adjoined my bedroom, now began to fill with strangers, travelling to and from the capital, and the thin wooden partition that separated us was insufficient to exclude the noise of so many voices. After awhile the confusion gradually subsided, by the greater part of the persons withdrawing to their several apartments, and the conversation assumed a more distinct and intelligible shape. The topic appeared to be the delegation sent from Canada on the subject of alleged grievances, and I was glad to find that, with the exception of one or two noisy illiterate persons, every individual deplored the agitation that had recently affected the colonies, and denounced the system of "grievance mongering" that had prevailed of late years, as having a tendency to retard the real improvement of the country, and discourage the loyal and respectable portion of the inhabitants.

Jist so, said a person, whose voice I at once recognised as that of Mr. Slick's—jist so, stranger you are jist about half right, and there is no two ways about it. Delegations are considerable nice jobs for them who want a ride across the Atlantic at the public expense, for nothin'; for demagogues, place-hunters and humbugs that want to make the na*tives* stare when they get back, by telling how big they talked, and what great things they did, to the great people and to the big-wigs to home. *I* did this,—*I* did that,—and so on. That's what Mackenzie did when he told his folks to Canada, when he returned from delegatin', that he seed the King, who was very civil to him, and took a glass of grog with him; and told him he was sorry he couldn't ask him to dine with him that day, for the Queen was very busy, as it was white washin' day to the palace, and they was all in hubbub.—For, Mac., said he (smilin' like a rael salt-water sailor), these leetle things, you know, must be done for kings as well as subjects, and women is women,

whether their petticoats are made of silk or cotton, and the dear critturs
will have their own way,—eh, Mac.! Our washin' we put out, but house
cleanin' must be done in the house or not done at all, and there is no
two ways about it: you understand one, Mac.? Tell my people, when you
return, if my governors don't behave better, d—n 'em, I'll hang one or
two of them as an example! Good-b'ye, Mac.—And some on 'em was
fools enough to believe the goney and his everlastin' lockrums, that's a
fact. Yes, delegations play the very old Nick with a country. They hurt
its credit, stop emigration, reform out decent folks, and injure its trade.
People are afeer'd of a country where there is agitation, for agitation is
what the doctors call in cholera the premonitory symptom; a sign that if
active measures are not taken, rebellion ain't far off. But you colony chaps
are gulled from year's eend to year's eend, hang me if you ain't. You are a
nation sight too well off, so you be, and if you was taxed like us Yankees,
or the ignorant British, and had to move round and mind your stops, so as
to make two eends cleverly meet together when the year is out, it would
be better for you, I guess. One half of you don't know what you are talkin'
about; and other half are goin' the whole figur' for patriotism.

Lord, I shall never forget a rise I once took out of an old Colonel, to
Bangor, the Honorable Conrad Corncob. He rose to be a gineral arterwards,
but then he was only a kurnel, and it's very odd, but you can tell a kurnel
as far as you can see him. They're all got a kind of school-master look, as
much as to say, I am bothered to death with my boys, and will wallop the
first one I catch like blazes that comes with his "please sir, may I go out."—
"Master, here's Pete a-scroudgein," and so on. It's all wrote as plain in their
face as a handbill. Well, he was ravin' about the disputed territory, a-blowin'
up Mr. Harvey, the Governor of New Brunswick, sky high, and say what
he would do agin' the Britishers, and, at last he says, a-turnin' to me and
a-rollin' up his eyes like a duck in thunder—Mr. Slick, says he, "dulce est
pro patria mori."—What in natur' is that? says I, gineral, for I've forgot
what little Latin minister larned me at night-school; and, in fact, I never
was any great shakes at it, that's a fact.—Why, says he, "it's a sweet thing to
die for one's country."—Well, I don't know, says I, what you may think, but
somehow or another, I kinder think it a a plaguy sight sweeter thing to live
by one's country; and besides, says I, I don't translate that are Latin line that
way, at all.—Possible? says he: I don't see no other meanin' to it at all.—I
do then, says I, and this is the way I turn it into English: "mori" the more

I get, "pro patria" by the country, "dulce est" the sweeter it is. And that's what I call patriotism in these days.—Says he, Mr. Slick and he looked all round to see nobody was within and then puttin' his fingers on his nose, says he, Mr. Slick, I see you are up to snuff, and that it ain't easy to pull the wool over your eyes; but atween you and me and the post, it wouldn't be a bad thing to be on full pay as a gineral for the winter months, when a body can't do no business in the timber line to home, would it? and my two sons on the staff, one on 'em with the rank of captain and the other of major; do you take?—To be sure I do, says I? I take well enough; and if them Maine folks will be such almighty "maniacks," as I call 'em, as to send out troops to the Brunswick line, you'd be a fool if you didn't make your ned out o' them as well as anybody else, that's a fact.—But, Mr. Slick, said he, mum is the word, you know; keep dark about it, and I'll show you how to put the leake into folks; and then turnin' round and puttin' himself in the fix of Webster, Clay, and some o' them great-guns, he made as if he was addressin' of an assembly of citizens. Now, said he, I'll show you how I talk into them about the boundary. "Will you sell your birth-right, my fellow citizens? will you sell your birth-right to the proud and insolent British? I await your answer. Will none speak? Then none will be so base. Will you tamely submit to have your sacred soil polluted by benighted foreigners? No; let Maine answer indignantly, No; let Florida echo it back; let the mountains and valleys, the lakes and the rivers, take it up, and reverberate in thunder; No. No, fellow citizens, let us rather rally round the star-spangled banner of our great and glorious country. Let us, choosing that day that is consecrated to fame by the blood and heroism of our ancestors, the great day of independence, plant our flag on the terri*tory*, and rampart it round with the bodies of our free and enlightened citizens. 'Dulce est pro patria mori.'"— And then he bust out a-larfin', and staggered like over to the sophy, and laid down and haw-hawed like thunder.—Well, Slick, said he, when he came too, what darned fools mankind are, to be so easily gulled by that are word patriotism! ain't they? It fairly beats all, don't it?— Now, strangers, said the Clockmaker, that's pretty much the case with delegations. As long as them missions arc profitable things, delegates will be as plenty and grievances as thick as hops. If I was the minister I would receive them folks very civilly, and attend to their business if they had any, *and was recommended by the Governor:* but I never would encourage agitation, and hold out a premium for it, by rewardin' *agitators themselves* with appointments. *A trade won't be followed long that ain't a profitable one, that's a fact.* I'll tell you a story.—Do, said the company; let's hear your story: and the motion of the chairs indicated a closing in of the listeners round the speaker.—About forty years ago, or thereabouts, I think it is, said Mr. Slick, if my memory sarves me right, there was a rebellion to Ireland. Patriots were as thick as toads, arter a rainstorm; they was found in every man's path a'most, and they stirred up a tempestical time of it, you may depend. They began with grievances and speech-makin', and all that are sort of thing, jist as they did t'other day to Canidy, and it eended the same way. It was put down arter a good many poor deluded critturs lost their lives in the field. Then came the day of reckonin', and they caught some o' the leaders and hanged them, tho' most of the first chopmen cut and run, as they always do in such like cases, considerable cranky. Among the rest that they nabbed was two brothers, the two Shears's. Well, folks pitied these two men a good deal, too; they said they railly was in airnest, and had no private eends to sarve, like most of the patriots, but was led astray by artful men. They said that nothin' could excuse the horrid murders, and blood, and distress caused by their doin's; but still, somehow or an other, there was so much courage and darin', and eloquence, and elevation of mind like, about these men, they did raily grudge the gallus its due, that time, anyhow, and kind o' sorter felt as if they'd a-been glad if they had got off. But no. Nothin' would do. Government said a just severity would be marcy in the eend, for it would deter men from follerin' sich a bad example, and they was jist hanged and beheaded. It excited quite a sensation like. People felt considerable streaked about it, pitied 'em, mourned 'em, and, as usual, forgot 'em. Well, last summer I was to Dublin, and, arter I had finished my trade there, havin' a little time on my hands, I goes about to see the Castle, Custom House, College, and what not of curosities; for Dublin is worth seein', I tell you; it takes the shine off of most cities, and, at last I heard, there was a place under St. Michan's church where bodies never decayed one mite or morsel, but kept as fresh as the day they died, and as sweet as a pot of butter in an ice-house. So, thinks I that's curious too; hang me, if I don't go and see it. I have heerd tell of such a thing, but I never see the like of that, and it must be worth lookin' at. So off I sot, with an old East India Captain, that was a-stayin' here, to the Shelburne Inn, to Stephen's-green—quite a spooney old boy as you'd see in a hundred—and when I got to the church, I hired the old saxton woman, or whatever they call her, to let me in. What does she do but lights two candles; one on 'em she gives me, and t'other one she keeps in her own hand, and onlockin' the door, down we goes into the vault. Well, there warn't any onpleasant smell in it at all, tho' the floor seem covered with fat crumbly black soil like, that felt greasy onder foot, and, as far as I know, might a-been human; and railly, as I am a livin' sinner, I hope I may die this blessed minit if the warn't jist as nateral as life. Well, there were three on 'em on the floor: two on 'em, that was men, had their heads off; but the third was a woman; and the coffins had rolled off and fallen away to powder; and they had nothin' over them at all, but there they laid on the floor like dead dogs, as naked as when they was born. Well, says I to the woman, says I, if that don't beat all, too: why nothin' has decayed about them men, but the chords of their necks. Their heads is off; how strange that is, ain't it? what made their heads go for it? and no other part? what on airth is the meanin' o' that?—Here another general move of the chairs in the bar-room showed the increasing interest of the company in his narrative, as they closed in still further, and contracted their circle.—Why, their heads ain't gone, your honor, said she (for all Irish people say your honor to you when there is anything to be got by it), they have got them in their laps, and are a-holdin' of them in their hands: see, and she lifted up one of their heads, and turned its ghastly face round towards me, and its eyeless socket stared horrid; while the mouth, all contracted, showed the teeth and looked wicked ugly, I tell you, with an expression o' pain and sufferin' that was dreadful to behold. I didn't get that head out o' my head one while, I tell you. It fairly harnted me; and I fancied I seed it arterwards, when I went to bed, for the matter of two or three nights, one arter the other. Dead bodies ain't very pretty things at no time; I can't jist say I am fond of them, and I 'most wonder somehow, how doctors don't get sick of them too. Brother Eldad was always a buyin' of them, jist for the pleasure of whitlin' of them, with his knife, and every draw and trunk he had, a'most, had an arm, or leg, or somethin' or another in it. I believe in my soul, he never buried one agin' that he dug up, for he seemed to owe the worms a grudge, so he did; but as I was a-sayin', they had their heads in their laps. Well, says I to the old' woman, says I, is that St. Dennis? for he is the only man I ever heerd tell of that ondertook to walk of with his head onder his arm arter that fashion—who onder the sun is he?—Why, says she, them two men are two brothers: they was hanged and beheaded in the rebellion; they are "*the two Shears's;*" hante they kept well

Patriotism

intirely. Now give that cratur next to your honor, said she, a prod with the foot and turn him over, and see how beautiful the corpse looks, where the air ain't come to the back.—No, says I, not I indeed; I always feel kinder onswoggled like, at dead bodies; it makes my flesh crawl all over, and I won't lay foot to him for nothin', a'most, for it's ondecent to kick 'em about with your foot that way, as if it was a carcass of pork.—Why they won't bite your honor, said she, tho' they do show their teeth; and by the powers, I am not afeered of any man that ever was, dead or alive; so I'll give him a roll over if you 'd like to see the other side of him. He, is as light as a baby, he is so dry.—No, says I, jist let him be; it don't seem jist altogether right. Let him be where he is. Well, then, said she, observe, your honour, how nateral the limbs look. See the great toe, how it forks out, strainin' as if seekin' for support for the body, when hangin; and the chords of the legs, how hard and crampt they be. The hands, too, are convulsed, and the fingers clenched in the agonies like of a violent death It's a beautiful sight entirely. People say they are great curosities, them, and that it's worth goin' many a long mile to see, and a crown piece to get a sight of them. Most gentlemen give me five shillings for my trouble; and once, Lord Argent gave me a sov——

Well, well, says I, a-stoppin' of her gab about the pay, for women in a gineral way never lose sight of the main chance one blessed minit—well, says I, "is this the reward of patriotism," to be hanged and beheaded, and then left kicking about here on the floor, like dead rats? Lawful heart! why don't them patriots (for some on 'em are the top of the pot now) why don't they clap 'em into a coffin, bury 'em decently and put a monument over and show their pity or their gratitude, if they have any. If it ain't fit to make a fuss about folks that was hanged and they actilly did desarve what they caught that time, why on airth hante they the decency to inter 'em privately, and jist put up a stone with their names on it, to show where they be, and who they be? It's enough to make a man sick of patriotism this, I'll be hanged myself if it ain't. It is hard to say which is wus, to see patriots forgit their country, or the country forgitten patriots, for it happens both ways.—Don't call it patriotism, said the Sea Captain, who stood all the time a-sniflin' and a snivelin' like a child, (he did, upon my soul!) don't dignify the crime o' rebellion, which is an offence against the laws of God and man, by such a name. The innocent blood which they caused to be poured out like water called for the just but heavy retribution of shedding their own.—Well, says I, them whose cause they took hold on might bury 'em, at any rate. It wouldn't hurt 'em one might or morsel to do that much, I am sure.—Patriots, said he, in gineral, are too busy in consartin' schemes for their own aggrandizement to have time to think of the dead, or care for the livin' either. The very name of patriot awakens no other idea than that of the cowardly assassin, or midnight incendiary. Patriotism, and the worst species of crime have become synonymous.— Call 'em Pat-*riots*, then, says I, if you please, or christen them anything you like; but they ought to be buried, anyhow.—So they had ought, said he. Poor unfortunate men! the victims of your own folly, and the villany of your more subtle and designing accomplices, I pity you—I pity you from my heart, and will ask permission to perform the last sad office for you, and see that your bodies repose in peace at last. Ah! my good friend, said he, had they read their Bible more, and seditious pamphlets less, they might have escaped this ignominious end. They would have observed the precept of the Psalmist. "Fear God, honour the King, *and meddle not with them that are given to change*."—Stranger, said I,—for I didn't see what right he had for to go for to preach to me,—as for fearin' the Lord, says I, I guess I was always brought up to that since I was knee high, or so, to a chaw of tobacco; and as for a king, we hante got none, and ain't likely to have one. We have nothin' but a President, and he is a divil outlawed, for he is nothin' but a miserable, dispicable Loco Foco. Now, says I, if you can find anywhere that an everlastin' miserable skunk of a Loco Foco is desarvin' of honour, why ———; but he wouldn't hear me out, but jist walked away a bit, a-sayin' of oh! oh! oh! as if he had a fit of the cholic, and a-wavin' of his hand up and down, as a freemason does at a funeral. The crittur was a considerable of a spooney, that's a fact; but, greenhorn as he was, he warn't far out in his latitude about politics, I tell you. Whenever I hear how sweet it is to die for one's country, patriotism, and such stuff, I always think of them two Shears's, and the re ward they got at the time, and now receive from posterity, "*for meddlin' with them that are given to change*."

VIII

TOO KNOWING BY HALF

INSTEAD of embarking at Windsor in the steamer for New Brunswick, as we had originally designed, Mr. Slick proposed driving me in his waggon to Horton by the Mount Denson route, that I might have an opportunity of seeing what he pronounced to be some of the most beautiful scenery in the province. Having arranged with the commander of the boat to call for us at the Bluff, we set out accordingly a few hours before high-water, and proceeded at our leisure through the lower part of Falmouth. Mr. Slick, as the reader no doubt has observed, had a good deal of extravagance of manner about him, and was not less remarkable for his exaggeration of language, and therefore I was by no means prepared to find a scene of such exquisite beauty as now lay before me. I had seen at different periods of my life a good deal of Europe, and much of America; but I have seldom seen anything to be compared to the view of the Basin of Minas and its adjacent landscape, as it presents itself to you on your ascent of Mount Denson; and yet, strange to say, so little is it known or appreciated here, that I never recollect to have heard it spoken of before, as anything remarkable. I am not writing a book of travels, and shall not attempt, therefore, to describe it. I am sketching character, and not scenery, and shall content myself by recommending all American tourists to visit Mount Denson. It is an old saying of the French, that he who has not seen Paris has seen nothing. In like manner, he who travels on this continent, and does not spend a few days on the shores of this beautiful and extraordinary basin, may be said to have missed one of the greatest attractions on this side of the water. Here, too, may be studied the phenomena of tides, that are only presented to the same extent in one other part of the world; while the mineralogist and geologist will find much to employ and interest him. It possesses, also, the charm of novelty. It lies out of the beaten track, and is new. In these days of steam how long will this be the case anywhere? While musing on this subject my attention was directed by Mr. Slick, who suddenly reined up his horse, to a scene of a different description.

There, said he, there is a pictur' for you, squire. Now that's what minister would call love in a cottage, or rural felicity, for he was fond of fine names was the old man.—A neat and pretty little cottage stood before us as we emerged from a wood, having an air of comfort about it not often found in the forest, where the necessaries of life demand and engross all the attention of the settler. Look at that crittur, said he, Bill Dill Mill. There he sets on the gate, with his go-to meetin' clothes on, a-doing of nothing, with a pocket full of potatoes, cuttin' them up into small pieces with his jacknife, and teachin' a pig to jump up and catch 'em in his mouth. It's the schoolmaster to home, that. And there sets his young wife a-balancin' of herself on the top rail of the fence opposite, and a-swingin' her foot backward and forrerd, and a-watchin' of him. Ain't she a heavenly splice that? By Jacob's spotted cattle what an ankle she has! Jist—look a rael corn-fed heifer that, ain't she? She is so plump she'd shed rain like a duck. Them Blue-noses do beat all in galls, I must say, for they raise some desperate handsome ones. But then there is nothin' *in* that crittur. She is nothin' but wax-work—no life there; and he looks tired of his bargain already,—what you called fairly onswaggled. Now don't speak loud, for if she sees us she'll cut and run, like a weasel. She has got her hair all covered over with paper-curls, and stuck thro' with pins, like a porcupine's back. She's for a tea-squall to-night, and nothin' vexes women like bein' taken of a nonplush this way by strangers. That's matrimony, squire, and nothin' to do; a honeymoon in the woods, or young love grow'd ten days old. Oh, dear! if it was me, I should yawn so afore a week, I should be skeerd lest my wife should jump down my throat. To be left alone that way idle, with a wife that has nothin' to do and nothin' to say, if she was as pretty as an angel, would drive me melancholy mad. I should either get up a quarrel for vanity sake, or go hang myself to get out of the scrape. A tame, vacant, doll-faced, idle gall! O Lord! what a fate for a man who knows what 's what, and is up to snuff! Who the plague can live on sugar-candy? I am sure I couldn't. Nothin' does for me like honey; arter a while I get to hate it like sin; the very sight of it is enough for me. Vinegar ain't half so bad; for that stimulates, and you can't take more nor enough of it if you would. Sense is better nor looks any time; but when sense and looks goes together, why then a woman is worth havin', that's a fact. But the best of the joke is, that crittur Bill Dill Mill has found out he "knows too much," and is most frettin' himself to death about it. He is actilly pinin' away so, that it will soon take two such men put together to make a shadow; and this I will say, that he is the first feller ever I met that actilly was "*too knowin' by half.*" But time progresses, and so must we, I guess.

The noise of the waggon, as Mr. Slick anticipated, soon put the young bride of the woods to flight, and a few hasty and agile bounds carried her to the house; but her curiosity proved quite as strong as her vanity, for the paper head was again visible, peeping over the window-blind. The bridegroom put up his knife with an air of confusion, as if he was half ashamed of his employment, and, having given a nod of recognition to Mr. Slick, turned, and followed his wife into the cottage.

That is the effect, said Mr. Slick, of a want of steady habits of industry. That man lives by tradin', and bein' a cute chap, and always gitting the right eend of the bargain, folks don't think it a profitable business to sell always to a loss; so he says he is ruined by *knowin' too much*.—Ah! said he to me the other day, I don't know what on airth I shall do, Mr. Slick; but I am up a tree, you may depend. It's gone goose with me, I tell you. People have such a high opinion of my judgment, and think *I know so much*, they won't buy nor sell with me. If I go to an auction, and bid, people say, Oh, if Bill Dill Mill bids, then it must be cheap, and it goes beyond its valy right away. If I go to sell anything, every one thinks I wouldn't sell it if I hadn't a very good reason or it, for I am *too knowin' for that*. If I offer to swap, I only stamp a valy on the thing I want, and put it right out of my reach; for the owner wouldn't let *me* have it at no rate, but doubles his price, and goes and says, Bill Dill Mill offered me so much for it, and everybody knows he only offers half a thing is worth. I can't hire a help for what anybody else can, for the same reason; and I had to marry before I was ready, or had quite made up my mind to it; for I knew folks would think twice as much of my gall as soon as they knew I was after her. Darn it, said he, if they said I was a fool, I wouldn't a-minded it a bit; or said it was luck, or anything. Indeed, I don't know as I wouldn't as lif they'd call me a rogue, as say for ever and ever, *Oh, he is too knowin' by half*. It's the divil, that's a fact. Before this misfortin came I used to do a considerable smart chance of business; but now it's time for me to cut dirt, and leave the country. I believe I must hang out the G. T. T. sign.—Why, what the plague is that? says I.—Gone to Texas, said he. What else on airth shall I do. I have nothin' to see to, and the day seems twice as long as it used to did.—Ah! says I, I have heerd folks say so afore, when they was jist new married. But I see what you want; you want excitement. How would politics do? It's a wide field, and some considerable sport in it, too. Agitate the country; swear the Church is a-goin' to levy tithes, or dissenters to be taxed to support them, or that the Governor is a-goin' to have martial law. Call office-holders by the cant tarms of compact cliques and official gang, and they will have to gag you with a seat in the council, or somethin' or another, see if they don't.—No, said he, a-shakin' of his head; poor business that; there is nothin' to be made by it, as far as I see, but inimies; and, besides, people are fond of a change; they get tired of professions at last, and jist as you are a-going to reap the advantage another feller outbids you, and carries off the prize. No, that won't do.

Well, preachin', says I, how would that answer? Take up some new pinte, and you will have lots of folks to hear you; and the more extravagant the better. Go the whole figur' for "religious liberty;" it has no meanin' here, where all are free, but it's a catchword, and sounds well. You don't want ordination now-a-days; it's out of fashion; give yourself a call; it's as good as any other man's call. A man that can't make himself a preacher is a poor tool, that's a fact, and not fit to make convarts.—Hem! says he, I was a-thinkin' of that, for ministers fare well in a gineral way, that's sartin; and a-travellin' about, and a-livin' on the best, and sleepin' in the spare bed always, ain't a bad move nother; but I hante the gift of the gab, I am afeerd, and I couldn't come it no how I could fix it.—Well, 'tis awkward, says I, to be thought *too knowin' by half, too*; did any one ever accuse you of bein' *too industrious by half*? What do you mean by that? said he, a little grumpy like.—.Nothin', says I, but what I say. Get a spinnin'-wheel for your wife, and a plough for yourself; work more, and trade less; live by your labour, and not by your wits; and the day, instead of being so 'tarnal long, won't be long enough by a jug-full. Instead of bein' "*too knowin' by half;*" you don't "*know half enough*," or you'd know that.

Fact, I assure you, squire; if that crittur had really been a knowin' one, the name of it wouldn't a-fixed his flute for him, for there is always a why for every wherefore in this world. There is a thousand ways for managing that. Now I got the name myself. Them tricks in the clock-trade I told you. I didn't think you would go right away, and publish; but you did, and it put people on their guard, so there was no doin' nothin' with them for some time hardly; and if I went to say a civil thing, people looked shy at me, and called out, "Soft Sawder." Well, what does I do? Instead of goin' about mopin' and complainin' that I was "too knowin' by half," I sot myself about repairin' damage, and gitten up something new; so I took to phrenology. "Soft Sawder" by itself requires a knowledge of paintin', of light and shade, and drawin' too. You must know character. Some people will take a coat put on by a white-wash brush as thick as porridge; others won't stand it if it ain't laid on thin, like copal, and that takes twenty coats to look complete; and others, agin, are more delicater still, so that you must lay it on like gold leaf, and that you have to take up with a camel's hair brush, with a little pomatum on the tip of it, and hold your breath while you are a-spreadin' of it out, or the leastest grain of air from your nose will blow it away. But still, whether laid on thick or thin, a cute person can tell what you are at; though it tickles him so while you are a-doin' of it, he can't help showin' how pleased he is. But your books played the divil with me; folks wouldn't let me do it at all arter they came out, at no rate; first civil word always brought out the same answer. Ah! now, that's your "Soft Sawder;" that won't do.—Won't it tho', says I. I'll give you the same ingredients in a new shape, and you will swaller it without knowin' it, or else I am mistakend, that's all. So now, when I enter a location, arter a little talk about this, that, or the other, I looks at one of the young grow'd up galls airnest like, till she says, Mr. Slick, what on airth are you a-lookin' at?—Nothin', says I, my dear, but a most remarkable developement.— A what? says she.—A remarkable developement, says I, the most remarkable, too, I ever seed since I was raised. —Why, what in natur' is that? says she.— Excuse me, Miss, says I, and I gets up, and puts my finger on her crown. What benevolence! says I, and firmness of character! did you ever!—and then, says I, a passin' my finger over the eye-brow, you ought to sing well, positively; it's your own fault you don't, for you have uncommon pitikilar powers that way. Your time is large, and tune great; yes, and composition is strong.—Well, how strange! says she; you *have* guessed right, I sware, for I do sing, and am allowed to have the best ear for musick in all these clearin's. How on airth can you tell? If that don't pass!—Tell! says I, why it's what they call phrenology, and a most beautiful study it is. I can read a head as plain as a book; and this I will say, a finer head than yourn I never *did* see, positively. What a splendid forehead you have! It's a sight to behold. If you was to take pains you could do anything a'most. Would you like to have it read, Miss? Well, arter hearin' me pronounce aforehand at that rate, she is sure to want it read, and then I say I won't read it aloud, Miss; I'll whisper it in your ear, and you shall say if I am right.—Do, says she; I should like to see what mistakes you'll make, for I can't believe it possible you can tell; it don't convene to reason, does it?

Nothin', squire, never stops a woman when her curosity is once up, especially if she be curious to know somethin' about herself. Only hold a secret out in your hand to her, and it's like a bunch of catnip to a cat; she'll jump, and frisk, and frolic round you like anything, and never give over purrin' and coaxin' of you till she gets it. They'll do anything for you a'most for it. So I slides out my knee for a seat, and says, it's no harm, Miss, you know, for Ma is here, and I must look near to tell you; so I draws her on my knee, without waiting for an answer. Then gradually one arm goes round the waist, and t'other hand goes to the head, bumpologizin', and I whispers—wit, paintin', judgment, fancy, order, musick, and every good thing a'most. And she keeps a sayin'—Well, he's a witch! well, how strange! lawful heart! Well, I want to know!—now I never! do tell !—as pleased all the time as anything. Lord! squire, you never see anything like it; it's Jerusalem fine fun. Well, then I wind up by touchin' the back of her head hard, (you know, squire, what they call the *amative* bumps are located there,) and then whisper a bit of a joke to her about her makin' a very very lovin' wife, and so on, and she jumps up a-colourin' and a-sayin'—It's no such a thing. You missed that guess, anyhow. Take that for not guessin' better!—and pretendin' to slap me, and all that; but actilly ready to jump over the moon for delight. Don't my clocks get fust admired and then boughten arter this readin' of heads, that's all? Yes, that's the beauty of phrenology. You can put a clock into their heads when you are a-puttin' other fine things in, too, as easy as kiss my hand. I have sold a nation lot of them by it.

The only thing agin phrenology is, it's a little bit dangerous. It's only fit for an old hand like me, that's up to trap, for a raw one is amazin' apt to get spooney. Taking a gall on your knee that way, with one hand on her heart, that goes pitty-pat, like a watch tickin', and the other a-rovin' about her head a-discoverin' of bumps, is plaguy apt to make a fool of you without your knowing of it. Many a bird has got fascinated so afore now, that, do what it would, it couldn't get away. It might flutter and struggle a little; but at last it would fall as helpless as anything, right down. But then a fool is a fool all the world over. For my part I am not afeerd of none of them. This squire, is what I call reason, and knowin' the world. A wise man is never taken at a nonplus. But Bill Dill Mill is a noodle, and such a one, too, as it would take seven fools and a philosopher to make, and even then they wouldn't make no part of a primin' to him. He has got everything to larn yet, that feller, for a crittur that is *"too knowin' by half" may know too much for other folks' good, but he don't know "half enough" for his own, that's a fact.*

IX

MATRIMONY

TALKIN' of that young bride of Bill Dill Mill, and phrenology, continued the Clockmaker, puts me in mind of a conversation I had with minister about women, jist afore I came down here, the last time. The old man was advisin' of me to marry, and settle down to Slickville, into what he called "a useful member of society." Poor old crittur! he is so good himself, he thinks no harm of no one, and looks on a gall as a rose without a thorn, or an angel in petticoats, or somethin' of that kind; but book-larned men seldom know nothin' but books, and there is one never was printed yet worth all they got on their shelves, which they never read, nor even so much as cut the leaves of, for they don't onderstand the handwritin', and that is—human natur'. On most subjects no man could advise better nor minister; but on the question of woman he is as dreamy as a poet, chock full of romance and nonsense, and actilly talks blank varse, where the rhyme is left out. It's considerable of a long yarn, but it will give you some idea what an innocent, pure-hearted, dear old crittur he is; indeed, among our ministers he is actilly at the top of the pot. He is quite "a case," I do assure you.

One arternoon, as we was a-sittin' together smokin', says he, awakin' up out of one of his bouts of cypherin' in his head, Sam, says he, it's most time you was thinkin' of settlin' yourself in the world. By all accounts you are considerable well to do now, and have made an everlastin' sight of money among the Blue-noses to Nova Scotia: you should look round for a help-mate, and pick yourself out a rael, complete, right-down good wife. There is nothin' like matrimony, nothin' like home, nothin' on airth to be compared to a vartuous woman. They are somethin' better than men, and somethin' jist a little less than angels, when you can fall in with one of the right kind. Oh, a right-minded, sound-minded, and pure-minded woman, is the greatest and best work of God. Man was made out of gross materials, of nothin' but clay and spittle; but woman, she was made out of the rib of man, twice refined and remoulded, as it were, from a substance that had been cleared of its dross by a process of previous formation. She was the last work of creation; the best, the most finished, the most beautiful. Man, is airthenware, coarse, rude, rough, and onseemly. Woman, is porcelain, a crittur highly finished and delicate. Man was made for knockin' about, he is tough and strong; but woman, to be taken care of and handled gently. What a sweet thing is innocence, Sam; how beautiful to contemplate, how lovely to associate with! As a philosopher, I admire purity in the abstract; but, as a man and a Christian, I love it when parsonified. Purity in a child, of such is heaven; purity in woman, of such also is the realms of bliss; but purity in man—oh, Sam, I am most afeerd, sometimes, there ain't much of it any where now a days, I snore: but matrimony, Sam, is a state ordained by God, not only to carry out his great purposes that is above our comprehension, but also for our happiness; yes, it is a nateral state, and a considerable of a pleasant one too, when well considered and rightly entered upon. Don't put it off too long, Sam; don't wait till the heart ossifies.—Ossifies! says I; why what the plague is that, minister?—Why, Sam, says he, you ought to be ashamed to axe that are question. I do believe, in my soul, you have forgot all you ever larned while tradin' among them benighted critturs in the British Provinces. Ossifies, means growin' into a hard substance like a bone.—Oh, says I, now I see, and that's the reason of the old sayin' when a man licks his wife like a sack, "I've got a bone to pick with you, my dear," says he, and shows the crittur's heart is ossified. There are some men, I know, that could find it the luckiest thing that ever happened them to have their hearts ossified, if it took that turn sometimes. You may rave as much as you please, minister, about purity, and porcelain ware, and vartue, and all that are sort of thing, till you are tired, but there are some women I've seed that have more of the devil and less of the angel in 'em than you are a-thinkin' on, *I* can tell you. Regular built bruisers too; claw your eyes right out, like a Carolina gouger, and walk right into you afore you know where you be.—Well, said he, p'raps so; it mought be the case since the fall, but that's mostly our own faults, our own bringin' of them up: but I was a-goin' to explain to you about the heart. As we grow old, it hardens, and loses its feelin.' When we are young it is as sensi*tive* as anything; you can't hardly touch it without givin' it pain or pleasure. It is so cute, and beats so strong and quick that it's sensations are plaguy powerful. Well, as we advance in years, the outer coverin' of it hardens, and gets as rough as the bark of a hemlock tree, and when you peel that off, then there is a hard, close, tough rind all round it, and inside that another, they call the inner *cu-tickle.* Ingratitude, and disappointment, and onkindness, and the wear-and-tear of the world, does this, so as to defend the heart from sufferin' pain all the time. I guess it's a wise provision of natur', a marciful dispensation that. If we don't feel so much pleasure, we feel less pain; we *have less and less heart,* until we get gradually weaned from airthly things, and put our affections on things above. The passions cease to play, and reason begins to dominate in their place. We are less the critturs of feelin', and more the subjects of wisdom. You apprehend me, Sam, don't you?— It's as plain as a pike-staff, says I, and as clear as mud. That ossified skin you talk of, puts me in mind of them nasty, dirty, horrid critturs, the Scotch and Irish peasants. They don't wear no shoes and stock but go barefooted, and their soles be as hard as the hoofs of jackasses; and them little, short-legged, hairy Highlanders kick every bit as hard, and twice as wicked, as donkeys too. They are shockin' critturs them, for if there's a part about a man or woman that's not fit to be seen at no time, it's the foot. Women that go that way, put me in mind of a divin' duck there is to Labrador, that has a red shank and a black-webbed foot; our sailors call 'em the immigrant ladies; and them ducks act exactly like the galls, too, a-flirtin' and a-frolickin' about like fun. You'll see a duck now, minister, sailin' round and round about her mate, ever so slow, to attract his attention, like; and when he sees her and makes up to her, smirkin' and courtin,' she jist downs with her head and ups with her legs, and away she dives right out of sight in no time, leavin' him alone, starein' and wonderin' like a fool. That gets his dander up immediatly and when he sees her come up agin, off he sets arter her hot foot, and she gives him the dodge agin; and when they get tired of that fun, they sail off together a-liftin' up their heads and a-gabblin' away like any thing, so pleased. Rompin seems kinder nateral to all created critturs, and the female is every where a-tormentin,' wicked, teasin, little toad. Natur is natur, that's a fact.—Well, Sam, said he, larfin, for a man that minds the main chance tolerable well as you do, I never seed one yet so amazin' full of nonsense as you be; you have such strange ideas as never entered into no soul's head but your own, I do believe: and yet, as you say, mirth and playfulness does seem kinder nateral: the Latin poet, Virgil, if you hante forgot all you ever larned to night-school with me, has beautifully illustrated that. He then said some Latin about a gall peltin' her spark with apples, but I misremember the words.—Perhaps he quoted these lines, said I,

> Malo me Galatea petit, Lasciva puella
> Et fugit ad Salices sed se cupit ante videri.—

Ay, said Mr. Slick, them's the very identical ones.—Now, says minister, that is natur', for he was natur's poet, was Virgil.—Natur', says I; I guess it is natur'. A little innicent rompin', (it must be innicent tho', minister, said I, and I looked up to him as demure as you please,) is what I call primitive and nateral, and I must say, I am shocking fond of a little of it myself.—You are right, said he, to say innocent, Sam, for nothin' that's not innocent ever gives real pleasure; nothin' that's impure can be happy. The fact is, I don't jist altogether like that word rompin'; it's a coarse thing, and a vulgar thing, and only fit for such benighted critturs as them in the British Provinces; say mirth, innocent mirth, and then I agree with you: that I do approbate. I delight in that; it's a sign of a sweet disposition, a pure mind, and a light heart. But mirth is different from rompin'. It don't admit, as rompin' does, of obstropolus noise, nor ticklin', nor screamin', and things that don't seem quite decent; call it mirth, and I won't non-concur you.—You may call it what convenes you, minister, says I, but still it's the identical same thing, that's a fact. It puts life into a body. It piques you, and raises your dander like: I must say, I like a romp dearly. Now, that's the reason married folks are so everlastin' striped; they never romp. It makes me feel skery of matrimony, to see it so heavy and sour: I don't wonder so many folks to Slickville have got the dyspepsy; the only thing I wonder at is, how they can digest it at all. I guess, now, if a married woman was to imitate that are divin' duck, give her husband the dodge now and then, and, whenever he came near hand to her, jist race off and let him chase her, she'd— Ahem! says minister, ahem! Sam, we won't illustrate, we won't enter into details, if you please; where was we when we got off into this rompin' digression.—Why, says I, you was advisin' of me to get married afore my heart got bonafied.—Ossafied, said he, I didn't say bonafied. I wish it was a bona fide one, that's a fact. True, Sam, marry airly, marry before the feelins' become blunted, and before you grow suspicious and cold. All our young emotions are good and generous; but we become jealous, selfish, and mean, as we advance in years. At first we see nothin' but the roses and flowers of life afore us, and our young eyes are so good, and our vision so cute, the colours all look bright and beautiful, and we can distinguish all the tints and shades ever so far off, as plain as can be. Well, away we go to gather them, to make 'em into garlands and weave 'em into wreaths, and never think of the ten thousand million of thorns that are onder the leaves, and are all over the bushes. Well, first we tear all our clothes to tatters, and then we prick our fingers, and inflammation and fester comes, and run 'em into our feet, and contraction and lameness comes; and scratch our little faces till the tears run down our cheeks and mingle with it. But that ain't the worst of it by a long chalk, neither; for many a time, jist as we pull the rose, and go to put it to our bosoms, away goes all the leaves, a-flutterin' off to the ground; it was too full-blown to bear rough handlin', and we get nothin' but the stem in our hand, and ever so many prickles a-stickin' into the skin. And if we do succeed, in gettin' the rose arter all, and take it to home, why, next mornin', when we wake up and look at it, oh, the leaves are all edged with brown and dirty yaller, and the sprig is all wilted, and it looks flabbergasted like, and faded, and it's only fit to be throwd out of the windur; for nothin' looks so bad a'most, as a wilted flower. Jist so is the world, Sam; only the world has its thorns for the heart, and that's more than the rose has; and who shall heal them? Philosophy may give its styptics, and religion its balm, but there are some wounds in *that* place, Sam—and he clapt his hand on his breast, and did look dreadful bad, poor old crittur, and I pitied him from the bottom of my soul, for I knowd what he was leadin' to—there are some wounds here, Sam, said he, that the eye cannot see, nor the hand reach; which nothin' a'most can cure. They may heal over and get cicatrised, and seem all right agin, but still they are so tender, you can't bear to touch them without wincin', and every now and then they open of themselves, like old scars do in the scurvy, and bleed, and throb, and ache, oh! how they ache!

When my elders discharged me, Sam, and reformed me out, and took a Unitarian in my place, I actilly thought my heart would a-burst with grief;—and his voice quivered and trembled like anything, and a great big tear-drop rose up in the corner of his eye, swelled, and swelled, till it bust, and run over, and trickled down one of the furrows of his cheek, but he wouldn't let on he know'd it, and wouldn't wipe it off, hopin' I wouldn't see it, I suppose. It actilly a'most made me pipe my eye to see him, it was so affectin'.— So, says I, I know it all, minister, says I; we won't talk of that;

what's done is done, but the loss is theirs, and it sarves them right. But it didn't stop him, he went right on.—For, oh! Sam, said he, the fountain of love lies in the deepest recesses of the human heart. It may cease to gush over, as it does in youth, when it is fed by a thousand rills of emotion. The wintry frosts of old age may dry up some of its springs, and the lacerations of ingratitude may drain off and limit its supply; but deep and far down is the well, Sam, where summer-heats and wintry frost cannot penetrate, and its water, what little is left of it in old age, is as pure, and sweet, and pellucid as ever, and there it remains till the temple that covers it, (that's the body, you see, Sam,) crumbled and mouldered by time, totters to its fall, and chokes it in its ruins. But, oh! Sam, if our friends, them that we dearly loved, basely desert us at last, and meanly betray us; if them we admitted to our confidence, and folded with affection to our bosoms, pour into that fountain the waters of bitterness, and pollute it at its source, better, far better that we had died first. I could have met my eend as became my vocation and my principles had the blow been dealt out by enemies, Sam; but, oh! it came from my friends, from them that I loved as brothers, nay, more than as brothers, as children. It was too much for my narves. It overpowered my strength, and I hid my face in my hands as Caesar did in his mantle, and wept like a child. *Et tu*, said I,—for I couldn't help a-thinkin' of that are old republican hero, for it was jist the way them are pretended reformers sarved him out—*Et tu,* says I, *et tu, Brute!*—You might well say a brute, says I, and if I had a-been near hand to them, I'd asarved them like a brute, too, I know. I'd a cropt their ears, and branded them on the rump, as they do a horse that's turned out on the common in the fall. I'd a marked them V. B. (the voluntary brutes!) hang me if I wouldn't. I'd a-kicked them till I kicked their western eends up to their shoulders, and made 'em carry 'em there like a mason's hod. "Sich a gittin' up stairs you never did see."— Sam, said he, you actilly frighten me, you talk so savage; it makes my blood run cold. Let us leave the subject, and go right back to what we was a-talkin' of; and he passed his hand over his face hard, as if to shove back the expression o' pain and sorrow that was there, and keep it out of view; and then, said he, a-lookin' up all bright agin, Where was we, Sam? for my mind goes a wool-gathering sometimes, and gets confused. Where was we?—A-talkin' of the galls, says I—exactly, says he; it's a pleasanter topic that, and the contemplation of the dear critturs softens our naturs, "*nec sinit esse feros*," nor suffers us to be ferocious. Nothin' tames a man like a woman.—I guess so, says I.—Yes, my son, said he, get married, and marry soon; it's time you were a-thinkin' on it now in airnest. Well, I feel most plaguily skeered, minister, says I, to try, for if once you get into the wrong box, and the door is locked on you, there is no escape as I see; and besides, women are so everlastin' full of tricks, and so cunnin' in hiden 'em aforehand, that it's no easy matter to tell whether the bait has a hook in it or not; and if you go a-playin' round it and a-nibblin' at it, why a sudden jerk given by a skilful hand may whip it into your gills afore you know where you be, and your flint is fixed as shure as there are snakes in Varginy. You may tug, and pull, and haul back till you are tired; but the more obstropolous you become, the faster the hook is fixed in, and the sorer the place is. Nothin' a'most is left for you but to come up to the line, and submit to your fate. Now if you go for to take a widder, they are shocking apt to know too much, and are infarnal sly; and if you take a maid, it's an even chance if you don't spile her in breakin' her in, and she don't bolt and refuse a heavy pull. If they are too old they are apt to be headstrong from havin' had their head so long; and, if they are too young, they are hardly way-wise enough to be pleasant. Which, now, do you recommend, minister, widdur or maid? Poor old crittur! I know'd well enough he didn't know nothin' about it, havin' had no experience among women any more nor a child; but I axed him to humour him, for most men like to be thought knowin' on that subject.—Why, says he, a-lookin' up wise-like, that's a matter of taste, Sam, some perfers one, and some perfers the other.—(So like human natur' that, warn't it, squire? You never heerd a man in your life, when axed about woman, say, that's a subject I ain't jist altogether able to speak on, and yet plaguy few know much more about 'em than that women wear petticoats, and men don't.)—It's quite a matter of taste, said he; but, as far as my experience goes, says the old man, I am half inclined to opinionate that widders make the best wives. Havin' lost a husband, they know the slender tenure we have of life, and are apt to be more considerate, more kind, and more tender than maids. At all events, there is enough in the idea to put them on equal tarms. I guess it's six of one and half-a-dozen of t'other, not much to choose any way. But, whichever it be, you must prove their temper first, and their notions; see what sort o'sisters and darters they make; try—but, dear me! how late it is, said he, a-lookin' at his watch, how late it is! I must go, for I have a sick visit. I still visit my dear lost flock, as if they hadn't abused me so ill, Sam. I forgive them, all of 'em. I don't harbor any hard thoughts agin' any of them. I pity 'em, and always remember 'em in my prayers, for our religion is a religion of the heart, and not of the head, as political dissent is. Yes, I must go, now; but I'll give you a word of advice at partin', my dear boy. *Don't marry too poor a gall, for they are apt to think there is no eend to their husband's puss; nor too rich a gall, for they are apt to remind you of it onpleasant sometimes; nor too giddy a gall, for they neglect their families; nor too demure a one, for they are most apt to give you the dodge, race off, and leave you; nor one of a different sect, for it breeds discord; nor a weak-minded one, for children take all their talents from their mothers; nor a —— * O Lord! says I, minister, how you skeer a body! Where onder the sun will you find a nonsuch like what you describe? There ain't actilly no such critters among women.—I'll tell you, my son, said he, for I'd like afore I die to see you well mated; I would, indeed! I'll tell you, tho' you talk to me sometimes as if I didn't know nothin' of women. You think nobody can't know 'em but them as romp all their days with them as you do; but them, let me tell you, know the least, for they are only acquainted with the least deserving. I'll gin you a gage to know 'em by that is almost invariable, universal, infallible. *The character and conduct of the mother is a sure and certain guarantee for that of the darter.*

X

THE WOODEN HORSE

NO person on entering the harbour of St. John, for the first time, could suppose that it was the outlet of one of the largest rivers on the American continent, as it is in no way to be distinguished in appearance from any of those numerous inlets of the sea that render the coast of the British provinces everywhere accessible to ships of the largest class. As soon, however, as he gets a view of this noble stream, and becomes acquainted with its magnitude, he feels that Saint John is destined by nature, as well as the activity and intelligence of its inhabitants, to become the next largest city to New York on this continent.

Sensible folks these Brunswickers, said Mr. Slick: rael right down men, of bisness, and no mistake. They don't take it all out in talkin', as some people do. If they have any politicks to do, they do it, as they load a vessel, as fast as they can to do it well, and a-done with it. They are jist a pattern to them Canada goneys to cut their garment by if they had the sense to follow it. I met old Jeremiah Sterling this mornin'; you have heerd tell of him, squire? he is the richest man in the city. He is an O. F. M. as we call Our First Men among us.—Well, says I, friend Jeremiah, how do you kinder sorter find yourself to day?—Why, kinder sorter, midlin', says he, Mr. Slick; what you call considerable nimble, and spry. We are gitten on well here, very well indeed. We have a good many 'sponsible men grow'd up here since you was this way, and our credit is good. We stand No. 1, letter A.—Well, says I, if it is, it won't be that way long, I can tell you; the less you talk about 'sponsibility the better the English marchants and Wall-street brokers will trust you, I know.—Why says he, what on airth are you a-talkin' about? I don't onderstand you; you are at your old trick of ridlin'?—Why, says I, responsible government, to be sure. Didn't you say you had a good many 'sponsible men grow'd up here, lately? —Well, that's notable, said he. Lawful heart! if that don't beat gineral trainin'! How could you suppose I meant such cattle as them? No, says he, come with me, and I'll indicate what 'sponsibility is, for the street is no place to talk over such matters in, and he took me into his countin' room, and touchin' a spring, opened a great iron door, and then onlocked another of the same kind, and showed me a great iron safe, on wheels like a gun-carriage. Well, it was chock full of doubloons and sovereigns, and splendid American eagles; it was actilly good for sore eyes to look at 'em! and then he opened another, filled half way up to the top with bank paper, notes of hand, bonds, and mortgages, and stuff of that kind. He stood for the whole endurin' space of five minutes a-contemplatin' of it without sayin' of a word, only smilin'. At last, says he, Slick, (and he let down the lid with a slam that smelt of thunder,) that's what *I* call *'sponsibility*. I didn't airn that little lop of specie a-talkin' over *politicks,* you may depend, but talking over customers. Your 'sponsible men want no indorsers, do you twig? Now, who has most interest in takin' care of that "stake," that it don't go for it by fire, or sympathisers, or what not,—me, or that are chatterin', jawin' watchman of mine?—Why you, says I, you, of course.—Exactly, says he; and so it is in politicks. *Them critturs that race about like a run away steamboat, callin' fire! fire! and disturbin' all honest folks in their beds, cuss 'em! they have nothin' to lose by a fire if it does come: but in the scramble they generally find somethin' or an other to pick up that they didn't work for.* Now them chaps, patriots, Durhamites, arsondaries, and what not, to Canady, remind me of our engine men. Any engine that gets to a fire first, if it's only a chimbly a-blazin', gets five pounds out of the pockets of the people. *Cryin' fire is a profitable trade in more things than one.*

Jeremiah was right, squire. It's a pity Government ever listened to colonial agitators. It was erroneous considerable. It would have been better for England, and better for the colonies too, if they hadn't, and that they'll find some o' these days, or my name is not Sam Slick. But John wants a commission o'lunacy taken out; the foolish old crittur actilly seems possest. Concession never stopt agitation since the world was first squeezed out of a curd, it only feeds it. Throwin' sops to varmint only brings 'em back agin; and when you have nothin' more to throw to 'em, they are plaguy apt to turn to and tare you to pieces. It puts me in mind of the wooden-horse to Java.

That time I took the whalin' trip, we stopt to Java: well, jist then there was a native chief there, that almost drove the Dutch off the island. He cut off their outposts, broke up their settlements, druv away their cattle, seesed their galls, and kicked up a regular built tornado. The Dutch governor, old Vandam, who was as fat and as heavy as a December bear, was fairly explunctified: he didn't know what onder the sun to do. He was in a most awful feese. All he could say when people came with news, was "Tousand Teyvils;" and the chief gave him news enough to say it all day long, until finally the outlaw-gentleman went by the nickname of "Tousand Teyvils." At last the Governor took a tub of tobacco, and a keg of good hollands, and a dozen of his best pipes, and shot himself up in his castle for two whole days and two whole nights, to study the ins and outs of the matter alone; for talkin', he said, always put him out like a wrong figur' in the first part of a sum, and he had to go over it all agin from the beginnin'. Well, at the eend of the two days and two nights the Governor opened the door and ordered in more pipes and more skidam and schnap-glasses, and then sent for his council, and nodded to them to set down; for he was a man of few words, was old Vandam, his maxim bein', that them that talked well was seldom good for nothin' else; and the councillors squatted low and didn't say a word. Then he looked at the liquor, and then at the glasses, and the servant filled them up chock full; and then he looked at the door, and the servant went out and shot it to after him. A Dutchman's eye don't often speak much; but when it has any expression in it, it speaks to the pinte, you may depend. Well, he motioned to them to drink, and they drank off their hollands and smacked their lips: for if his liquor warn't good, I want to know whose was, that's all.—Oh, mine Cot! says the Governor, takin' the pipe out of his mouth, and lettin' go a great long roll of smoke, as big as what comes from a steam-boat,—oh, Goten Hymmel! I have got von idea, and you shall see what you shall see; and he winked to them knowin' like, and sot down agin.

It was a long speech for the Governor; but he got thro' it, for he had made up his mind; and when once a Dutchman makes up his mind, I have always observed you might as well think of turnin' Niagara as turnin' him. Well, the councillors sot there awaitin' for the Governor to illuminate 'em on the subject of his idea, and drank and smoked till they drank and smoked all that was placed afore them, when the council always broke up. And when they rose to go, the Governor shook his head and said agin, —"You shall see varte you shall see." Well, next day I was woked up by a most riprorious noise in the street, folks beatin' drums and blowin' horns, and rattlin' arms and all sorts of things a'most; so I jumps out of bed in an all-fired hurry, and ups with the winder and outs with my head.

Hullo! says I, what in natur' is all this to do about? who is dead, and what's to pay now ?—Oh! says they, there is somethin' wus than galls in the bushes. The Governor komes out to the head of his army to fight Tousand Teyvils,—and they was very full of courage, was the Dutch, for they was more nor half shaved then. Says I to myself, there will be sport to-day, see if there ain't, and you had better go and see the fun. So, thinks I, I don't much care if I do; and I dresses myself as soon as I could and runs down and joins them.

It was a most mortal hot day, and people actilly sweated to that degree, it laid the dust: indeed, where I was, in the rear, it began to be muddy a considerable some. I actilly thought I should a-died with the heat, it was so brilein', and was beginnin' to repent comin', when orders came to halt; and glad enough I was to hear 'em, you may depend.

We campt near a most a-beautiful meddow at the foot of a mountain, with good shade and lots of nice cool water, and we turned to to wash and make comfortable. Presently the horns blew a long, lively blast, and in a few minutes they was answered by another from the mountain. Then ten mules was brought out, and loaded with money and goods and what not; and a captain and his guard proceeded with them to the mountains, along with one of the councillors, and in two hours time they returned, and then a gineral salute was fired by the whole line, for they had bought a peace with the na*tive* chief. Every one was delighted; they not only nodded to each other, but actilly spoke. Some said goot, others said fary goot, and some hot-headed young fellows said, tam coot. Then a report came Tousand Teyvils was to dine with the Governor; and an invitation came to me, as representin' our great nation, to be present at the feed too. Well, we all formed into line to see the chief that people was so afeerd on; for no one knew whether he was man or devil, no one havin' ever dared to show anything but a back to him; but he kept us waitin' for ever so long, for great men, I have obsarved, always arrive late at dinner; it's only common people that jist come to the time, or may be a few minutes before, to make sure. Well, while we was waitin the Governor goes into the dinner-tent to see all was right; and arter walkin' all round it ever so slow, he turns to the head waiter and gives a grunt, "Eu–gh," says he, which is the Dutch for it will do very well, I am satisfied with your arrangements. It is a beautiful language for a hot climate like Java is the Dutch, so little of it goes so far. It is like cayenne, the leastest spoonful in the world does the bisness. Then the Governor says, Casper, says he, (that was the feller's Christian name, and it's very odd I never seed a Dutch sarvant that warn't named Casper,) says he, yen I takes out my noshe-viper to blow my noshe after mit dog guesser (which is low Dutch for dinner, 'cause it sets the dogs guessing and barking like mad) that is a shine to you to do varte I told you for to do. Now, if you neglects, my coot Casper, then—and he drew his finger across Casper's throat—which is the Dutch for sayin I will have your head cut off.

Poor Casper lifted up his hand to put it on his heart; but he was so tarnation frightened, he didn't get it no higher than his breeches; and thrustin' it into his pocket, which was big enough to hold a quart bottle, he bent over it and bowed down to the ground, which is the Dutch way of sayin' I onderstand you, old boy, and will take devilish good care to mind my eye and save my head. Jist then the guns fired a salute, which was a sign Tousand Teyvils was a-comin'; and sure enough there he was, a regular snorter by buth and edication, a tall, strappin', devilish, handsome feller, with a cap and plumes stuck sideways like on his head. Well, as he marched along in the double line, folks seemed as amazed as if they was jist born, and hung back like as if it was old Scratch himself agoin' to give 'em a taste of his breed, and they looked as skeered as if they had seed a rifle lookin' at 'em eend ways; and Tousand Teyvils curled up his upper lip, jist as you have seed a pugdog do his tail, with a slight twitch of his nose too, as much as to say ain't you a pretty set of mean-spirited rapscallions to come and buy your peace like cowards, instead of fightin' it out to the bat's eend like brave men? Cuss you! you hante an idea above your nasty, muddy, stinkin' canals and flag-ponds; and all you care for is your tarnal schnaps and tobacco. Phew, you paltroons, how you stink of sour crout!

He had a most audacious eye, I tell you: it looked exactly as it was forged out of lightnin'; it warn't easy to look into it, that's a fact. It seemed to say, I am a pickaxe, and will dig you out of your hole like a badger, I hope I may be gouged, if I don't. Well, the Governor advances two steps to meet him, which is a great way for a governor to go, especially a Dutch one, and takin' him by the hand and bowin', says he,— "Mine goot frient—my prave frient," and then he suddenly began to stop, and his eyes swelled, and the whole expression of his countenance altered, and the water came to his lips, and he began to lick his chops, as if he was a boa constrictor, and was a-goin' to slaver him for swallerin' whole.

I never see such a treacherous face afore. Tousand Teyvils didn't seem to like it nother, for he cut this mummery short by sayin',—"How am you was," (for he didn't speak good Dutch at all,) "how is you been, my old Bullock?" and he squeezed his cornstealers till the old gineral began to dance like a bear on red hot iron.

When he got clear of him, he blowed his fingers as if they was scalded, and howled and moaned like a wounded dog. It was pitiable to see him, for he was a caution to behold. If all the crooked Dutch oaths he muttered that time was straightened out, they'd reach across the Hudson, I do believe.—Oh, mine Cot! says he, to Casper, who came in for orders (and it railly did seem to hurt him beautiful), how shall I use my noshe viper? I can't blow my noshe no more as a child, my nails have grow'd one whole inch longer. Varte shall I do? Est ist sharder (I am sorry).

Well, arter a while they all sot down, and they eat and drank, and drank and eat, till all was blue agin; they fairly pulled off their coats to it, as if they were in rael wide-awake airnest; and arter the cloth was removed, says the old Governor,—Mine hears, (which means my dummies, or fellers that hear but don't speak,) mine hears, fill your glasses. Well, they all filled their glasses and rose up.—I have von toast, said he, ahem! and he took out his noshe-viper (which is the Dutch for a pocket-handkerchief) and tried to blow his nose, but he couldn't for his fingers were all lame, they was crushed so; and then he took his left hand that arn't squeezed, and you may depend that are wind-instrument, his nose, let go in great style, it sounded like a conch-shell. That was the signal: in rushed Casper and the guard, and come down on poor Tousand Teyvils like fallin' stars, and tied him hand and foot, and carried him in old Vandam's carriage down to town, and rowed him off to a fortified rock at some distance from the land, where they imprisoned him like Buonaparte, and where he is livin' to this day chained like a dog. Fact, I assure you.—Coot, farry coot, tam coot trick, the company all said agin; and then they turned to smokin' and drinkin' till all was blue agin. They didn't get drunk, tho' they had a considerable of a muddy time of it too, because nothin' will make a Dutchman drunk; but they sucked in the gin till they couldn't move hand or foot, or hear, or see, or speak, but sot bolt upright, starin' and gapin' like a house with the windows and doors knocked out. Now, instead of bein' ashamed of such a nasty, dirty, unperlite, sneakin' trick as that they played poor Tousand Teyvils, they boasted of it; for nothin' ever I seed made Dutch man ashamed, except forgettin' to carry his bag of tobacco.

Tam dat old tief! dat Tousand Teyvils, said the old Governor, (and he blarted like a calf jist weaned, as if somethin' was the matter of him; but what can you expect of a Dutchman?) "Ich Rharter," which is the Dutch for, I guess; Ich Rharter, when he next has de high favour to shake hands mid a governor, he don't squeeze his hand like von lemon: and they all said "Ach yaw!" which is the Dutch short-hand way for sayin' that is a capital joke of his highness the Governor. Well, there was great rejoicin' to Java over this bloodless victory, and the Governor ordered a pint of gin, a pound of tobacco, and two pipes to be sarved out to each soldier in camp for his bravery; and two days arterwards there was a grand review of the Dutch army. Pretty lookin' soldiers they were too, squire, it would have made you died a-larfin' to have seed them. Either they had fell away greatly in that hot climate, or hadn't fatted up as they intended to do afore they died, for their trowsers hung so loose on 'em they could have stowed away their knapsacks, 'coutrements, and all in 'em, instead of carryin' them on their backs. Howsumdever, they was satisfied: and if they was, seein' that they had to carry them and not me, I didn't see as I had any right to find fault, do you? for my rule is to let every man skin his own foxes. Well, they marched, and counter-marched, and fired, and all that are sort of work, jist as if they was in airnest; and the boys shouted, and the women smiled, and the blacks grinned, and all went on swimmingly, like a house a-fire. Presently a great heavy piece of ordnance was fired off, and a booth was thrown open, out came a'most an almighty big wooden boss, a London brewer's shafter would'nt make the smallest part of a circumstance to him. He had a splenderiferous saddle-cloth, that nearly covered his body, all trimmed with gold, and a bridle all of polished worked steel, reins and all; and he was led by ten soldiers, five on one side and five on the other, and mounted by a *native* rider superbly clad. His very jacket must have cost enough to set up a common man like me in the world. The hoss looked so big and so fierce you'd think these ten men couldn't hold him; but as he was on wheels, I guess they pulled him instead of holden of him. Well, every now and then the hoss, that had machinery in it, would up-head and snort and neigh, jist like natur', and out came gingerbread, and tarts, and sugar-candy, and fruit, and all sorts of good things. Such a scramble you never did see, fellows tumblin' head over heels, and fighting and quarreling for a share of the goodies. Well, then he'd progress a little a-further, and then go thro' the same menouvres, and move his head as exact like a live hoss as ever you did see in all your life, and then came the pure gin. Oh, dear, it was as good as a play to see them holdin' their hands, cocoa-nut shells and hats to catch the liquor as it came from the hoss.

Rejoicin', like everything else in the world, must have an eend at last (and Dutch rejoicin' don't last long at any time, as far as ever I seed, especially when there ain't no smokin' in it), and so did their review. The people all went home pleased. The wooden hoss was a grand idea. It was worked out by General Vandam himself, that time he shot himself up in his castle for two whole days and two whole nights, a-studyin' over this matter of Tousand Teyvils, and shows plain enough, to my mind, that a Dutchman can think, arter all, if you only give him time enough.

The day arter the review I walked out over the exercisin' ground, and there lay the poor old hoss, his ribs broke in, his body ripped up, and his tail pulled out. While I was musin' over the fate of the hoss, who should I see but a little nigger boy. So says I, come here you little imp of darkness, you spawn of the old one, you, and tell me how this is? Is Tousand Teyvils loose again? Who killed the Governor's hoss?—Why, says he, massa, (for he spoke very good English, as he lived as help to a gentleman that kept a bumboat,) him Dutchman comed here last night in crowds, with carts and hogsheads and kegs, and they got old horse and patted him, and "soff sawdered" him, (you know dat word, massa, him Yankee word all same as blarney.)—Yes, says I, I have heerd tell of him afore. — Well, they coaxed him. Come, good hoss; beautiful hoss; a little drop more skidam; dat is good hossy; a little more sweetmeat, dat's a pretty hoss! Well, dey holdy up his head, and lift up him tail; but no, dat no go—hossy no gib any. At last him Dutchmen get angry. Dunder and Blitzen! he say, if you no gib him by fair means you gib him by foul: and wid dat dey fall too and rip him up, to see what is in him. Well, massa, you see dem old iron chains, and rusty wheels, and dem ugly pipes. Well, dat is all dey found dere. Den dey turn to and abuse old Gobernor like sin. Tam old Gineral, dey say; he one old big coward, one "Erbarmlick!" (dat's Dutch, massa, for awful bad,) one Erbarmlick cheat! Tousand Teyvils worth a hundred such old fools and knaves! He no solda that. Oh, massa, noting a'most was too bad for him tongue to say of old Gobernor.—Well, says I, here's sixpence for you, you young suckin' Satan you, now make yourself scarce; and he scampered off as smart as a two year old.

Now, squire, said the Clockmaker, it's a considerable of a long story that, and I am most afeerd I have tired you; but *John Bull* and his *Colony Patriots* remind me of them Dutchmen and their wooden horse. As long as he will neigh and whinner and hold up his head, and give 'em cakes and candy and sweetmeats to eat, and skidam to drink, they are full and runnin' over with praises and professions of loyalty; but as soon as he stops, then those same patriots, those M'Kenzies and Papineaus and divils have knifes ready to rip him up. *John Bull don't know and don't valy his rael friends enough.* All are well disposed to him, except them noisy critturs that run about, as old Jeremiah says, cryin' fire—fire! but, cuss him, he is so near-sighted he never sees a whip till he feels it. *The railly loyal people, like railly religious people, don't talk of it for everlastin'ly. They seldom make professions, unless called for, and ain't found rebellin' like patriots, even when provoked. Their loyalty hante a condition to it like a mortgage. It ain't cupboard love, like that of the Dutchman to the Wooden Horse.*

XI

THE BAD SHILLING

IT was late at night when we arrived at one of the frontier towns of the state of Maine, which, to avoid local offence, I shall designate as Quimbagog. There was so much noisy disputation relative to politicks and religion in the coffee-room of the inn, that I retired early to bed, with a bad headache, and not without some misgiving, that by visiting Maine first I had entered the States, to use an expression of the Clockmaker's, by the wrong door. In order that the sketch which I am now about to give may be fully understood, it may be necessary to request the reader to recollect that Mr. Slick *is a Yankee*, a designation the origin of which is now not very obvious, but it has been assumed by, and conceded by common consent to, the inhabitants of New England. It is a name, though sometimes satirically used, of which they have great reason to be proud, as it is descriptive of a most cultivated, intelligent, enterprising, frugal, and industrious population, who may well challenge a comparison with the inhabitants of any other country in the world; but it has only a local application.

The United States cover an immense extent of territory, and the inhabitants of different parts of the Union differ as widely in character, feelings, and even in appearance, as the people of different countries usually do. These sections differ also in dialect and in humour as much as in other things, and to as great, if not a greater extent, than the natives of different parts of Great Britain vary from each other. It is customary in Europe to call all Americans Yankees; but it is as much a misnomer as it would be to call all Europeans Frenchmen. Throughout these works it will be observed, that Mr. Slick's pronunciation is that of the *Yankee*, or an inhabitant of the *rural districts* of New England. His conversation is generally purely so; but in some instances he uses, as his countrymen frequently do from choice, phrases which, though Americanisms, are not of Eastern origin. Wholly to exclude these would be to violate the usages of American life; to introduce them oftener would be to confound two dissimilar dialects, and to make an equal departure from the truth. Every section has its own characteristic dialect, a very small portion of which it has imparted to its neighbours. The dry, quaint humour of New England is occasionally found in the west, and the rich gasconade and exaggerative language of the west migrates not unfrequently to the east. This idiomatic exchange is perceptibly on the increase. It arises from the travelling propensities of the Americans, and the constant intercourse mutually maintained by the inhabitants of the different states. A droll or an original expression is thus imported and adopted, and, though not indigenous, soon becomes engrafted on the general stock of the language of the country. In using the term "language of the country," I mean that of the classes in humble life, of which Mr. Slick is a member, as I hope I have never been so misunderstood as to render it necessary for me to say, that I have no intention of imputing these idioms to any other. This explanation, while it accounts for an erratic man, like Mr. Slick, occasionally using some few phrases which are not native Yankeeisms, will enable the reader the better to understand the difference between the plebeian of the west and the east, as exhibited in the following sketch.

During the stroll after breakfast on the following morning, Mr. Slick said, Did you never mind, squire, how hard it is to get rid of "a bad shillin'," how everlastin'ly it keeps a-comin' back to you?—I said, I had never experienced any difficulty of that kind, never having endeavoured to pass one that I knew was spurious.—No, I suppose not, said he, because you are a careless kind of a man that way, and let your shillin's desart oftener than they had ought to. But what would I have been, had I been so stravagant? and as to passin' bad money, I see no harm in it, if you have given valy for it, and received it above boord handsum, in the regular way of swap, trade, or sale. Cheatin' is givin' a thing of no valy for somethin' that is. Now, a bad shillin' that has cost you as much as a good one, can't be said, no how you can fix it, to be a thing of no valy. S'pose any gentleman that keeps a pike was to give you a bad shillin' in change, you would have a right to pass it then, cause it had cost you a shillin'. The odds make the difference—do you take? I'd like, he continued, to go into committee with you on that matter (as we used to say to the house of Rip's), but there ain't time for it jist now, as the pirate said to the hangman when he was a-tyin' of the knot. Howsumdever it is so, and there is no two ways about it. I fell in with a bad shillin' last night, arter you went to bed, that I thought I had parted with to New Orleens five years ago, for ever. I had been sittin' down talkin' over roads and travellin', and the clearin's, and what not to Nova

Scotia, last night, with a gentleman that owns a free-trader to Quimbagog, the Honorable Lucifer Wolfe. I misremembered him at first, and I don't think I filled his eye chock full nother, for he sar*tain-ly* didn't know me when we first began our palarver. He was a tall man, over six foot high, all bone and muscle, and not an ounce of super*flu*ous flesh on him. I seed at once be warn't a na*tive* of Maine, but a ringtail roarer from the West. He was all made of fox-traps and bears-claws, and as springy as a saplin ash. Havin' been a considerable some in the African trade, a dealin' in niggers, he was very swarthy like, wore a most ungodly pair of whiskers, and had more hair than head, tho' that was none of the smallest nother. His eyes was full and hawk-like, and close together, but they squinted awful; one on 'em mounted guard on his tumbler and t'other on you, as if his fightin' and drinkin' liked keepin' company. His nose was hooked and thin, like the back of a jacknife; and a scar across one side of his face from the cut of a sword or a boardin'-pike, made the plump part of the cheek to scuttle down to the level of his jaw, and gave him a very savage kilniferous kind of look. He wore his neckcloth loose like a sailor's, which showed a rael bull-dog neck; and, as he turned his head on its hinges, you could see the silver hilt of a bowie knife that laid hid onder the cape of his coat, ready for use. I couldn't help a-thinkin of sister Sall when I seed it, for she used to say she liked things that appealed to the heart. I wonder whether she'd call a bowie knife pathetic or not, for few things sink as deep as they do. Then the two large padded flaps like watch pockets to his frock coat, showed pistols was concealed there. His shirt had two or three large gold brooches in it, and a chain of the same genuine material, as thick as a gall's finger, was suspended round his neck as a watch-guard, and his waistcoat was made of spotted calf's skin, tanned with the hair on, and the shaggy side showin' out. He looked half landsman half seaman, with a strong dash of the fire-eater. Altogether he was a caution to look at, that's a fact. All at once he recollected my phiz, and jumpin' up and catchin' hold of my hand, which he squeezed as if it was in a vice, he roared out—Why it ain't possible! said he. Lawful heart alive, if that airn't you! Where on airth did you spring from, since you gin' over livin' whar you used to did? Whar do you lead your life now? Why, you have become quite a big bug lately by your writins': penmanship, I take it, is a better bisness than clock makin'; but come, let's liquor; I want to wet up; the sight of an old friend warms my heart so, it makes my lips dry. What will you have? cocktail, sling, julip, sherry cobbler, purl talabogus, clear sheer, or switchell? name your drink, my man, and let's have a gum tickler, for old acquaintance, somethin' that will go down the throat like a greased patch down a smooth rifle. Well, says I, I am no ways pitikilar; suppose we have brandy cocktail, it's as 'bout as good a nightcap as I know on. Done, said he, with a friendly tap on the shoulder that nearly dislocated my neck; I like a man that knows his own mind. Most of our folks make as much fuss about choosing, as if their throats had any taste in them, and they actilly knew the difference; but they don't, that's a fact. New England rum takes the skin clean off, and they can't taste nothin' that's weaker. I'll go and speak for it to one of the gentlemen to the bar.—With that he swiggled his way thro' the crowd, to the counter, and, says he, Major, says he, I guess you may let one of your aidy-conks bring us a pint of cocktail, but let it be letter A, No. 1, and strong enough to loosen the hinges of a feller's tongue.—Well, we sot down and chatted away till we finished our liquor, and now, says he, Slick, answer me a few questions, that's a good feller, for I am a free-trader now. I have got a'most an angeliferous craft, a rael screemer, and I'm the man that sez it. The way she walks her chalks ain't no matter. She is a regilar fore-and-after. When I hoist the foresail she is mad, and when I run up the mainsail she goes ravin' distracted. I can beat her up the harbour, when there is rips, raps, and rainbows under her bow; ay, walk her like a lady right into the wind's eye. Chips! chips! and they know it a-bed. Heavens and airth! jist lookin' at her will take away the breath from them white-livered, catfish-mouthed, dipt lookin' scoundrels the Brunswickers. She goes right on eend like a rampin' alligator. She'll go so quick she'll draw their wind out: go ahead! cock-a-doodle-doo! And he crowd like a rael live rooster.—Go ahead, steam boat—cock-a-doodle-doo! and he smashed my hat in, most ridikilous over my eyes, a-flappin' so with his hands, like wings. It was a caution to see, that's a fact. Now, said he, Slick, my bully, I think I see a smart chance of doin' a considerable stroke of business to Nova Scotia, in the smugglin' line.

Is it true the British have made Hudson in Nova Scotia a free port? —It is.

Is it true that from Parsboro' at the head of the Basin of Minas, up to Windsor, it is thirty-five miles ?—It is.

Is it true the tide runs out so, you can lay aground anywhar you darn please, on the mud-flats, with safety?—It is.

Is it true you ain't bound to call at no custom house till you get up to Windsor?—It is.

Is it true they can't see you to Windsor till you come within two miles of it?—It is.

Isn't Windsor almost clear across the province, no more than thirty-five miles from Halifax Basin?—It is.

Then, says he, a-givin' me a most powerful slap on the thigh with his open hand, enough to make a beefsteak tender; then, said he, and he grinned like a red-hot gridiron, the crittur was so pleased, I defy all the Blue-noses, John Bulls, Brunswickers, and devils that ever was, to prevent smugglin'. Old Nick is in the die if, in thirty-five miles of river and basin, you can't find an honest feller on one side or another of it, near whom you can lay aground by accident and run your goods. I am intarmined to fill that are country, called Nover Scotiar, with smuggled goods as full as a dog is full of fleas, ay, and as hard to be cotched, too, as them nimble-footed little gentlemen be. Ain't the British awful fools, too? said he; they do beat all: I actilly believe they are the biggest fools livin' this day, on the blessed airth.—Well, says I, I won't say they are jist the biggest fools nother, for them are colony chaps are pretty much of a muchness with them, six of one and half-a-dozen of t'other, and no great to choose nary way. But the next time, friend Wolfe, clinch the argument on your own thigh, that's a good soul, and not on mine, for I feel it tingle clean away down to the tip eends of my toes: and now I'll tell you somethin' you ain't axed yet, for you don't know all things, cute as you be. They used to have to the east, when I fust know'd it, an excise officer and a custom house officer to each port; now, I hear it is talked of to have one man to do the work of both (cause savin' is popular), and he will be kept so busy he won't have time to leave his home one etarnal minit, so there won't now be no custom-house at all in a manner, and that only for form's sake. It's a free-trade now, a'most, and we are a-goin' to have the whole supply afore long, see if we ain't; and one thing I have often remarked, Yankee trade brings Yankee notions. All we got to do, is, to be quiet. They call all change reform, them fellers; it's a sort o' party catch-word they larnt from the English, and all changes they make will help us and hurt them.—The devil a hair I care, says Lucifer, what they do. I am no politician, and I hate politicks. I am no great hand at makin' laws; but one thing I do pride myself on: I never seed the law yet that could tie my hands, for I am a rael scroudger: I can slip them thro' any clauses you please. Build up four square walls of laws round me, and I'll whip thro' the keyhole. The way I'll run goods into that are country is a caution to steam-boats and rail roads, and them plaister diggin', shingle weavin', clam-feedin' Blue-noses, may do their prettiest, cuss 'em. I'm for free-trade, and them that wants a fleece for revenue must first catch the sheep, that's my maxim; and if he is cotched, why he must jist submit to be sheared, that's all, for bein' such a born fool. But no one hadn't better go foolin' with me, for I've got a loadin' iron, "speechifier" by name, that never missed her man since Lucifer Wolfe owned her. She'll let daylight shine' thro' some o' them Blue-noses, I know, so they can't tell a sneeze from a blow'd-up boat, she's so quick on the trigger. I'm a good-natured man, but it don't do to rise me, I tell you, for it's apt to make me sour in hot weather.

But come, said he, that cocktail and your news is considerable excitin', and has whetted my appetite properly; I guess I'll order supper. What shall it be, corn bread and common doin's, or wheat bread and chickin fixin's? But we must fust play for it. What do you say to a game at all-fours, blind-hookey, odd and even, wild cat and 'coon, or somethin' or another, jist to pass time? Come, I'll size your pile.—Size my pile! says I, why, what the plague is that? I never heerd tell of that sayin' afore.—Why, says he, shell out, and plank down a pile of dollars or doubloons, of any size you like, and I'll put down another of the same size. Come, what do you say?—No, I thank you, says I, I never play.—Will you wrestle, then? said he; and whose ever throw'd pays the shot for supper.—No, says I, since I broke my leg a-ridin' a cussed Blue-nose hoss, I hante strength enough for that. —Well, then, we are near about of a height, says he, I estimate, let's chalk on the wall, and whoever chalks lowest liquidates the bill.—If it warn't for the plaguy rhumatiz I caught once to Nova-Scotia, says I, a-sleepin' in a bed the night arter a damp gall lodged there, I think I would give you a trial, says I; but the very thoughts of that foggy heifer gives me the cramp.

I jist said that to make him larf, for I seed he was a-gettin' his steam up rather faster than was safe, and that he could jist double me up like a spare shirt if he liked, for nothin' will take the wiry edge of a man's temper off like a joke: he fairly roared out, it tickled him so.—Well, says he, I like that idea of the damp gall; it's capital that: it's a Jerusalem bright thought. I'll air my wife, Miss Wolfe, before the fire to-night; I hope I may be kicked to death by grasshoppers if I don't. I'll heat her red-hot, till she scorches the sheets. Lord! how she'll kick and squeell when I spread her out on the close-horse. How it will make her squinch her face, won't it? She nevers hollers unless she's hurt, does Miss Wolfe, for she is a lady every inch of her, and a credit to her broughter-up. A damp gall! Come, that's good! it accounts for some on 'em bein' so wretched cold. But, stop, said he, it's no use a-sittin' here as still as two rotten stumps in a fog. I'll tell you what we'll do; here's two oranges, do you take one, and I'll take the other, and let us take a shy among them glasses to the bar there, and knock some o' them to darned shivers, and whoever breaks the fewest shall pay for the smash and the supper too. Come, are you ready, my old coon? let's drive blue-blazes thro' 'em.—No, says I, I'd be sure to lose, for I am the poorest shot in the world.—Poorest shote, said he, you mean, for you have no soul in you. I believe you have fed on pumkins so long in Conne'ticut, you are jist about as soft, and as holler, and good-for-nothin', as they be: what ails you? You hante got no soul in you, man, at all. This won't do: we must have a throw for it. I don't valy the money a cent; it ain't that, but I like to spikilate in all things. I'll tell you what we'll do,— let's spit for it; and he drew his chair up even with mine. Now, says he, bring your head back in a line with the top rail, and let go; and who ever spits furthest without spatterin' wins.— says I, you'll laugh when I tell you, I dare say, but I've gin up spittin' since I went down to Nova Scotia; I have, upon my soul, for nothin' riles them Blue-noses more. Spittin' would spile a trade there as quick as thunder does milk. I'm out of practice. They'll swaller anything, them fellers, they are such gulls, but they keep all they get: they won't let out, for they are as hard as the two sides of a grindstone.—Well, then, what the plague will you do? said he.—Why, says I, a-takin' up the candle, and a-yawnin' so wide and so deep you could hear the watch tickin' thro' my mouth, I'll guess I'll go to bed, says I, for I hadn't the leastest morsel of sleep in the world last night.—Mr. Slick, says he, a-risin' up, and a-clappin' both arms a-kimber, lookin' as fierce as a wild-cat, and jist crowin' like a cock agin, give me leaf to tell you, Mr. Slick, says he, that you are no gentleman, and he show'd his teeth as wicked as if he could grin a nigger white.—I never said I was, said I, so we won't quarrel about that.—But I'm not a-goin' to be baulked that way, said he; you'll find me fist a leetle the ugliest colt you ever undertook to brake; there is no back out in me, for I'm a snappin' turtle, so you'll fight or play, that's flat, and no two ways about it, so take your choice, for I feel most intierly wolfish and savagerous, and have half a mind to give you a tickler in the ribs that will make you feel monstrous amiable, and set you a-considerin', I tell you.—Says I, friend Wolfe, for I seed there a was a smart chance of a row, play I won't, so there is an eend of that matter, and as you are a-goin' to embark considerable capital in the smugglin' line, to Nova Scotia, (and I put my finger on my nose and winked that there might be no mistake about what I meant,) I guess it would be jist about as well for us not to quarrel. So don't kick afore you are spurred—do you take? Lord, it laid his bristles in a minit that, for the crittur's feelin', like some people's respectability, was all in his pocket.—Ah, said he, spoke like an honest man, that, and not like a cussed Yankee pedlar, and they ain't no better than an onsarcumcised Ingian, or an odoriferous nigger. There is some sense in that; give us your flipper, old boy; but let's have a drop of wet to drown it. I never sleep well unless words is either foughten out or washed out, and grog makes me feel as good-natured as a sooped eel.—Lord, how glad I was to find it takin' that are turn, for I was actilly in a piled-up agony and the chilly ague began to crawl all over me. Only thinkin' of fightin' such a ring-tail roarer as that, nearly broke two of my ribs short off. What shall it be, said I.—Apple toddy, said he.—Apple toddy then let it be, said I; and I ordered a pint o' the best, and so we slinged. Arter discussin' it out, we parted, on the best possible tarms, for ever I hope: *but cuss them bad shillin's, they are always a-comin' back to you,* there is no gettin' quit of them at no rate, for they won't take the mitten if you do try to cut them.

Such is the loose, good-for-nothin' loafers, cheats, smugglers, and outlaws, squire, the Blue-noses are a to have among them, by their beautiful free ports, for the trade won't pay regular marchants, and, unless I am much mistaken when once these "bad shillin's" are imported they'll find it no easy matter to drive them out of circulation agin. The advantage is all on our side. The reason why Windsor hasn't growd more of late years is, they have had a lot of poor little miserable coasters, that either didn't know the way, or was afraid to go beyond the American lines, so Windsor built Eastport. Now they have got bigger vessels, are makin' money hand over hand in airnest, and jist as they have got it to work right, they must have a reform free port, and give the carryin' trade to us. If it warn't that puppies can't see till they are nine days old, one would wonder they were so blind; but the wust of it is, they are plaguy apt, afore they do find their sight, to get their ears cropt and their tails cut. It reminds me of father and neighbour

Outhouse Pipes. Father had a hundred acres lot in the rear of his farm, that was used as a pastur, and a capital one it was too, well watered, well shaded, and well covered with beautiful white clover, and sweet grasses, and what not; but it cost considerable to keep up the fence round it. So, said he, one day, to Outhouse Pipes, neighbour, says he, that partition fence costs a great deal of time, money, and trouble, every year, and poles is gittin' almighty scarce, I'm a-most afeerd we shall run out of wood afore long, suppose we pastur in common, and let that fence down, the poles would do for other fences, and be quite handy. Well, says Pipes, quite careless like, so as not to let father see how pleased he was; well, says he, I was a thinkin' myself it would be more neighbourly, and every bit and grain as good too. I don't care if I do. Well, what does Outhouse Pipes do, for his stock was more nor twice as large as father's, what does he do, but turns in all his cattle, hogs and sheep, and father's pastur' being the best, they all in course went into his field, and when dry time in summer come, his tarnation lookin' cattle, cross bull, and breachy oxen, 'most worried all father's dairy cows to death, and finally druv 'em all out into the township barrens. There never was no findin' them when you wanted them, and in a little while they fell off in the milk, got thin and mangy, and looked like old scratch. Well, bimeby father got tired of this fun, and wanted Outhouse Pipes to fence again on the division line; says he, I guess you have eat sour grapes, and your sons' teeth are on edge, ain't they? He said it warn't reasonable at all to be so peskily whimsical and crotchical; that it was none of his seekin' to pastur' in common; that we had used up all his share of the poles, and didn't know where to get any more; and, arter five years' 'crastination, vexation, and trouble, father, to eend the dispute, went and put up the whole line himself, his own and neighbour Pipes, too. Cuss them cattle, Sam, says father, they have done me more nor a hundred pounds damage, but I guess, when a man has *a good field of his own, containin' all he wants in the way of feed, shelter, and water, he had better snug up his fences strong and tidy, and keep it to himself.* But father's trouble warn't eended so easy as he was a-thinkin' on. Havin' once got a taste of the good grass, the nasty onruly brutes of Outhouse's were for everlastin'ly a-breakin' in and chasin' our beasts from one eend of the pasture to the other. As for father, poor old soul, he spent most of his time a-runnin' and a-hollerin' arter them stray critturs, and drivin' of them out. Well, if this don't beat the bugs, he'd say! What a spot o' work this is sartainly. They are like *a bad shillin'* them breachy devils, you can't git rid of them at no rate. Put them out as often as you please, they are for everlastin'ly a-comin' back to you.

I am a-thinkin', said the Clockmaker, the Blue-noses will find that arter a while, usin' the trade in common with us is like father's pastur', their neighbours have two craft to their one to put in it, and bein' the strongest of the two, will gradually drive them off altogether, while shutting them out again is easier talked of than done, and that when actilly debarred the onruly ones will occasionally break in and cause tarnal trouble and expense. *Changing one thing for another is not always reform, as they have found out to England, to their sorrow, in more things than one.* But them who change often and unnecessary, are apt sometimes to find to their cost, when it's too late, that they have incautiously got hold on "*a bad shillin'*."

XII

TRADING IN BED

DURING one of our former journeys a circumstance occurred, that I did not understand at the time, but which Mr. Slick now explained to me. On our return from Chester in Nova Scotia to Windsor, we stopped at a small house on the road side, near a sawmill, for the purpose of feeding our horse, and in the course of a conversation which it appeared to me was designedly introduced, relative to the stream and the adjoining timber-land, Mr. Slick extolled the " water power" "mill privilege" betterments and convenience and value of the place in terms of such extravagant praise, that the owner proposed to sell it to him, an offer which was immediately accepted.

You see, said Mr. Slick to him, I ain't jist prepared to pay you right down on the nail in hard pewter, not expectin' any such trade, but "*I'll bond it;*" that is, do you bind yourself in a bond to give a title, upon my payin' you five hundred pounds within two years. If I pay it, why then the land is mine; and if I don't do so, why there is no harm done: you take, don't you?—Well, I don't know as I do, said Blue-nose (who appeared puzzled at this novel mode of selling property, in which the bond was to be given to the wrong man). Why don't you give me a bond, said he, for the purchase-money, and I'll give you a deed? I'll trust *you,* for you are good for more nor that.—Why, I'll tell you, said the Clockmaker. It's altogether for your advantage, and saves trouble and expense, you see. Accordin' to your plan, if I didn't pay my bond when it's due, why you'd lose the land: now this way, you don't part with the land till you get the money; for you hold on till you are paid and finger the cash. It's safer and better for *you,* and I must say I do like a fair deal. So now, do you take the pen and write the bond yourself to prevent mistakes, and I will tell you what to put into it. The bond was accordingly written, duly executed, and delivered, and we proceeded on our journey. As this transaction had taken place some time ago, and never again been referred to by Mr. Slick, it had nearly escaped my memory; but the opportunity having now occurred of making an advantageous use of it, he unfolded his object without reserve.

We are now, squire, said he, in the state of Maine, the head-quarters of land spekilators, and I'll put off my Chester friend's bond to an advance. I never had no notion of buyin' that are feller's land. I don't want it no more nor my old waggon does a fifth wheel. I've been spekilatin' on his capital. If I don't sell the bond, lose nothin', for I have paid nothin'; if I sell it, I gain all I can get for it. It is one of the best and prettiest modes of trading I know on; but the difficultest part is all to do yet, and that is to sell it. Anybody can put the leake into a Blue-nose, or a John Bull, for they are a primitive, unsuspectin' sort of folks, not jist exactly up to snuff; but to walk into a down east-land jobber requires great skill, I tell you, and a very considerable knowledge of human natur' and of bisness. If your hook ain't well covered, and the bait well chose and suited to the season, they won't so much as look at it. If you pull at a nibble, you never get another one, for there is nothin' so bad as eagerness. A quick eye, a steady hand, and cool temper, is not do withoutable. Tantalise 'em, play 'em on and off, let 'em see the bait and smell it, then jist raise it a little out of sight till they have to look for it, and then let it float down stream for them to foller, and when they get to it, snub it short till they pass it, and have to turn back and make up agin' stream. They don't see so clear then for the drift stuff, air bubbles, and what not; and when you find them makin' right at it full split with their mouths open, slacken up a little, and jist as they snap at it, draw it forward an inch or so, and then rest a bit. The next grab they make they will take in the bait, hook, sinker, and all, and maybe a part of the line, then give it a back pull (not forrard, for that is blundersome, and may pull it out agin p'raps, but back) with a short turn of the wrist, and it whips the hook right into the jaw. O, it's beautiful play, that! it sharpens the wit, pints the eye teeth, and raises a man in the scale of intelligence. I never see a human yet, unless he was one of our free and enlightened citizens, that had the science—never, and I must say my hand is 'most out. I want prac*tice*; for in them British provinces the folks are as simple as the partridges be, and they are so tame and so stupid, it's no fun a-goin' out a-gunnin' arter them, for you can shoot 'em like hens at a roost. Floorin' one of them afore the eyes of the others never starts the flock, it only 'mazes them.—But stop, said he, tapping me on the shoulder, stop, squire, and look out o' that are winder. Do you see that are tall, limber-timbered, slinky-lookin' man with the blue cloak and two long black cords a-hangin' from it with almighty big tassels a-danglin' to the eend of it like the lamp-rope there, a-carryin' part of the cloak, folded on one arm like a Roman senator, and t'other arm kimber, with his hat cockaded military like?—well, that is General Conrad Corncob. He is the greatest spikilator in these parts. He made a hundred thousand dollar in eastern lands last year, and ten thousand to New Brunswick this season. He thinks no small beer of himself, that man, and boasts that he never put his foot in it in his life. If I don't lighten him of two thousand dollars afore to morrow mornin', say my name is not Sam Slick. I'll walk right into him, tight as he is, I know. I'll bam him so he'll be a caution, I hope I may be shot, if I won't. There is nothin' like fishin' for the leadin' trouts of the hole—no, nothin'; there is some fun in that, somethin' worth holdin' out the landin'-net for—beautiful spots of gold on them fellers—lick, it makes my mouth water. It's excitin'—it's dreadful pretty; it caps all, that's a fact. I shan't see you now agin till mornin', squire, for it's considerable well on in the evenin' now, when daylight's down, and I shouldn't wonder if I had "*to trade in bed*" afore I bring *him* to tarms; so good-night. I'll play possum with you in the mornin', and be ready to start with you as early as you please.

The following morning Mr. Slick put a small piece of paper in my hand, and said, with a smile of triumph on his face,—Read that, squire, if you please.—"To the cashier of the Bangor Bank. Sir, please to pay to Samuel Slick, Esq. two thousand dollars and ninety cents, and charge the same to yours, &c. Conrad Corncob, Lt. Gen."—I did him, said he, exultingly, I did him; but it was no easy matter, I tell you. I had to play him up and down stream more nor once, and shift the colour of the fly till I tempted him; but he is bagged for once, anyhow. It was a'most a-difficult piece of bisness; and I must say, tho' I say it that shouldn't say it, that I don't think there is another man this blessed day in the States would have done it but myself, not one. But come, we must be a-movin'; and as we drive on, I'll tell you how it was.

Arter I left you, I seed him in a line with the stable; so I jist walks out and makes for the hoss-stalls, lookin' down in a hurry like, and seemin' chock full of bisness, and not lettin' on as if I know'd that he was there, for there is nothin' like a non-committal, and he calls out,—Why, Slick, if that ain't you, as I am alive! why, how do you do, eh? who on airth would have expected to have seed you here.—So I looks up, 'mazed like, like a feller that's lost his road, and, says I,— Stranger, you have the advantage of me, I guess.—Possible, said he, not know me? oh, for ever!—Why, says I, I know

your voice, and know your face, and *ought* to know your name; but——.
—Well, if you think you *ought*, said he, you *shall*. Don't you mind Gineral
Conrad Corncob, him that was kyurnal last war on full pay?—Corncob?
says I. Let me see, said I. Corncob—Corncob!—and then I scratched my
head, like a dog in sarch of a flea,—oh! ay! to be sure I do, and glad to
see you too.—I thought, said he, Slick, you was down to Nova Scotia, a-
tradin' among them tatur-headed Blue-noses; and d—n them fellers, they
talk rather warlike about the boundary line. I shouldn't wonder if they'd
like a war, the villains; for they'd find it a plaguy sight easier, I estimate, to
come and grab our vessels than build them for themselves. Halifax always
goes ahead by a war. Have you done anything out of the clock line down
there lately? Is there any room there for a spec' in the land way on a large
scale?—Well, I jist look'd up at him and eyed him hard in the face, without
sayin' of a word for a space, dubersome like, as if it was a dangerous thing
to let one's tongue run too fast, and then said, a-holdin' of my head down,
as if I had concluded to keep dark,—Well, I must say, said I, I haven't done
bad in clocks, that's sartain.—Fire and tow! have you done anything in the
timber line? said he, for that is a rising property.—Well, I made as if I didn't
hear him, so as to 'cite his curiosity, and, says I,—Gineral, that are boundary
line will cause trouble yet, I reckon. You Maine folks have been talkin' a
leetle too fast lately, a leetle too much bush. You won't frighten Blue-nose
so easy as you are a-thinkin' on, I tell you.—Well, says he, we've talked and
bragged so much lately about it, I'm tired and sick of the subject; but I see
you have made a hit, I know you have, you are so infarnal costive. I've seed
folks carry a heavy secret afore to-day.—What is it?—Governor Fairfield
has been too rash, and talked too big, says I. We have suffered in the eyes of
foreigners. — The devil take the eyes of foreigners, and Governor Fairfield,
and the boundary too, says he. Fire and tow! your spec', what is it? And
he opened his cloak and put his arm inside of and walked on.—What's
the tune, said he, two or three hundred thousand dollars, eh?—Well says
I, gineral, there is no evadin' you, you are so everlastin' cute. I believe you
could see a hole in a millstone if it was no bigger than the pint of a needle,
providin' you picked it yourself. Who told you I had made a spec? tell me
now how it leaked out.—Oh! says he, I knew it from your manner, I hope
I may be shot if I didn't. Fire and tow! It tante no easy matter to blind
me.—Well, then, says I, I *have* made a spec', gineral, that's a fact, and such
a spec', too, as ain't often made now-a-days nother. It's a top sawyer one, I

do assure you; but I can't avail it. I am afraid this Britisher that's here will be the ruin of me yet; for he has made me promise to make tracks with him this summer, and I am 'most afeerd I shall lose the chance of gettin' up a company by it, and it's a pity, too, for there ain't such a location atween the poles hardly. I got it for half nothin', a mere song; it's grand, that's sartain. Now, says I, if you would give me a little advice how to work it, I'll give you some hints about property in Nova Scotia that will clear two hundred per cent.; but it's a long story, and walls have ears, so I will turn in with you, if Miss Corncob, your wife, ain't here, and we'll talk it over in bed. If we can agree, I will give you an agency that will be worth while.—Well, says he, do, for there is nothin' like "*tradin' a-bed*," and I will council you to the best of my abilities; but is it refuge or superfine clear stuff, or only marchantable.—Oh! says I, there is no mistake, it's for myself, and not to put off agin; it's the rael solid thing, and not holler, or lackered, or plated, but jist genu*wine*. If it was a barn, there would be no need of advice, I reckon; but it's how to go the whole figur'.

Well, arter walkin' about a trifle from the house, for a while, and talkin' about indifferent subjects, we took jist a dust of rael good mint julip, and turned into bed.—Says he, Slick, excuse me, but I must turn my back on you, for, as I chews a good deal, I'd have to spit across you in the night, which ain't very genteel, so I can't lay spoonbill fashion.—Now for the spec'.—I seed his curiosity was up, so not to appear in a hurry, I said, Gineral, says I, nothin' but bisness would ever make me sleep with a man. I got frightened out of a year's growth once, by goin' to bed with a Britisher. It was second or third stage out of Buffalo, Canady way. When I arrived it was late to night, and I had to dig thro' the woods considerable sharp to get there at all. The house was full, and every bed had two in it, all 'xcept one, and that an Englishman had, who carried on and swore so 'bout sleepin' two in a bed that they gave him one all to himself, more to save the bother, of havin' a quarrel with him than out of any love for him; for them English are the devil when travellin', they give so much trouble, and do what you will are never satisfied.—Exactly, said the Gineral, most commonly their manners are rude, overbearin', and tyrannical. They want their flints fixed for 'em as we did last war; but, fire and tow! let's have your spec' afore we get a noddin'; I shall go for it soon, for I am considerable sleepy, I tell you.—Well, says I, so they jist told me to take up with the Englishman, and I ondressed in two-twos, outs with the candle, and into bed in no time. The crittur was a-lyin' with his back to me, a-snoring like a bull, and more nor once I had a-mind to wake him, so that we might have a fair start for it; but then, I thought it would only eend in a fight, so I let him be. But jist as I was a-droppin' off to sleep, the crittur fell too and kicked like a jackass. Lord, I thought he would have kicked me out of bed, or broke my leg, he kicked so like all possessed. Thinks I to myself, what on airth shall I do? shall I give him a slockdolager onder the ear and wake him up, or shall I turn to and kick him in return agin? I didn't actilly know what to do; at last I gets upon my knees, gist lays hold of him by the shoulders and turned him over, with his face to me, and his back to the outside of the bed. Now, says I, kick away till you are tired, will you, my hearty, and you won't hurt nothin' but the wall. Well, if he didn't snore and kick away in great style, it's a pity, but as he didn't touch me no more, I dropped off a-sleep, and left him a-batterin' away at the wall with his heels like a paviour's rammer. In the mornin' he was quiet enough; but oh, such an ugly ungainly lookin' beast I never seed. He had his mouth wide open, a-showin' of his snags of teeth like a hoss when he sneezes, and there was dry froth on his nose and lips from snortin' so. His eyes was open too, (for some men sleep with their peepers open, like the Dutch overseer of the niggers with the glass eye, in the sugar-house,) and they stared like the eyes of an owl, and had jist sich a glassy, filmy, onmeanin' look. His hands, like most Britishers, was as white as chalk, but the nails was blue, and so was his lips. The nostrils were pinched in, and his nose looked pointed, altogether he was a perfect pictur' of an ugly man. Hullo, shipmate, says I, how's your heels this mornin'? I guess you must have hurt 'em agin' that are wall last night, for you kicked like all vengeance; but he was as sound as a top. With that, I throw'd down the clothes on *my* side, and was a-gittin' out of bed, when one leg touched him, and his skin was so cold and so clammy; I turned round and took another survey of him, and then put my ear close to his mouth, and I hope I may be shot if he warn't as dead as a herring. He was, I swear. It was an apperplexy fit he had, that made him kick so, like mad. It made me quite sick; I didn't get that crittur's ugly mug out of my thoughts for one while, I know. It was horrid now, warn't it?—Well, fire and tow! it was horrid, that's a fact, said the Gineral, and if your bed-fellers are apt to be so confounded on-lucky, I must say I'm 'most afeerd to go to bed with you. I don't like to hear about them things at night, they kinder skeer away sleep and set me a dreamin'; let's hear about your Nova

Scotia estate: what is it like?—We had a crowner's inquest on the body, says I, and the crowner, who was a bit of a wag, returned a vardict, "died of fright, a-sleepin' along with a Yankee." He did, upon my soul. Fact, I assure you.—Who the plague cares, says Corncob, what the great fat porter-drinkin' hog died of; do, for gracious' sake, let him be. Did you say your land was in Nova Scotia or New Brunswick? Come, gin' over foolin', that's a good feller.—I seed he was very anxious to hear about the bond, so to tease him and pique him, says I, I had another curious adventure once with a man in bed.—What a devil of a long-winded feller you be, Slick, says he; why don't you come to the pinte at once? if you want advice, ax it; if not, let's go to sleep, for your stories are dismal. Fire and tow! I shall see that dead man in a night-mare yet.—Well, says I, this one will make you larf, anyhow, for it took a different turn from t'other one altogether. When I fust went out in the clock line, up Huron way, I used to be subject to the cramp, violent fits of the cramp, and nothin' a'most gave me relief but holdin' up a roll of stick brimstone in my hand, and I used to place it every night onder the pillar of my bed to have it handy. Well, one night (and most sincerely cold it was too) I was a-bed along with Plato Frisk, a jumpin' Quaker, a terrible cross-grained cantankersome crittur as ever I seed. He had a beard like a goat, it hung down to his waist a'most, and he had the power of raisin' it up with his chin, and whiskin' it as an ondocked crittur does its tail. A switch of it across your face was as bad as a blow from a bunch of stingin' nettles; it made it smart agin, like all wrath. It was a caution to look at. His nose was long, thin, and rounded, like the shape of a reapin' hook, and his eyes as black and small as a weasel's; they looked like two burnt holes in a blanket, they was so deep. He actilly was an awful lookin' crittur, as shaggy as a two-year old, and jist about as ontamed too. Well, I woke up in the night half dead with the cramp, and screamin' like mad, and I jist out fin and felt for the brimstone, and I no sooner seized it than Frisk he roared like a bull too, and folks came runnin' and troopin' in from the other room, to see what on airth all the hubbub was about; and I hope I may die this blessed minit if I hadn't got him by the nose in mistake for the brimstone (a'most an endless one it was too), and was a squeezin' away and a-hangin' on to it like grim death to a dead nigger. It made me larf so, when the lights come in and I seed the ugly faces the goney made, that it cured the cramp, hang me if it didn't. Well, the Gineral he haw-hawed right out, like thunder.—Why, Slick, said he, what a droll feller you be! that was a mistake done a–purpose, I know it was, for you was always full of the devil when a boy; but for gracious' sake let my nose alone, at any rate, for I hante much to spare, I tell *you*. Upon my word you ain't over safe to sleep with, are you? But, fire and tow! let's go to land, as the feller said when the boat upset, let's get to land. Let's have bisness first, and jokes arterwards.—Well, there is reason even in roastin' an egg. I know'd I might push this too far, and that it was time to stop afore he smelt a rat. So I jist began at the beginnin', by tellin' him the land warn't for sale at no rate, but for a company, in shares, to be called " Chester Lakes Mill Company," and to be incorporated like other companies, so that they needn't pay their debts if they hadn't a mind to. Then I laid out afore him how grand the water powers was, and what noble timber there was all around on the Queen's land that was to be had for takin', and the great lakes for raftin' of it, and Windsor river for shippin' of it, and Mahone Bay on t'other side for exportin' of it, and so on, and then offer'd him a bonus of four hundred dollars, and a commission of ten per cent. to sell shares. All the time I was a talkin' of this, I heerd old "fire and tow" a-workin' of the weed in great style, and when I got this far, he put out his hand and felt onder the pillar for his baccy. I seed he was a beginnin' to nibble at the bait, and that he was fairly on the scent, and I calculated I should have him afore long, if nothin' didn't skeer him. Says he, why not sell out and out and have done with it? I think I could show you how to put it off.—Sell it, says I, catch me a-sellin' of it! why it's onfit for sale.—Onfit! says he: how so? I thought you said it was particular jam.—So it is, says I, and that's the reason it's onfit; it's the rael right down thing itself.—You know best, says he, but if I was to presume to offer an opinion to a man o' your judgment, I should say, sell. Companies is cumbrous, full of liabilities, and troublesome. Sales is short and snug, and they eend the bisness, so you can turn the money quick, and are ready for a fresh start.—Exactly, says I, when it's a bam sell by all means; but when it's got a bottom my rule is to hold on.—Says he, look here, Slick.—What on airth is the use of lookin', says I, for it's as dark as Egypt; I can't see if I do look.—Fire and tow! said he, listen, if you can, for you are like a sheep's head, all jaw. I'll give you two thousand dollars at a word, for your bargain; what do you say now, go or no go? Say the word, bargain or no bargain!—I'll give you an answer in the mornin', Gineral, says I. I don't want to part with it, and I must sleep upon it. The fact is, selling shares to a company would bring more nor twice that are sum. Let me cypher over it a little, for I have got hold of a rael pitikilar smart chance, and the right eend of the rope too, and if I am too greedy to turn it at once, I know I shall repent it to my dying day.—No, said he, I like a man to be up to the notch, and stand to his lick-log; salt or no salt, say the word, or it's no offer.—Dear, dear, said I, you put the leake into everyone, a'most, Gineral; other men beat the bush, but you catch the bird; say ninety cents more, for I have made a vow I wouldn't look at two thousand dollars, and it's yourn.—Fire and tow! then, done, said he, and now I'll show you how I do business; and with that he jumps out of bed and lights a lucifer, and openin' of his desk, says he, write you a short assignment of that bond, Slick, and I will write the cheque; and in less than twenty minutes the bond was in his trunk, the cheque in my portmanter, and we was both in bed agin, back to back, as sociable as you please. Well Gineral, says I, as you say business fust and jokes arterwards, now I'll tell you another story of two fellers sleepin' in one bed, a'most as good as t'other one.

The house they was a-sleepin' in took fire, and they jumps up in an all-fired hurry, and seesin' one pair of trousers atween them, half asleep and half awake as they was, each put a leg in it, and they rolled down stairs tied together kickin' and' squeelin' like two pigs, and were half trod to death and 'most killed. I'll tell you how it was.—Do be quiet, says he; I believe in my soul you'd talk all night; and when I larf so much, I can't go to sleep arterwards, it sets me a-coughin' so. Good-night, and he was off in a hand gallop of a spore in a little less than half no time.—Thinks I to myself, (half larfin' in my sleeve till I a'most snickered agin,) you are right, Gineral, bisness first, and jokes arterwards; that's jist exactly what you have been doin', only you don't know it. You'll find this night's work a capital joke some o' these days, or I am mistakened, that's all. You'd rather a-had the dead Englishman here alongside of you in bed than me, I know. You might a-got an odd kick from him, but I'll be hanged if you'd a-been *bit*. The crittur hadn't sense enough for that at no time. Oh! it was done pretty, that, squire; it made me feel good all over. It was what I call work manlike. Bed is the place for doin' bisness in arter all. You ain't bound to hear all that's said in bed; and if you hesitate, and boggle a little, why it looks sleepy like, and not stupid. There ain't time too for chafferin' and higglin' too long; and a funny story throw'd in for spice, keeps a feller in good humor. Then there ain't no fear of interruption or observation, and nothin' to distract attention. Bundlin' or courtin' in the new clearin's is done the same way.

It's the best place for makin' a sarmon in too, or an oration, or any difficult piece of bisness; but as for dealin' and traffikin' that requires skill, depend on it, squire, if you are only wide awake and duly sober, there is nothin like *"tradin' in bed."*

XIII

KNOWING THE SOUNDINGS,
OR POLLY COFFIN'S SANDHOLE

THE reckless speculation occasioned by an equally reckless issue of paper money, which has of late years appeared in the United States, has had a far more injurious operation than any one who has not carefully watched its progress and effects could possibly suppose. The first apparent change it produced was to raise the price of real and personal property far beyond their value, and to cause the unhappy delusion, that this feverish excitement was a healthy condition. That a great alteration had taken place was obvious to all; and those who were profiting by it, found it by no means a difficult task to make men believe it was the natural result of republican institutions, of a free trade, a fertile soil, and an intelligent spirit of enterprise. In this opinion they were unfortunately confirmed, by finding the liberal party among the English and the Colonists constantly repeating the same absurd theory, and contrasting the high prices of the United States with the sounder and more rational condition of Canada, as a proof of the superior advantages of elective governments over a monarchy. They all affected to be unable to attribute the difference in the price of land on the opposite sides of the boundary line to any other cause than the ballot, universal suffrage, and annual elections. The consequence of all this has been, that the Americans have suffered immense losses in their trade, while the colonists have suffered no less in their peace and happiness, by the introduction of wild theories of government by those whose rank and influence gave a mischievous weight to their opinions. In the States however, the great pecuniary loss they have sustained is by far the least injury they have incurred from this unfortunate error. *They have suffered in their morals.* A wild and unprincipled speculation like this has no pretension to be dignified by the name of trade or enterprise. It is one of the worst species of gambling, inasmuch as it originates in deception, and is contaminated with fraud throughout. The preceding sketch, which is *founded on fact,* shows with what care even clever and experienced men like General Corncob can be duped, when their caution is disarmed by the eagerness of speculation; and how readily a man like the Clockmaker can reconcile himself, by the aid of a little sophistry, to a fraudulent transaction.

Had you no compunction, said I, Mr. Slick, in palming off upon the General that worthless bond, and in taking from him so large a sum of money as two thousand dollars without giving him any equivalent whatever? Compunction, said he, in great astonishment, why no, squire, why should I? This ain't tradin', it's spekilatin'. It makes all the difference in the world. For instance, I make a throw, you see, and he buys it. Well, if it wins, he gets whatever we raffled for, and if he don't, he loses, that's all. Great gains cover many losses. If one land spekilation in ten turns out well, and is rael jam it makes a man's nest. Oh, no! if it was trade, why honor bright! but it tante, it's spekilatin'; and you might as well call loo, or put, or all-fours, or any other game trade. It tante givin' valy for a thing, *it's buyin' a chance*. Now, there is no more harm done in settin' off a chance to advantage than in platin' a candlestick, or gildin' a frame. It's puffin', that's all, and that's done every day everywhere; so it is in smugglin'—do you suppose there is any harm in that? If you smuggle clever, you win; if you don't, it's seized, and there is an eend on it; you lose the trick, but the game is not immoral.

It would be difficult to believe that so sensible a man as Mr. Slick could be the dupe of such shallow nonsense, if daily experience did not prove how much easier men can deceive themselves, where their interest is concerned, than satisfy others, and how soon the morals of a country are damaged by this sort of national gambling. The explanation was disagreeable. I was reluctant to permit him to lower himself in my opinion, and I changed the conversation by a reference to colonial subjects. These were topics on which I admired to hear him talk, as his observations were generally correct, often original, and, always amusing.—Yes, said he, I must say, without a morsel of vanity, I estimate I have picked up a few notions of men and things in a gineral way that every one can't boast of. Now, there's them colonies and colony chaps, Lord, I know their ins and outs better than they do themselves. Oh, dear I wish I had the berth Lord Sir John Russell, Queen's Prime Minister for immigrants has, for jist one month. The way I'd show him how to handle the ribbons ain't no matter, I know. I'd larn him how to set on the box, how to hold the whip atween his teeth, and to yawk the reins with both hands, so as to make each hoss in the team feel he had a master that was none o' the scariest, and that wouldn't put up with no nonsense. A cross-grained, ongainly crittur wouldn't frighten me by layin' down and refusin' to draw, I tell you. I'd jist start the rest of the cattle into a handsome lope, and give him a drag over the gravel till I scratched his hide for him a considerable sum, and see how double quick he'd get tired of that fun, up on his pegs, and go as quiet as a lamb. Lord, I'd come down on him like a duck on a June bug; I'd make him wake snakes, and walk his chalks, as the western folks say, I know. Nothin' vexes an onruly beast like takin' no notice of him, but jist movin' on as if it was all the same to you what he did, as you know how to fix his flint. I have an idea that no man can be a good statesman that can't drive well. There's a great deal to be larned from hosses. Natur' is natur', that is a fact; but the natur' of a hoss ain't human, that's all, and he can't talk; study *him*, therefore, and man comes easy arter that. There ain't no part of a hoss I don't know, stock, lock, or barrel. No man can't cheat me in a hoss. As for a John Bull, or a Blue-nose, I never seed one yet that I couldn't walk right into like a pumkin-pie. They are as soft as dough, them fellers. No, sir; a steady arm and a light hand is what is wanted, not givin' them their head one minit, and curbin' them the next, and most throwin' 'em down. That's no way to drive, but jist the way to spile their temper; but bein' afeerd on 'em is the devil, it ruins 'em right off. Oh, dear! if I was only alongside Lord Sir John on the state-box, I'd teach him in six lessons so that he could manage them by whisperin'; but you might as well whistle jigs to a milestone as to an Englishman, they are so infarnal sot in their ways. The first thing to know how to get safe into port is to study the soundings. I mind a trick I played once on old "Tarnal Death," as we called Captain Ebenezer Fathom, the skipper I went to South Sea with. He know'd every inch of the American coast as well as he did of his own cabin; and whenever he throw'd the lead, and looked at what sort of bottom it showed, he know'd as well where he was as if he was in sight of land. He did beat all, that's a fact, and proper proud he was of it too, a-boastin' and a-crackin' of it for everlastingly. So, afore I goes aboard, off I slips to a sandpit on Polly Coffin's betterments, where they got sand for the Boston iron foundaries, and fills a bag with it and puts it away in my trunk. Well, we was gone the matter of three years on that are voyage afore we reached home; and as we neared the Nantuckit coast, Captain Ebenezer comes down to the cabin and turns in, and says he, Sam, says he, we are in soundin's now, I calculate; run on till twelve o'clock, and then heave-to and throw the lead, for it as dark as Comingo, and let me see what it fetches up, and, tarnal death! I'll tell you to the sixteenth part of an inch what part of the thirteen united univarsal worlds we be in.—I will you bet, says I, you do?—I'll bet you a pound of the best Varginy pigtail, says he; for I am out of baccy this week past, and have been chawing oakum until my jaws fairly stick together with the tar. Yesterday, when you turned in, I throw'd out a signal of distress, and brought a Britisher down on us five miles out of his way; but, cuss him, when he found out I only wanted a pig of tobacco, he swore like all vengeance, and hauled his wind right off. What tarnal gulls and fools they be, ain't they? Yes, I'll bet you a pound of the best.—Done, says I, I'll go my death on it you don't tell; for I never will believe no soul can steer by the lead, for sand is sand everywhere; and who can tell the difference?—Any fool, said he, with half an eye, in the pitchiest, inkyest, lampblackiest night that ever was created. I didn't get here into the cabin by jumpin' thro' the skylight, as national officers do, but worked my way in from before the mast. Tarnal death to me! a man that don't know soundin's when he sees it is fit for nothin' but to bait shark-hooks with. Soundin's, eh? why, I was born in soundin's, sarved my time out in soundin's, and made a man of in soundin's, and a pretty superfine fool I must be if I don't know 'em. Come, make yourself scarce, for I am sleepy; and he was a-snorin' afore I was out of the cabin.— Well, at twelve o'clock we hove-to, and sure enough found sand at fifty fathom, as he said we would. What does I do but goes and takes another lead and dips it into the water to wet it, and then stirs it in the bag of sand I had stowed away in my trunk, and then goes and wakes up the skipper. Hollo, shipmate! says I, here's the lead: we have got a sandy bottom in fifty fathom, as you said.—Exactly, says he, didn't I tell you so. I can feel my way all along the coast when it's so dark you can't hear yourself speak. I know every foot of it as well as if I made it myself. Give me the lead.—As soon as he took it and looked at it, he jumpt right up an eend in bed.—Hollo! said he, what the devil's this? give me my spec's, that's a good feller, for I don't see as well as I used to did.—So I goes to the table and hands him his spectacles, and says I, I knew you couldn't tell no more than any one else by the lead. That are boast of yourn was a bam, and nothin' else. I'll trouble you for your pound of Varginy pigtail; jist enter it in the log, will you?—Heavens and airth! said he, a-mutterin' to himself, old Nantuck is sunk, an airthquake, by gum! What a dreadful pretty piece of bisness this is!—He looked as white as chalk: his eyes started most out of his head, and his hair looked a hundred ways for Sunday. Lord, how frightened he looked, he was quite onfakilised.—Tarnal death to me! says he, bring the candle here agin; and then he wiped his eyes fust, and then his spec's, and took another long look at it, as steady if he was a drawin' a bead on it fine with his rifle.— After a space, he jumps right out of bed on the floor, and bawls out as loud as thunder to the hands on deck,—" 'Bout ship, boys! said he, 'bout ship for your lives, as quick as wink! old Nantuck has gone for it as sure as rates, it has by Gosh! I hope I may die this blessed instant minute of time if that are lead hasn't gone right slap into old Aunt Polly Coffin's Sandhole. What a spot o' work this is! Poor old Nantuck!" and he was jist ready to cry a'most, he seemed so sorry.—Stop, says I, captain, I'm 'most afeerd I've made a mistake; I do believe I've gin you the wrong lead: look at this, a-handin' up to him and a-showin' of him the right one.—Ah! says he, fust a-smilin' and then bustin' out in a hoss-laugh, you thought to catch me, Sammy, did you, my boy? but it's more nor you nor any livin' soul can. None o' you can put the leake into me where soundin's is consarned. I defy all creation to do that. Nothin' but an airthquake can do that. "Let her off two pints, and hold on that way till daylight." Nobody had better not go foolin' with me; and then he swung round and fixed for a nap, agin makin' a chucklin' noise, half grunt, half larf. Catch me, catch the devil, will you? Think I don't know the bar grit from Polly Coffin's Sandhole? Oh! of course I don't, I don't know nothin', nor ever did; I never had no eyes nor no sense nother. Old folks never know nothin', and never will; so, tarnal death to you! teach your grandmother to clap ashes, and your daddy how to suck eggs, will you?

Now, squire, I know the soundin's of them are colonies as well as Captain Ebenezer did Nantucket bottom, and could put his royal highness Lord Sir John Russell up to a thing or two he don't know, that's a fact. He ought to go and see for himself, how else *can* he know whether folks are drawin' the wool over his eyes or no, or whether it's proper to 'bout ship or not? Do you think he could tell now, or any other British minister that ever stood in shoe-leather, from the days of old Captain Noah of the Ark whaler downwards, how many kinds of patriots there are in the colonies? no, not he. It's a question that would pose most men, unless they had sarved an apprenticeship to state teachin'. Well, there are jist five.

Rebel patriots, mahogany patriots, spooney patriots, place patriots, and rael genu*ine* patriots. Now, to govern a colony, a man ought to know these critturs at first sight; for they are as different from each other as a hoss is from a jackass, or a hawk from a handsaw.—*A rebel patriot* is a gentleman that talks better than he fights, hante got much property in a gineral way, and hopes to grab a little in the universal scramble. He starts on his own hook, looks to his rifle for his support, and shoots his own game. If he got his due, he would get a gallus for his reward.—*A mahogany patriot* is a crittur that rides like a beggar a-horseback: you'll know him by his gait. As soon as he begins to get on a bit in the world, he is envious of all them that's above him, and if he can't get his legs onder the mahogany of his betters, is for takin' his better's mahogany away from them. To skin his pride over and salve his vanity, he says he is excluded on account of his politicks and patriotism, a martyr to his vartue. This chap mistakes impedence for independence, and abuse for manliness: he is jist about a little the dirtiest and nastiest bird of the whole flock of patriots. This feller should be sarved out in his own way: he should stand in the pillory and be pelted with rotten eggs.—*A spooney patriot* is a well-meanin', silly Billy, who thinks the world can be reduced to squares like a draftboard, and governed by systems; who talks about reforms, codifyin', progression, schoolmasters abroad, liberality, responsibility, and a pack of party catch words that he don't know the meaning of. This chap is a fool, and ought to go to the infarmary.—*A place patriot* is a rogue: he panders to popular prejudice, appeals to the passions of the mob, and tries to set them agin' their richer neighbours, and attempts to ride on their shoulders into the government, and to secure place will sacrifice every thing that is valuable, and good, and respectable. He is a philosopher in his religion, and a rascal in his philosophy. He is wilful, and acts against conviction. This man is the loudest and most dangerous of all, and should go to the workhouse.—*The true patriot* is one who is neither a sycophant to the Government nor a tyrant to the people, but one who will manfully oppose either when they are wrong, who regards what's right, as minister said to me, and not what is popular; who supports existin' institutions as a whole, but is willin' to mend or repair any part that is defective.—Why, Mr. Slick, said I, in the most unfeigned astonishment, I never heard a republican hold such language before: why, you are a Tory, if you only knew it. Are you merely talking for effect, or do you really mean what you say? for your picture of a true patriot is nothing more or less than a picture of a consistent Tory. Any person must see the resemblance to the Duke of Well——. —Why, squire, said he, interrupting me, you don't know our soundin's from Polly Coffin's Sandhole as well as I do, or you wouldn't ax that are question, at no rate. I am a Federalist when I am to home, tho' I somewhat guess you are a Consarvative; but a monarchist in a republic, and a republican in a monarchy is jist about on a par,—a pair of rebels that ought to be chained together, that they might have time to argue it out. Our government suits us best, yourn suits you best; a good citizen stands by his own. I don't care who looks like the pictur'. I drawed one of a true patriot, and you may give him what nick-name you please; but I hante done yet. I want to show you the soundin's of the colonial Tories, for mind, I ain't no party-man. I don't care a snap o' my finger who's up or who's down; I'm a *Yankee,* and my name is Sam Slick; at least, they tell me so. Now, the colonial Tories, compacts, officials, divine succession men, cliques, or whatever, they are,— for they have as many aliases as the Spanish pirate had that was hanged to Boston,—are about the best folks goin', to my mind, to trade with, and the nearest up to the notch; yet there are three sorts of them.

Whole hogs, who won't hear of no change, good or bad, right or wrong, at no rate. These critturs are of the donkey breed. They stick their head into the fence, and lash away with their heels right and left, till all is blue agin.—*Fashionable ones*, who don't care much about politicks, but join that side because the upper-crust folks and bettermost people are that way of thinkin': jackdaw birds, that borrow feathers to strut in. If the great men or the governor was a radical, these critturs would be radical too. *They take their color from the object they look up to.*—Then there is the *moderate ones*: now extremes meet, and a moderate colonial compact chap and a true patriot are so near alike it would puzzle a Philadelphia lawyer to tell 'em apart. I shouldn't like to let on that I said so; for, cuss 'em, if it hadn't a-been for them the patriots or reformers, winter afore last, would have throw'd Canada into our hands as slick as grease; and I wouldn't a-said to others what I have said to you for nothin' a'most. Now, if I was John Russell, (for them almighty long tails worn afore a man's name instead of behind it, always bother me, and it comes handier to me not to use them), if I was him, I'd jist slip off on the sly to the provinces without sayin' of a word, and travel as plain Mr. Russell, (and, I guess, nobody would take him for a lord unless he told 'em so, for he ain't overly tall, that's a fact,) and jist take the soundin's of these folks myself. He'd hear the truth then, for some patriot folks say *one thing to a governor and another to the world*. He'd know, too, when influence *was character*, or when it was *trick*. When he returned again to home, to the state-house in Downin'-street, and a colonist brought him a lead to look at, he'd tell with half an eye, like Captain Ebenezer, whether it had sand on it from the *rael bottom*, or *Polly Coffin's Sandhole*.

If them jawin' Jacks to Parliament had half the sense my poor old mother had, they'd know what to say when them patriot critturs come home, with their long lockrums about grievances, with an everlastin' lyin' preface to it about loyalty. They'd say, as she used to did, poor old crittur, to me when I boasted what a good boy I was a-goin' to be: *Sam, she'd say, I'd a plaguy sight sooner see it than hear tell of it*. It puts me in mind of what an Ingian once said to a British governor afore our glorious revolution. He was a great hand was the Britisher (like some other folks I could tell you of) to humbug with talk, and was for reformin' everything a'most, and promised all sorts of things, and more too, that he did not mean; but all his speeches *would read both ways*, so that he could intarpret them as he liked: so, which ever way things eventuated, he was always right. *A regilar politician that!* One day he called his red children together, as he called the Ingians, and made *them* a speech too. It was a beautiful speech, I tell you, all in bad English, that it might be understood better and sound Ingian-like. Bimeby, when he had done, up rises an old chief, a rael salt, and as cunnin' as a fox, for he was quite a case that feller, and, says he, Mr. Gubbernor.—Let my son speak, said the Governor, and his great father will open his ear and hear him, and he will keep his words in his heart; and he clapt his hand on his breast, and looked as spooney as a woman does on her first child.—Very good jaw that, Mister Gubbernor, said he; you speak 'um dam well; now, Mister Gubbernor, try and *actum* well, for that is more better.—That's exactly the language John Russell ought to hold to colony patriots when they boast of their loyalty; he should say, "actum well, for that's more better still." Whenever he does that, I shall think he knows "the rael soundin's from *Polly Coffin's Sandhole*;" won't you, squire?

XIV

AN OLD FRIEND WITH A NEW FACE

HAVING travelled this day from Parnassus to Thebes,[1] a distance of thirty-five miles, we concluded to remain where we were, although there were some two or three hours of daylight yet to spare, and to resume our journey on the following morning. Thebes is a small town, nor does there appear to have been any grounds whatever for supposing that it could, by any possible contingency, ever attain the size or imitate the splendour of that whose name has been thought so appropriate as to be transferred to this little assemblage of wooden houses and log huts. The town appeared to have been abandoned by its inhabitants for some temporary purpose, for the houses, though all closed, bore marks of recent occupation. The shops and taverns were open, as if in readiness to receive the returning population, while the scaffolds, heaps of mortar, and unloaded waggons of timber, all exhibited signs of a hasty desertion of the work men. The silence and melancholy that reigned through the streets constituted the only point of resemblance to its great prototype. So unusual an occurrence naturally excited my curiosity, and upon inquiring its cause, I was informed there was a gathering, or a religious bee, at a short distance, which was most numerously attended by people from a distance as well as the immediate neighbourhood; that there was a great "stir," and a preacher of more than common eloquence, called a "Corcornite," who was breaking up all the old congregations, and proselyting the whole country to his new notions.

It is a nervous fever, said my informant, the innkeeper, with an air of satirical severity. All nations have their peculiar excitements. The Chinese have their opium, the South Sea people their chew-chew, the Dutch their skidam, the Indians their tobacco, and the Irish their whiskey; but we have a combination of them all—we go ahead of most folks in that line. We have rum, strong tea, baccy, politicks, and fanaticism. We are the most excitable and excited people in the world. One mistake, stranger, naturally leads to another. Them are Puritans that came out of your country to this, proscribed all amusements, all innocent festivities, all gaiety of the heart, and held that the more wretched and melancholy they were the more acceptable they would be to the Lord. They were no half-measure chaps them. When they began to dissent from the Church they went the whole figur'. They gave up all the Church allowed, and retained all the Church disapproved. The Church prayed for the King; they beheaded him. The Church thought a cheerful countenance betokened a happy heart; the Puritans called it the face of a malignant, and so forth. Well, what was the consequence of all this? why, as pretty a set of hypocrites was begotten as you'd wish to see. I take your Cromwell to be jist a superfine sample of them, and the breed is tolerably pure yet; cold, canting, sour pharisees, who appropriate heaven to themselves, and quietly consign all the rest of the world to the devil. This feeling has tinged every one of the hundred thousand sects that have sprung up to oppose the old Church of Old England. I am a colonist by birth myself; I was brought up an Episcopalian, and so was my wife; but my children have all seceded. One is a Hixite, another a Universalist, a third a Unitarian, and a fourth a Socialist. Religion, instead of being a bond of union in my house, is the cause of discord, and doctrinal points are never-ending sources of dispute and disagreement. Christianity, sir, is fast giving place to philosophy, and we are relapsing into what these new lights call "rational thinkers," or, in plain English, Atheists. It makes me sick to think on it; but you had better go and see for yourself, and then tell me if such disgraceful work is religion. This fellow that is drawing such crowds after him, belongs not to any of the great sects of Episcopalians, Methodists, Baptists, or Papists, but is called a "Corcornite." His doctrine is simply this, that a state of future punishment exists, but exists only for those who do not embrace his creed,—a comfortable sort of faith, which, I fear, his sect is not the only one that propagates.

The meeting was held on the betterments of a new settler, near a bridge, to which several roads led, and which, from its central situation, was easy of access from various parts of the country. Waggons, gigs, and cars without number, were stationed near the fences, and along the line of the forest, the horses belonging to each carriage being unharnessed and severally fastened by a halter to the axletree for security. Here and there were tents and booths, giving the field the appearance of a military encampment; and on the edge of the woods, and under the shade of the giants of the forest, were numerous conical wigwams, made after the fashion of the Indians, and resembling one of their summer fishing establishments. In the centre of the clearing was a large barn, which was filled by a mixed and mottled multitude of people listening to the wild declamation of the preacher, whose voice was occasionally heard over the whole field, as he screamed out his frightful denunciations. Groups of men were scattered about the field, seated on the huge stumps which here and there dotted the surface of the ground, or perched on the upper rails of the wooden fence, discussing business or politicks, or canvassing the doctrines or merits of the preacher; while others were indolently lounging about the refreshment booths, whiling away the time with cigars and mint julip until they should be joined by their fair friends at the hour of intermission.

After some difficulty, Mr. Slick and myself forced our way into the barn, and fortunately obtained standing room on one of the seats, from which we had a view of the whole interior. One preacher had just ceased as we entered. He was succeeded by another, a tall, thin, and rather consumptive-looking man, who had a red silk pocket-handkerchief tied about his head, and wore no neck-cloth. There was something quite appalling in his look. There was such a deep dejection in his countenance, such a settled melancholy, such a look of total abstraction and resignation to the endurance of some inevitable fate, that I was forcibly reminded of the appearance of an unfortunate criminal when led out for execution. Instantly all was hushed, every eye was upon him, and every ear in anxious solicitude to catch the almost inaudible whispers that fell from his lips. Now and then a word was heard, and then a few unconnected ones, and shortly a few brief sentences or maxims. Presently his enunciation was clear and distinct, and it gradually increased in volume and rapidity until it became painfully loud, and then commenced gesticulation, emphasis, and raving. It was one unceasing flow of words, without pause or interruption, except for an occasional draught of water from a stone pitcher that was placed beside him. Even this, however, was insufficient to prevent exhaustion, and he removed his coat. He then commenced the great effort of his eloquence, a description of the tortures of the damned. It was a studied and frightful piece of declamation, in which he painted their wild demoniac shrieks, their blasphemous despair, their unquenched and unquenchable thirst,—the boiling, steaming lake of brimstone—their unwilling tenacity of existence, and increased sensibility of pain. When all the figures of speech and all his powers of imagination were exhausted, he finished the horrible picture by the introduction of fallen angels, who, with expanded wings, hovered for ever and ever over this awful abyss, whose business and pleasure was, as the boiling of the infernal caldron brought any of the accursed to the surface, with spears of heated glowing metal to thrust them deeper and further into the burning flood.

The groans, screams, and hysterical laughter of the female part of the audience was so frightful and appalling an accompaniment to this description, that my feelings became intensely painful, and I was about leaving the building, when his voice suddenly dropped from the unnatural pitch to which he had strained it, and sunk into a soft and seductive tone, in which, in the mildest and gentlest manner, he invited them to accompany him to Paradise, which he described, after the manner of the Mohammedans, as an abode furnished with all the delicacies and pleasures most suited to their senses and corporeal enjoyments. He then represented the infernal regions as the doom of those who belonged not to the "band" of which he was the head, in the absence of its persecuted founder, "Corcoran," and invited his hearers to fellowship.

Enough, said I, to Mr. Slick; and more than enough. I am disgusted and horrified; let us go.—I most wonder you staid so long, said he; it is awful hot here, and that crittur talked so of sulphur I've actilly got the taste of it in my mouth; my tongue is all warped and curled up like singed shoe-leather. I must have a brandy cocktail to cool it. But I've seen that feller afore; I know his, voice and the cut of his jib as well as anything, but to call his name out, to save my soul alive, I can't. They call him Concord Fisher, but that is not his rael name, that's a bam. Where on airth have I seen that goney, for seen him I have, by gum!

The following morning, he said,—Who do you think that are preacher was, squire? I told you I know'd I had seed him afore, for I never forgot a face yet; tho' names are considerable slippery, and it ain't jist so easy to keep hold on such soapy things. It was that everlastin' skirmudgeon, Ahab Meldrum; it was, I swear. Last night, jist as I was a-turnin' in, who should slip into my room, but Ahab.—Sam, says he, I seed you to the great "stir," and know'd you in a minit; you are jist the man I want to see, for I need your advice; but, for the love of Heaven give me some brandy and water, for I am e'en a'most dead,—and he gave a kind of tan-yard grin that went right straight to the heart.—We have to preach tee-totalism here, for nothin' else will go down; but it's easier to preach than to prac*tise* that: give me some grog, or I shall die.—It sarves you right, says I, for bein' such a 'tarnal hypocrite: why the devil don't you take your grog like a man, if you need it, above-board, off-hand handsum, and let them that don't like it, lump it, that's my way; I don't approbate no nonsense. Well, I goes and gets some brandy and water, enough to make a nightcap for two, and, says I, swig away till you are tired, now, will you; you are safe with me; I won't blow you, you may depend. Well, I pitied the poor crittur too, for he looked as pale and as white about the gills as a scalded nigger; I actilly thought he would have fainted, he was so weak. Take a drop of it neat, says I, water only spiles it; and I poured him out a gill of the pure grit, which brought his color back and revived him a bit. When he come to, says I, Ahab, what onder the sun brought you here? what made you leave Alabama? You was gittin' on like a house a fire there, a soft-sawderin' the women there, with your new rule in grammar, that the feminine gender was more worthy than the masculine, and the masculine more better nor the neuter, and so forth. I hope you hante been illustratin', eh? no more Polly Bacons, I hope, eh? you was always a sly feller that way: what was it?—Sam, says he, I've been a fool, and it sarves me right; I was doin' the smartest chance of preachin' there of any man in the state, and I throw'd it away like an ass. I am punished enough, anyhow; spare me, for I am as weak as a child, and can't stand Jobeing. Spare me, that's a good crittur, and don't you bark agin' me, too, or it will drive me crazy; and he put his hand to his face and bo-hood right out.—Why, you poor crittur, says I,—for a touch of old times come over me, when we was boys to school together and I felt kinder sorry to see him that way, lookin' so streaked—why you poor crittur, says I, you've worn your self out a-screachin' and a-screamin' that way, and yellin' like a ravin' distracted bed bug; let me mix you a pitcher of egg-nog, stiff enough to stick to your ribs as it goes down, and it will make a man of you agin' in two-twos. So away I goes and gets a lot of eggs and sugar, and some brandy, and mixes up a dose that would float a dollar a'most, and made him drink it: now, says I, for your new rule in grammar; how did it work?—Well, says he, it's no use concealin' anythin' from you, Sam; it didn't turn out well in the eend, that's a fact. People began to talk considerable hard and Lynchy about their galls comin' so often to a single man to tell their experience, and to wrastle with the spirit, and so on; and the old women began to whisper and look coonish, and, at last—for I don't want to go into pitikilars, for it ain't an overly pleasant subject—I got a notice to make myself scarce from Judge Lynch, and, as I know'd a little grain more about the matter than they did, and guessed the secret would soon be obleeged to be known, I felt my jig was up, and I jist took the hint and made tracks. Then I hooked on to the Corcornites, and here I am among them, I must say, rather takin' the lead. Folks actilly *do* say I take the rag off quite, all along up and down Maine and Varmont, and a piece beyond; but I can't stand it; I shall die; the excitement is too much for me. I have endured more already than a dead nigger in a doctor's shop could stand. Livin' so long in a hot climate, I hante strength for it, and I am fairly used up and worn out. What do you think of Socialism? it seems as if it would go down, that. It's gittin' kinder fashionable. Owen writes me word he has been introduced to Court to England, of which he is proper proud, and a nation sight of people patronise it since, a complete swad of them. He says it will trip the heels of the Church yet, let the Bishops do their prettiest for Socialists have votes as well as other folks, and must be courted, and are courted, and will be courted all through the piece. He seems quite up in the stirrups, and jist dares them to prosecute him. I have had liberal offers from the sect here, for whatever is the go to Europe will soon be the chalk here, and to tell you the truth, I feel most peskily inclined to close with them, for them rational religionists live like men and ain't so everlastin' strait-laced in matters of the heart as others be, nother. In fact, they are jist about the most liberal sect I know on. Now, tell me candid, has it a bottom, or is it a bam? Will it stand, or will public opinion be too strong for it? for I don't want to embark on board a leaky ship; when I spikilate I like to have the chances in my favor.—Well, Ahab, says I, you make me crawl like all over, to hear you talk so loose, so you do; what a devil of a feller you be, you are actilly bad enough to be nigger-in-law to old Scratch, you are so bad; you have tried every sect there is, a'most, and now you talk of turnin' infidel, as coolly as of turnin' into bed. Give up preachin', you ain't fit for it, nor never was, and more nor that, you hante strength for it. If you don't mind, you'll go for it yet. Go where you ain't known, and either go tradin' or go farmin'.—Too hard work, Sam, said he, too hard work; but Socialism strikes me as rather genteel, while the work is light, the pay good, and *religious liberty* great. Jist hand me the brandy tho', that's a good feller, please. I must take some clear, for that egg-nog is cold and heavy on the stomach,—and he drank off near about half a pint without winkin'. No, said he, no ox-carts for me, Sammy, boy; no, nor baccy, nor cotton nother; they are low, very low, them. Corcoran,

"What do you think of Socialism?"

the head of our sect is in jail. They are a goin' to give him a birth in the
states prison. It's all day with him now; and I must say it kinder sarves him
right for not takin' up his killock, when he seed he was a-gitten into such
an almighty frizzle of a fiz. What's the use of legs but to absquotilate with,
like a jumpin' bull frog, when traps are sot for you. What I want to know
is, whether So—so—social—Socialism ca—an stand or no?—Not much
better than you can, I expect, says I, for he was blind drunk now, and as
dumb as a wooden clock, two years old, and I lifted him on the bed with
all his runnin' riggin' on, and there he was this mornin' when I got up,
a-snorin' like a sizeable buffalo. Oh, squire, said the Clockmaker, that are
Ahab has made me feel dreadful ugly, I tell you. Old times kinder touches
the heart; I look on my old class-mates like brothers, and I don't feel sorter
right when I see one on 'em actin' like old Scratch that way. *A bad man
is bad enough, the Lord knows; but a bad minister beats the devil*, that's as plain
as preachin'.

1. I have used these names, instead of the real ones, as well on account of
avoiding local offence, as of their absurd adoption in the States.

XV

THE UNBURIED ONE

As we approached Boston, Mr. Slick said, Ah, squire! now you will see as pretty a city as we have this side of the water. There is a good many folks worth seein' here, and a good many curosities of natur' too. There's the State House, and Old Funnel, and Charleston College, and the Market-place, and the Wharf they give to the British steamer (an act of greater liberality p'raps than you'll find, I estimate, in the world), and ever so many things. Then there is Mount Auburn. Lord, the French may crack and boast as much as they please, about their "Pair O'Shaise," but it's no touch to it. Why, I never was so disappointed in anything in all my life, since I was broughten up, as that are Paris buryin' ground. *It looks for all the world like an old ruined town, where the houses are all gone, and the porches, and steps, and dog-kennels are left.* It hante no interest in it at all, except the names o' them that's buried there; but Mount Auburn is worth seein' for itself. It's actilly like pleasure ground, it's laid out so pretty, and is the grandest place for courtin' in I know on, it's so romantic. Many a woman that's lost one husband there, has found another in the same place. A widower has a fine chance of seein' widders there, and then nobody ever suspects them of courtin', bein' that they are both in black, but takes 'em for mourners, and don't intrude on 'em out of pity. I'll go a bet of a hundred dollars the women invented that place, for they beat all natur' for contrivances, so they do. Yes, squire, if you have a mind for a rich young widder, clap a crape weeper on your hat, and a white nose-rag in your hand, and go to Mount Auburn, and you'll see some heavenly splices there, I tell you, in some o' them are shady walks, that will put all the dead in creation out of your head a'most. Them saller lookin', garlick eatin' French heifers, you see to "Pair o' Shays," may have better top gear, and better riggin' in gineral than our galls, and so they had ought, seein' that they think of nothin' else but dress; but can they show such lips, and cheeks, and complexions, that's all, or such clinker-built models? No, not them, nor any other women of any other nation in the univarsal world. If they can, it's some place that's not discovered yet, that's all I can say, and you must go a leetle further than the eend of the airth to find them, for they ain't this side of it. You must see Mount Auburn to-morrow, squire, that's a fact; but then, leave your heart to home, to the *Tre*mont, as folks do their watches when they go to the *thea*tre to London, or you will lose it as sure as you are born. O, there is a sartain somethin' about Boston that always makes an American feel kinder proud. It was the cradle of our liberty. The voice of our young eagle was first heard here, and at Bunker's Hill, which is near the town, it gave the British the first taste of its talons.

> Newbury port's a rocky place,
>   And Salom's very sandy,
> Charleston is a pretty town,
>   But Boston is the dandy.

I guess the English must feel most awful streaked when ——

To divert him from a topic on which his national vanity always made him appear ridiculous, I observed, that I believed there was but one opinion among strangers about Boston, who were always much pleased with the place, and its society, but that I was not myself fond *of cities as cities*. Long streets, and broad streets, said I, walls of brick and mortar, and stones heaped on stones, have few charms for me. Even architectural beauty is, after all, but the effect of a judicious arrangement of poor materials. It is good of its kind, but not one of those things I most admire. It may have many component parts of beauty, it may combine lightness, strength, proportion, and so on. The general effect may be good, criticism may be satisfied, and the eye dwell on it with complacency. You may be willing to concede to it the usual terms of praise. You may say it is grand, or magnificent, or exquisite, or beautiful. You may laud the invention, the judgment, and skill of the architect; you may say, in short, that your artificial and acquired taste for architectural beauty is gratified and content, (an admission, by the by, which, it is very rare to hear,) but still it is but the work of the hodsman and mason. I do not mean to underrate its importance, because, as a great part of mankind must dwell in cities, and all must live in houses, few things are of greater consequence than the appearance of those cities and houses; and order, symmetry, and the general adaptation of the parts to each other, and to the whole, are matters of deep interest to us all. I merely mean to say, that the most beautiful building is but a work of art, and that, as such, it gives me less pleasure than many other works of art, and that it falls so immeasurably short of the works of nature, of which I am a great admirer, I fear I do not derive all that pleasure from it that it is capable of affording. I like cities, therefore, not for themselves, but as a gregarious animal for the greater number of my own species they contain, and for the greater opportunity they afford me of meeting the *idem velle* and *idem nolle* people, among whom, only, we are told, by a very competent judge, is to be found true friendship. But, even in this case, I am not sure I do not lose in quality as much as I gain in quantity; for I fear that though there be more refinement in the citizen, there is less heart than in the countryman. Before you can impart its brightness to steel, you must harden its texture, and *the higher the polish the more indurated you will find the substance*. By this process it loses its pliability and acquires brittleness, and its strength is diminished in proportion to its beauty. It is a gay deceiver. It flatters your vanity by its devotion to yourself. Its smooth and brilliant surface will reflect your image while present, but the very operation of refinement has destroyed its susceptibility of an impression. It is your own smile that is returned to you, but it refuses to retain it when you cease to look upon it. As a lover of nature, therefore, I love the country and the man that inhabits it. I find more of beauty in the one, and of generous impulses in the other, than I find in cities or in courtiers.

I reciprocate that idee, said the Clockmaker. Give me the folks that like "human natur'" and "soft-sawder." Them critturs in towns, in a gineral way, have most commonly cut their eye teeth, and you can't make nothin' of them. There is no human natur' in them to work on; and as for soft sawder, they are so used to it themselves, it seems to put 'em on their guard like. They jist button up their pockets, and wrinkle up their foreheads, and look on you with their eyes wide apart, on-meanin' like, as if they warn't attendin', and bow you out. Nothin' makes me feel so onswoggled as one of them "I guess-you-may-go kind of stares;" it's horrid. But as for country folks, Lord, you can walk right into 'em like nothin'. I swear I could row a boat-load on 'em cross-handed right up agin the stream in no time. Boston is a fine town, that's sartin, tho' I won't jist altogether say it better nor Edinboro', nor Dublin nother; but it's ———. Talking of Dublin, said I, reminds me of the singular story I overheard you telling some countryman in Nova Scotia of the remarkable state of preservation in which the dead

bodies are found under St. Michan's church, and especially the anecdote of
the two Shears's; was that a fact, or one of your fanciful illustrations given
for the sake of effect?—Fact, squire, I assure you, said he, and no mistake:
I seed it with my own eyes no longer than two years agone. Gospel, every
word of it.—You mentioned there was a female exhibited with them in
the same perfect state: who was she?—Oh! she was a nun, said he; she had
been there the matter of the Lord knows how many years a-kickin' about,
and nobody knew her name, or who her folks were, or where the plague
she come from. All they know'd was she was a nun that wouldn't let no
one see so much as the colour of her eyes while she lived, but made up
bravely for it arter she was dead. If you had only a-heerd how it made the
old sea-captain rave like a mad poet at the full of the moon, it would have
made you laugh, I know. I sot him a-goin' a-purpose, for nothin' pleases
me so much as to see an old feller try to jump Jim Crow in an oration.
So, says I, captain, says I, that are nun warn't a bad lookin' heifer in her day
nother, was she? a rael, right down, scrumptious-lookin' piece of farniture,
and no mistake; but what in natur' was the use of her veilin' her face all
her life to keep off the looks of sinful carnal man, if they won't veil her
arter she is dead, and no one wants to look at her. Oh, dear! oh, dear! if she
could only wake up now and see us two great he fellers a-standin' starin' at
her full in the face, what an everlastin' hubbub she would make, wouldn't
she? If she wouldn't let go, and kick, and squeel, and carry on like ravin',
distracted mad, it's a pity, that's all. I say, Miss Stranger, said I, a-turnin' to
our female guide, and a-chuckin' her onder the chin, now what do you
estimate is the first thing that are gall would do in that case—would she
——? but the old ongainly heifer pretended to take a fit of the modest all
at once, and jist turned towards the door, and by bringin' the lamp closer
to her body, threw the corpses and that corner of the cellar into darkness,
and then axin' us if we'd like to see the next vault, led us right up into
the churchyard. When we got out into the air says the old sea-captain,—I
agree with you, Mr. Slack.—Slick, sir, if you please, is my name.—Oh!
I beg your pardon, Mr. Clack, then.—No, nor Mr. Clack nother, says I;
it's Slick—Sam Slick is my name! a-raisin' of my voice till the buildin'
actilly gave an echo agin, for the crittur was as deaf as a shad. I am from
Slickville, Onion county, Conne'ticut, United States of America.—Well,
Mr. Slick.—Ah! now you have it, said I; you've got it to a T.—To a T! said
he, (the old soft horn,) how is that? I really don't onderstand how you have

a T in it at all.—Oh dear! said I, no more we have; it's nothin' but a sayin' of ourn, a kind of provarb; it's a cant phrase.—Ah! cant is it? said he, with a face a yard long: then you must permit me to observe, that you are one of the very last men, judging from your remarks, that I should have supposed to have had anything about you approaching to cant; but I fully concur with you that the exhibition of this female is not decent. I should not have observed myself, unless you had called my attention to the corpse, that it was a female. No, I suppose not, says I, and there's not one mite or morsel of cant in that, I suppose, at all. How innocent we are not to know a hawk from a handsaw, ain't we?—Speak a little louder, said the old man, if you please, sir, for I have the misfortin' to be a leetle hard of hearin'.—I was a-sayin', sir, said I, that I don't know as I should nother, if that are woman that showed 'em to us hadn't a-said, beautiful crater, your honor, that same nun must have been in her day. The jontlemen all admire her very much entirely. They say she looks like a statue, she does.

Well, well, said the captin, kinder snappishly, whoever she was, poor crittur! the exhibition is improper. She has the reputation of having been a nun, who, whatever may be the errors of their creed that induce them voluntarily to quit a world into which they are sent with certain social duties to perform, have at least the merit of a sincere devotion, and their motives are to be respected. As in life they are scrupulous in the observance of all the most minute proprieties of conduct, they, of all others, seem to have the greatest claim to be exempted from this degrading exposure after death. Decay, however, has now commenced, and will soon remove all trace of humanity. Corruption, according to that beautiful idea of Scripture, will assert its claim of kindred, and the worm proclaim himself her brother. Alas! where now are the gay and thoughtless crowd that thronged to witness the gorgeous and solemn spectacle of a young, beautiful, and innocent sister, assuming that veil that was to separate her from the world for ever? Where are the priests that officiated at the altar?—the sisterhood that rejoiced in receiving?—the relatives that grieved at surrendering this sacrifice? and they, too, whose voices pealed forth the hymn of praise, and poured out the tide of sacred song to the echoing aisles—where are they? All, all have passed away! and none, no, not one, is left of all that assembled crowd to disclose her lineage or her name. Their rolls have perished with them, and all that now remains is this unclaimed, unknown, nameless one. Poor thing! has indignant humanity asserted its rights? hath the vindictive world rejected thee, as thou rejected it? or why art thou here alone, unhonoured and unknown? Alas! is there no distinction between the gallows and the cloister? is it fitting that thou, whose life was a life of penance and of prayer, whose pure mind communed only with heavenly objects, should now consort with convicted criminals, and that thy fair form should be laid with the headless trunks of traitors? Ah, me! thou has returned, poor houseless thing! to thine own, and thine own knows thee no more! I have seen the grave open to receive its tenant, and the troubled sea its dead, and the green turf and the billowy wave fold them in its bosom, to sleep the sleep that knows no waking. All have their resting-place, save thee! Ambition has its temple, and wealth its tomb, while even the poor are cared for; but thou, how is it, fair one, that thou alone of all thy sex should be left the "unburied one?" the greedy sexton's show, and the vile scoffer's viler jest. Who art thou? History can find a place for treason and for crime; could it afford no space for self-denying virtue such as thine? Was, there no pious hand to grave thy name on unpretending, monumental stone? none of all thy father's house to perform the last sad rites of affection—to restore to the earth what was earthy—to the dust, dust—and ashes to ashes? All, all are silent and even tradition, garrulous as it is, has but one short word for thee—a nun!

Arter spinnin' this yarn, the old sea-captain turned off to examine the tombstones in the church-yard, and I mounted the car to the gate and drove off to the hotel. There was some feelin' and some sense too in what he said, tho' he did rant a few, warn't there? but as for his goin' to make believe he didn't know she was a woman, that is what I must say, now, I call a most superfine bam that. Old fellers always *think* young ones fools; but young fellers sometimes *know* old ones is fools. Now who'd a-thought, squire, he continued, that that are old boy would have flowed right off the handle that way for nothin' at all, at seein' that queer, parchment-colored, wilted, old onfakilised nun. I think, myself, they might as well bury her; and if they'd ship her out to minister, I don't make no doubt he'd bury her hisself in Mount Auburn; or to brother Eldad, and he'd stick her up in a museum for a show, as they do mother Barchell at Surgeon's Hall to London; but as for her name, who the plague cares what it is? I am sure I don't. I wouldn't give a cent to know, would you? It sounded kinder pretty, that talk of his too. Lord! I wish sister Sall had a-been there; if she had a-been, he'd a-sot her a-boohooin' in no time, I know, for she is quite romantic is Sall, and a touch of the pathetic is what she does love dearly. Whenever she comes across a piece of dictionary like that are, she marks it with a pencil, and gets it by heart, and goes a-spoutin' of it about the house like mad.—Ain't that fine, Sam, says she? ain't it splendid? it's sublime, I declare; it's so feelin' and so true.—And if I won't go the whole figur' with her, she gets as mad as a hatter.—You hante got no soul in you at all, Sam, says she, I never seed such a crittur; I do believe in my heart you think of nothin' but dollars and cents.—Well then, I say, says I, don't be so peskily ryled, Sally dear; but railly now, as I am a livin' sinner, I don't jist exactly onderstand it; and as you are more critical than I be, jist pint out the beauties, that's a dear love, will you, and see if I don't admire it every mite and morsel as much as you do, and maybe a plaguy sight more. Well, I get her to set down and go over it all ever so slow, and explain it all as clear as mud, and then she says,—Now do you see, Sam, ain't it horrid pretty?—Well, says I, it does sound grand like, that I must say—and then I scratch my head and look onfakilised—but how did you say that was, dear? says I, a-pintin' to the top line; I don't jist altogether mind how you explained that.—Why, you stupid crittur, you! she says, this way; and then she goes over it all agin word for word. Now do you onderstand, says she, you thick head, you? Ain't that beautiful? don't that pass?—Yes, says I, it does pass, that's a fact, for it passes all onderstandin'; but you wouldn't jist explain once more, would you, dear? and I looks up wicked and winks at her.—Well, now, if that ain't too bad, she says, Sam, I declare, to make game of me that way.—If I hadn't a-been as blind as a bat, I might have seed with half an eye you was a-bammin' of me the whole blessed time, so I might; but I'll never speak to you agin, now, see if I do; so there now, and away she goes out of the room a-poutin' like any thing. It's grand fun that, and don't do a gall no harm nother, for there is nothin' like havin' a string to a kite, when it's a-gittin' away up out of sight a'most, to bring it down agin. *Of all the seventeen senses, I like common sense about as well as any on 'em, arter all; now, don't you, squire?*

XVI

DEFINITION OF A GENTLEMAN

ON our arrival at Boston we drove to the Tremont House, which is not only one of the first of its kind in the United States, but decidedly one of the best in the world. As our time was limited we proceeded, as soon as we could, to visit the several objects of interest in the city and its neighbourhood, and among the rest Bunker's Hill, where, Mr. Slick observed, "the British first got a taste of what they afterwards got a belly-full." The hill was surmounted by an unfinished monument, which, he said, it was intended should exceed in height the Monument in the city of London, as the Yankies went a-head of the English in everything.

As his father had been present at the battle, it was natural the Clockmaker should feel a pride in it; for, by proving our army to be both mortal and fallible, it had a great effect on the subsequent events of the war. In his exultation, however, he seemed to forget that he was talking to a British subject, who, if he now had any feeling on the subject, could only have wished that the prudence of the general had equalled the bravery of the King's troops. As Bunker's Hill was the scene of a victory won by British soldiers under the most difficult and trying circumstances, I was pleased to see the erection of this monument, as it is a tribute to their valour which they have justly merited. Why the Americans should have thought of putting it there I am at a loss to know, when there are many other places where their gallantry was not only equally conspicuous but crowned with signal success. In this case, however, they have not merely selected a spot where they were defeated, but one which is, perhaps, more remarkable than any other on this continent for that indomitable spirit and reckless courage that distinguishes the English.

On an examination of the ground it would appear, that a slight detour would have enabled the troops to have routed the rebel army with great ease and but little loss, and at the same time effectually to have cut off their retreat. Instead of adopting this obvious mode of attack, the troops were ordered to charge up the steep ascent of this hill upon an enemy securely protected by their entrenchments, a service which they performed under a most murderous fire, which from the nature of the ground they were unable to return with any effect. This successful effort is as deserving of commendation as the conduct of the officer in command is of reprehension, in thus wantonly sacrificing his men, out of mere bravado, in the attainment of an object which could be followed by none of the usual consequences of a victory. A monument to perpetuate the recollection of this gallant feat of those intrepid men, by whomsoever erected, is a most desirable thing, and it is to be hoped that means will not be long wanting to complete it in the same handsome style in which it is begun.

On our return to the hotel, as we passed the bar, Mr. Slick, according to his usual custom, stopped to take some refreshment, and when he joined me again, he said,—Squire, do you know Peter Barr to Quaco, where we stopt one night? Well, he is Bar by name and Bar by natur', for he is the waiter to a-most excellent one, the Reneficacious House. I reckon he is the most gentlemanlike man in all New Brunswick. He sar-*tain*-ly is a polished man that; his manners are about the best I ever fell in with. It does one good to see him enter a room, he does it so pretty; in fact, I call him as near about a finished gentleman as I know on, don't you, now?

I said I had seen the person he alluded to, but it was not customary to call servants finished gentlemen, and that I had never heard the term applied in that manner before; that he was no doubt a very attentive and civil waiter, and I believe an honest and excellent servant, but that finished manners referred to a very different state of society from that of the attendants on a bar room.

Ah, said he, now there peeps out the pride of the Englishman and the effect of your political institutions. Now with us we are all equal, and in course the polish extends very considerable thro' all the different grades of society, especially among them that live on the sea-board.

How, said I, can you have different grades if you are all equal? I do not exactly comprehend that.—No, said he, the fact is you do not understand us. Now, take my grade; it's what you call a clock pedlar in the scorny way you British talk of things, merely because my trade extends over the whole country; but take my grade (I won't speak of myself, because "praise to the face is open disgrace.") Well, I estimate they are as gentlemanlike men as you will find in the world, and the best drest too, for we all wear finer cloth in a gineral way than the British do, and our plunder is commonly more costly than theirn: this arises, you see, from our bein' on a footin' with princes and nobles, and received at all foreign courts as natur's noblemen, free and enlightened citizens of the greatest empire on the face of the airth. Now, I could go where despisable colonists couldn't go. If I went to France I should go to our Embassador and say, Embassador, I've come to see the ins and outs of Paris; and a nasty, dirty, tawdry place it is, it ain't to be named on the same day with Philadelphia, New York, or any of our first shop cities; but, as I *am* here, I'd like to see some o' their big bugs,—show us their king, he kept school once to our country, but we kinder thought he didn't speak as good French as the New Orleans folks; I wonder, if he has improved any. Well, he'd take me and introduce me to the palace without any more to do about it, and king and me would be as thick as two thieves, a-talkin' over his old scholars, frog soup, and what not of the ups and downs of refugee life. *Embassador* darsn't refuse *me*, or we'd recall him for not supportin' the honor of the nation. *King* darsn't refuse *him,* or we'd go to war with him for insultin' the Union—fact, I assure you. Creation! If he was to dare to refuse, he'd see our hair rise like a fightin' cat's back. We wouldn't pine and whine about it as the English do at gittin' their flag insulted by the French and us great folks, and then show their spunk on them outlandish petticoated Chinese, like a coward that first refuses a challenge and then comes home and licks his wife to prove he ain't afeerd; no, not we indeed, we'd declare perpetual non-intercourse with France, as the only dignified course, and they might keep their silks and champaigne for them as wants them, we can manufacture both of them as good as they can. Now this gives us a great advantage over the natives of Europe, and makes it work so that any man of my grade (I don't speak of the upper-crust folks, because them that eat their pork and greens with silver forks are the same all the world over, all they have to larn is how to spend their money ginteelly, but of my class, that has to larn fust how to make it and then how to keep it,) is ginerally allowed to be as much of a gentleman as you'll see in any rank in Europe, partikilarly when he sets out to do the thing in best style. Of course, when people are at their work they must have their workin' dress on, but when they ondertake to put on their bettermost clothes and go the whole figur', I want to know where you'll see a better drest man than one of my craft, take him by and large, from his hat clean away down to his pump-shoes; or a man more ready when his dander is up to take offence at nothin' a'most, and fight or go to a first-rate hotel and pay five dollars a bottle for his wine. Country folks will be country folks, and can't be expected to be otherwise, seein' that they don't go out of the bush, and can't know what they don't see; but a tradin' man, that roams from one eend of the States to t'other eend of the provinces, a-carryin' his own wares in his own waggon, and a-vendin' of 'em himself from house to house, becomes a polished man in spite of his teeth, and larns to despise spittin' on carpets afore company or whitlin' his nails with a penknife, as much as count this or lord that. There is a nateral dignity about them, arising from the dignity of freedom. So there is about the Ingians; minister used to say, there was an ease and elegance of motion about an Ingian that nothin' could give a white man but constant intercourse with the best society, and was seldom equalled and never surpassed even at courts. The crittur is onconstrained. They go on the *nil admirari* system, he used to say (for, poor old man, he was always introducin' neck-and-crop some fag-eend of a Latin line or another, his head was chock-full and runnin' over with larnin'). The meanin' of that is, they don't go starin' and gapin' about the streets with their eyes and mouths wide open, like musketeer-hawks, as if they never seed anything afore. Now, that's the way with us. No man ever heerd me praise any thing out of my own country that took the shine off of anything *we* had.

I've often heerd the ladies say to England,—Why, Mr. Slick, nothin' seems to astonish you here: you don't seem to praise anything; you have no curosity about you. What do you think of that noble structur', St. Paul's Church?—Pretty well, said I, jist as if we had a thousand such; but it's gloomy and not so big as I expected.—But Westminster Abbey, says they, don't that surprise you? for you have no abbeys in America, and we think that must appear to you very wonderful.—Well, says I, quite cool, like a corney-sewer, it's costly, but onconvenient for a large congregation. The finish is rather gimcrack, and so is its farnitur', and them old tattered banners in the chapel look for all the world like old rags we tie to sticks in the corn-fields to Slickville to frighten away the crows. They ain't fit for a meetin'-house like that are; and if they must have flags hung up in it, as we do them we took from your frigates in a ball-room, they might as well have new ones.—Oh! says they, did you ever? Then, says they, the delightful parks round the noblemen's seats, ain't they very beautiful? you must be astonished at them, we think. Were you not struck on entering them with —— Struck! says I; oh yes! and most delightfully skeered too. I am a narvous man, and sometimes sing out afore I am hit. Few people is so skittish and shy so bad as I do. Struck, indeed! No, Miss, I warn't struck. I'd like to see the best lord that ever trod in shoe-leather strike me for enterin' his park, or so much even as to lay the weight of his finger on me. I'd soon let him know there was a warrant out arter him. Heavens and airth! I'd chaw him right up like mincemeat, titles, stars, garters, and all. I'd knock him to the north eend of creation in less time than a cat takes to lick her paw. *Struck!* why the very thorts of it sets my blood all in a gallopin' boil. I don't think he'd take the trouble to do it a second time; for I'd make him cut dirt as if he heerd a whole team of thunder bolts arter him. *Me* struck, and *him* alive to brag of it! Well, I sorter guess not. No one never struck me, Miss, since I first sot foot in England, nor for many a long day afore nother. That pleasure is to come yet. Strikin' a stranger ain't thort friendly with us, and I didn't think it was the fashion here.—Why, Mr. Slick, says they, hante you got that word "struck" in the States? it means astonished, strongly affected.—Oh yes! says I, to be sure, "struck up all of a heap;" it's common when used in jinein' hand that way, but, never stands alone except for a blow. The truth is, I know'd well enough what she meant when she said it, but I answered that way jist to give her a high idea of my courage; for I suppose she thought honor was only found in Europe, and mainly among officers, the bulk of whose business is to fight when they can't help it. Then, says I, to answer your question, Miss, I have seed a nateral park, says I, to home, stretchin' clean away across from the Atlantic right slap thro' to the Pacific Ocean all filled with deer, and so big, these English parks of dwarf trees look like a second growth of sprouts on the edge of a potato diggin' in a new clearin', or a shelter grove in a pastur'. Then, says I, your lakes is about as big as our duck-ponds, and your rivers the bigness of a siseable creek when there is no freshets.—But, says they, we know natur' is on a large scale in America, and your rivers and trees exceed in magnitude anything of the kind in Europe; but look at the beautiful English landscape, the rich verdure, the high cultivation, the lawns, the shrubberies, the meadows, and the groves, so interspersed as to produce the greatest and best effect.—If the sun ever shined on it, said I, it would be scrumptious enough, I do suppose; but it's heavy, melancholy, and dull; it wants light in the landscape, and you hante water to give it, nor sun nother.—We are sorry, says they, England has nothin' to please you.—Haven't you tho', says I,—for it don't do to run down everything

either, especially to the ladies,—so, says I, haven't you tho'. Oh! says I, the
ladies, I must say, are quite equal to ourn. It was a whopper, that tho', but
they didn't know no better; and who has a better right to lie than them
that pays taxes? It wouldn't be patriotic to say they were superior, and not
perlite nor true, nother, to say inferior, but they *are* equal, says I, that's a
fact; and that's no poor compliment, I can tell you, for our ladies lick! but
I say nothin'.

Now that's what I call about right, squire. To go wanderin' and starein'
about and admirin' of everything, shows a man has nothin' to home worth
braggin' of or boastin' about, or hasn't seed nothin' of the world. It would
make Europeans vain, and, cuss them, they are vain enough and proud
enough already, especially the English; besides, it tainte good breedin',
and ain't patriotic. I like to sustain the national character abroad, and give
foreigners a proper idea of our enlightenment and freedom. Bein' stumpt
is a sure mark of a fool. The only folks among us that's ever nonplushed, is
them just caught in the woods, and some o' them, I will say, are as ignorant
as a Britisher; but then it's only them as never seed nothin' but bears and
Ingians. I mind once a gall we hired as a house help. They was agued out
of the west was her family, and them that the Ingians left the fever was
doin' for; so they cut and runs and come to Slickville. Well, she stared and
pawed at everything a'most, and actilly was the most ongenteelest crittur
ever was broughten out from among the rattlesnakes. Father axed her one
day at dinner to hand him some bread.—Did yau baul for anything, old
man? says she, or was it the old woman that yelled? for you and granny
Slick speak so much alike, I can't tell, unless I see yaur jaus a-movein',
which it is.—I asked for some bread, says father.—Well, what does she do
but ups with the head of the loaf, and stretchin' out her arms, takes aim
and let's fly right at him; and, if he hadn't a-been pretty act*ive* in fendin'
off, it would have hit him right in the face, and takin' his nose off so clean
he wouldn't have missed it till he went to blow it.—Why, Suckey, says he,
what on airth do you mean by that are! why don't you hand it?—Hand
it? says she; I never heerd of such a way as that. Father always says pitch,
and when we want a thing we always shy it. How onder the sun could yau
onload a cart of bricks if you didn't pitch and catch? why it would take
a month of Sundays. If people always carried everything that everybody
wanted, they might be a-carryin' to all eternity. Didn't I pitch the loaf fair
for yaur breadbasket? where the plague would yau have it, eh?—Then she

was always axin' what a thing cost.—Is that solid silver? said she, a-lookin'
at one of our spoons.—To be sure, said I, rael genu*wine*, and worth five
dollars.—Well, I want to know, said she: yau don't. Half a dollar would buy
a spoon, and four dollars and a half two lambs. Why yaur' silver spoons are
a rael airthquake; what a power of money they do swaller up!—Then she
got hold of the gilt pictur'-frame I had minister's likeness in.—Dear, dear,
said she, how grand! Now, is that all solid gold and no bam? why it would
buy Deacon Hiram Grumble's overshot sawmill at little big Snipe Swamp;
it would, I vow, timber-ranges and all. Why it would be a forten to a poor
gall like me. I'd gin all I have in the world for that, or ever shall have; but,
then, all I have is a featherbed, a side-saddle, a yearlin' colt, and a rifle. Now
declare solemn, that's a good soul, Sam, is that all solid, clear gold, without
cheatin', or only pinchback, like the earrings that stingy beast Pardon Brag
gave sister Ambrosia when he was snuffin' ashes with her afore they was
married?—Why, you foolish crittur, no, said I, it ain't. Who ever heerd tell
of a gold frame—Ay, ay, my young coon, said she, or a silver spoon either.
I'll take my, davy it's only pewter, and good enough too. I guessed yau only
said so to appear grand.—She knowed no better, poor crittur, for she was
raised to the swamps to the west among the owls and catamounts, and
warn't much more nor half-baked at no time nother. We couldn't make
nothin' of her, her independence was so great, and her ways so countrified.
When she come, she had but one frock, and when she washed it at night,
she laid a-bed all day for it to dry, she did, upon my soul.

One time we had a tea-squall to our house, and Susan handed about the
tea. Well, she got thro' this well enough; but what does she do arterwards
but goes round among the company with the sugar-bowl in one hand,
and the cream-jug in the other, sayin', How are yau off, yau stranger with
the factory-coat, for sugar? and old woman with the yaller petticoat, shall
I milk yau, and so on? When she came to me I couldn't hold in no longer,
and I bust out a-larfin. "Kiss my foot, will you," said she, " Mr. Sam, and
mind what I tell yau, if yau go for to cut any of yaur high shines with
me, I'll fetch yau a kick in yaur western eend that will give yau the dry
gripes for a week, dod drot my old shoes if I don't, for yau are a bigger
fool than I took yau to be." She felt equal to any of the company, and so
she was, *p*olitically speaking, and nothin' darnted her. It tante more nor half
convenient always, but it's the effect of our glorious institutions. She felt
conscious she might be the mother of a president of our great nation, and

it infused a spirit in her above her grade. In fact, no one, male or female, can forget that fact, that their child mought be an Albert Gotha for eight years. As for me, he said, I never was abashed before any man since I was knee high to a goose; I hope I may be skinned if I was. I do actilly believe, if your Queen was to ax me to dine with her, I should feel no more taken aback nor if it was Phoebe Hopewell. The fixin's of the table mought be a little grain different from what I had ever heern on, seein' that she is so much richer than I be; and havin' lords to wait behind cheers at dinner would seem, at first, strange, I do suppose, but I should jist cut my eye round like wink, and see how others did, like a well-bred man, and then right and left and down the middle, as they did, as onconsarned as if I had been used to it all my life. Afore you go, I'll pint out to you some smart men in the same grade as myself, travellin' clock venders, or in the tin line, who are men of great refinement in dress, and considerable taste in hoss flesh, and parfect gentlemen, who pride themselves on having the handsomest gall, the best trottin' beast, and the dearest coats in the city, and wouldn't let no man say boo to them for nothin'. Let a British duke ax one o' them to a party without fust callin' and gittin' introduced, as one of them did to another citizen of ourn not long ago, and see if he wouldn't make him a caution to behold. I'd trouble an old gouty lord to go a-hobblin' up stairs afore 'em, a purpose to keep 'em back, and mortify 'em, 'cause they were Americans. I guess they'd give him a lift with the tip eend of their toe that would help him to mend his pace, that's all. What your idea of a gentleman is I don't know, but I suppose nothin' onder an airl is one in your eyes; but my idea of a gentleman is jist this, one who is rich enough, willin' enough, and knowin' enough, when the thing has to be done in first-rate style, to go the full figur', and to do the thing ginteel. That's what I call a gentleman.

XVII

LOOKING UP

THE Clockmaker had an extensive and accurate knowledge of human nature. The wandering life he had led, and the nature of his business, which sent him into every man's house, afforded him a favourable opportunity of studying character, a knowledge of which was the foundation of his success in life. Like most clever men, however, he prided himself less upon what he did, than what he did not, know, and was more ambitious of being considered a man of fashionable manners, than a skilful mechanic, an expert salesman, or a shrewd, intelligent man. It was one of his weak points, and the more remarkable in him, for it was natural to suppose that his quick perception of the ridiculous, and his power of humour, would have enabled him to see the absurdity of such a pretension quicker than most men. Admitting the truth of his assertion, that all men, women, and children, are open to the influence of his universal and infallible soft-sawder, I have no doubt that a dose of it skilfully applied to him on this point, would have proved the accuracy of the remark, by showing that he was no more exempt from its operation than the thousands of dupes whose caution he had disarmed, and whose favour he had won by it himself.

Yes, squire, he continued, it's a great advantage we possess is manners. It enables us to visit the log-huts of the down east settler, and the palace of the nobles on free and easy tarms, to peddle in the one, and do first chop in the other. I rather pride myself on my manners, for I have seed more of the world than most men. That, you see, has provided me with small-talk for the women, and you might as well be without small change in tradin' as small-talk in courtin' the galls. There is nothin' a'most pleases womenkind like hearin' men talk glib to them, unless it be to hear the sound of their own tongues. Then, I larnt psalmody to singin' school, and havin' naturally a good voice, can do base to the nines, and sing complete. Beautiful tunes some o' them meetin' house ones are too. There is old Russia; now that's one you never get tired of; and Washington's march is another, and so is Jim

Crow Zionised. Lookin' on the same musick book with the ladies brings heads together, and if you don't put your hands on their shoulder or their waists you can't see straight, or stand steady to read. Many a match has been made afore now in the night singin' schools. There is where I got my first lesson in manners, tho' father was always a-preachin' up of manners to me too. Father, you know, was one of the heroes of Bunker's Hill. He was a sargeant at that glorious battle, and arterwards rose in Slickville to be a kurnel in the militia. He had quite a military air about him had the old man, and was as straight as a poker at seventy, and carried his head as erect as the cap of a gate post. He always used to say, march,—halt,—right wheel,—left wheel,—quick step, and so on, to his hosses, to the last. He used to say you could always tell a military man by his walk, his talk, and his manners. In his walk he was stately, for it looked hero like; in his talk, he swore a few, for it was the way of the camp; and in his manners, he was humble servant to the ladies, and haughty to the men, because one you fought for, and the other you fought with. Poor old man, he was always a-dingin' this lesson into my ears. *Always look up, Sam; look up in manners, and look up in politicks.* In manners, said he, a man that looks down ain't safe at all. It's a sure sign of roguery and treachery. Such a crittur will either lie, cheat, or steal, or do some bad thing or another, you may depend. Never trust a man that don't hold up and look you in the face; such a crittur knows his heart is bad, and is afeerd you should see into it thro' them are winders, his eyes. Have nothin' to do with him on no account. Look at Lawyer Slyware: well, he is the most pious lawyer and the most extortionate man in all Slickville. You'd think butter wouldn't melt in that feller's mouth, and yet, when he is onder the protection of the court, there ain't anything too bad for him to lay his tongue to in abusin' folks, and where money is consarned, he is mean and onreasonable. Some folks say his piety is jist a cloak, and nothin' more, to hide his claws; how that is, I won't say; but this I know, he looks down, and looks sideways, or any way but right up like a man at you full in the face, and such corn-crackers as that, let them be who they may, arn't over safe in the dark, or in the woods, I know. You recollect old Southey Crowe, don't you? Well, I'll tell you a story about him. He was one of those down-lookin' skunks I was a speakin' of, and a more endless villain, p'raps, there ain't this blessed day atween the poles than he was; but you musn't let on to any one about it that I said so, for he has left some children behind him that are well to do in the world, and different guess chaps from him altogether, and it would be a sin and a shame to hurt their feelin's by a revival; but it's true as gospel for all that.

When minister was first located here, to Slickville, he thought his hoss was the most everlastin' eater he ever seed, for he used to eat more nor any two hosses in all the town, and, says he, to me, one day, *kuy*mel, says he, what's good for a hoss that has an onnatteral appetite, do you know? says he, for my hoss eats near a ton of hay a month.—It's worms, says I; nothin' will make a hoss eat like the botts.—Well, what's good for botts, said he? —Well, says I, chopped hoss-hair in their oats ain't a bad thing, nor a little tobacco, nother; but I'll look at him and see what it is, for I never heerd tell of a hoss eatin' at that rate, at no time. Well, the next mornin' I goes out to the stable along with minister, to see the boss, and there had fallen a little chance of snow in the night, and there was the tracks of a man quite plain, where he had carried off hay, and the seed and dust of the clover was scattered all about after him. Minister, says I, there's the botts sure enough; they have carried off the hay by wholesale, but they've took it afore the hoss got it tho', and no mistake: look at them are tracks.—Dear, dear, said he, only to think of the wickedness of this world; who on airth could that be that was so vile?—Southey Crowe, said I; I'll put my head agin' a cent it's him, for in a gineral way, I suspect them rascals *that look down always*. These are dark nights now, I guess, for it's in the old of the moon, and jist the time for rogues to be up and doin'. I'll keep watch for you to-night, and see who he is. I'll catch him, the villain, see if I don't.—Well, don't use your sword, nor your pistols nother, *kuy*mel, said he; don't apprehend him, nor slay him, or hurt him, but jist admonish, for I'd rather lose hay, hoss, and all, than not forgive the poor Sinner, and reclaim him. Oh, how my heart rejoices over a repentin' sinner!—says I, for I felt my pride touched at his talkin' that way of an officer's sword, as if it was nothin' but a constable's thief sticker, and had half a mind to let the hay go to old Scratch, for all me;—Minister, said I, in a dignified manner to him, my sword, sir, has been draw'd in my country's cause, and it shall never be disgraced by a meaner one. It is consecrated to everlastin' fame, and not to be defiled by the crop and gizzard of a scoundrel. Well, at night, I takes my lantern, the same I had to dress by in the wars, and goes and off shoes, and hides away in a vacant boss-stall near the door, and I had hardly got all snugged away in the boss litter, and done swearin' at the parfume of it, (for it ain't pretty to sleep in,)

when, who should come in but Southey Crowe. Well, he ups into the loft
in little less than half no time, and pitches down a considerable of a lock
of hay, and then ties it up in a bundle fit for carriage, and slips it over his
shoulder like a knapsack, so as to have his hands free to balance with in
runnin', and to help him climb the fences. Well, as soon as he was ready he
goes to the door, and opens it; but his bundle was a little grain too wide,
and stuck a bit, and jist then, I outs candle, and sets fire to his load in several
places. As soon as he sees the light, he gives a jerk, forces the bundle thro'
the doorway, and runs like old Nick himself, as fast as he could cut dirt,
for dear life, and fancyin' there was some one a-pursuin' of him; he never
stopt to look behind him, but jist streaked it off like a greased thunderbolt.
At last, the poor crittur was singed in airnest, and 'most suffocated, and he
yelled and screamed most awful; he was a caution to hear; and the faster he
ran, the faster the flame burned, till at last the chord give way, and down
fell the burnin' bundle. A few days arterwards he came to minister, and
confessed that he was the man, and said Heaven had sent down fire to
burn the hay on him as a warnin' to him of the punishment to come for
robbin' a minister. Well, what does minister do, the old goose, but ups and
tells him human means was used, as it was my lantern. He said he didn't
want to encourage superstition by pious frauds, and I don't know what all.
It made me hoppin' mad to see him act so like an old fool. Well, what was
the consequence of all this nonsense? Why, Southey got over his fright,
seein' the Devil had no hand in it, and went right at stealin' agin. He was
one of them fellers *that always look down, was* Southey. Cuss 'em, there is
no trustin' any of them.

  Then he used to say, always *look up in politicks, Sam*. Now we have two
kind of politicians, the *Federalists* and the *Democrats*. The *Federalists look
up*, and are for a vigorous executive, for republican institutions such as
Washington left us, for the state-tax for religion, and for enforcin' law and
order—what you may call consarvitives, p'raps; and *they* appeal to men of
sense and judgment, and property, to the humane, liberal, and enlightened
upper classes, and they want to see the reins of Government in the hands
of such folks, because then we have some security things will be well
administered. Then we have the *Democrats*, elders that *look down*; who try
to set the poor agin the rich, who talk of our best men with contempt,
and hold 'em up as enemies to their country; who say the Federalists are
aristocrats, tyrants, and despots, and appeal to the prejudices and passions

of the ignorant, and try to inflame them; who use the word *Reform* as a catchword to weaken the hands of the Government, to make everything elective, and to take all power of good from the venerable senate (whose voice they call an aristocratic whisper), under pretence of restraining their power for evil. These are mob politicians. They first incite and discontent the mob, and then say the people must have a change of officers; and when they get into office, they sacrifice everybody and everything to keep in. This comes *o' lookin' down.*

These party leaders call the mob *their tail*, and they know the use of a tail too as well as neighbour Dearborne's rats did. Neighbour Dearborne used to wonder how it was all his casks of molasses had jist five inches draw'd off, exactly, and no more, out of each cask. His store was well locked, and well barred, and fastened up all tight and snug every day, and he was fairly stumpt to know how the thieves got in, and why they stole no more than jist five inches out of each; so what does he do but goes and gets up on the roof of the store, and watches thro' the sky light. Well, he watched and watched for ever so long, all to no purpose, and he was jist about givin' it up as a bad job, when he thought he seed somethin' a-movin', and he looked, and what do you think he *did* see? Why, a few great, big, overgrow'd rats come crawlin' along the tops of the casks, and they jist dipt their tails thro' the bungs into the 'lasses, and then turned to and licked 'em off clean. They did, upon my soul!

This is jist the way in politicks. Democrat or liberal leaders make the same use of their followers, *their tail*. *They make use of them to get a dip into the good things, but they lick all up so clean themselves nothin' was ever seen to stick to the tail.* See, too, what a condition religion is got into among these *down-lookin' gentry.* The Bible has got turned out of the common schools all thro' Slickville, because it offends the *scruples of them who never read it, and don't know what it contains.* To be religious is out of fashion now, it ain't liberal. It ain't enough with these demagogues to let every man worship his own way, but you must lock up the Bible from schools for fear it will teach little children to be bigots. Now, Sam, minister would say, see here: these same critturs, all over the world, belie their own politicks in their own conduct. Let one of our democrat-movement men go to England, or any place where there are birds of the same feather, and ask credit for goods, and take a certificate of character from the patriots, demagogues, and devils to home, and see what his reception will be. Sorry, sir, but have more orders than we can execute; don't know these people that have sartified your character; may be very good men, but don't know them. Busy, sir,—good mornin'. But let a man *look up*, and take a recommendation from the first pot-hooks on the crane; from the Governor and select men, and the judges, and minister, and me, the honourable Colonel Slick, commander-in-chief of the militia forces (a name well known in military circles), and see what they'll say.—Ah! this damned Yankee, (they *will* swear a few, for they are as cross as a bear with a sore head since the lickin' we give them last war,) *he* comes well sartified, most respectable testi-*mo*-nies, all upper-crust folks. High characters all. We can trust *him,* he'll do: t'other feller's papers were *rather* suspicious; this one's will pass muster.—And yet, Sam, our democrat liberals tell the poor ignorant voters that these men whose *sartificates will pass all the world over, all the same as if they was onder oath, ain't to be trusted in politicks at home.* He on them, they know better, and I wish with all my heart they was shipt clean out o' the State down to Nova Scotia, or some such outlandish place.

I fixed one feller's flint that came a-canvassin' the other day for a democrat candidate, most properly. Says be, *Kuy*mel, says he, did you hear the news, that infarnal scoundrel Coke, the mayor, is nominated for governor; he is a cussed Federalist that, he is *no friend to his country*; I wouldn't vote for him for a hogreave.

Upright magistrate, warn't he? says I.—Why, yes, to give the devil his due, I must say he was.

Brings his family up well, don't he?—Well enough.

Good neighbour, ain't he?—Why, yes; but what's that to do with it? he ain't *no friend to his country.*

Not a bad landlord, is he? I never heerd of his distressin' his tenants, did you?—Why, no, I can't say I did; but what's all that when it's fried?

A good deal of money passed thro' his hands, did you ever hear of any complaints?—I made no inquiries. I dare say if there was, he hushed them up.

A great friend to intarnal improvements, ain't he—rail-roads and them sort of things?—And well he may be, he owns a good deal of land in the state and it will benefit it. The devil thank him!

Sees a good deal of company to his house: was you ever there?—Why no, says he, your Federalists are too proud for that; but I wouldn't go if he was to ask me; I despise him, for he is *no friend to his country.*

Ah! says I, the cat's out of the bag now. This is mahogony patriotism; but who is your candidate?—Well he is no aristocrat, no federalist, no tyrant, but a rael right down reformer and democrat. He is a friend to his country, and no mistake. It's Gabriel Hedgehog.

Him, said I, that there was so much talk about cheatin' folks in his weights?—That was never proved, said he; let them prove that.

Exactly, says I, your objection to Coke is, that you never got so far as his front door yet; and mine to Gabriel Hedgehog, that I wouldn't trust him inside of mine at no rate. The Federalist, it appears, is an upright, honorable, kind, and benevolent man, discharging all his public and private duties like a good man and a good member of society. You say he is a friend to intarnal improvement because he owns much land; for the same reason, if for no higher or better one, he will be a friend to his country. *He has got somethin' to fight for, that chap, besides his pay as a member and his share of the plunder.* I always *look up in politicks.* Them are the sort of men to govern us. Your man's honesty is rather doubtful, to say the least of it, and you and him want to level the mayor, and all others above you, down to your own level, do you? Now, I don't want to cut no one down, but to raise up (we had cuttin' down enough, gracious knows, at Bunker's Hill, Mud Creek, and Peach Orchard, in cuttin' down the British). Now, I know, it's easier to cut others down than to raise yourselves, but it tante so honourable. Do you and Hedgehog turn to and earn the same reputation the mayor has, and as soon as you have, and are so much respected and beloved as he is, I'll vote for either or both of you, for my maxim always is *to look up in politicks.*

Now, says I, friend,—attention—eyes right—left shoulders forward—march! and I walked him out of the house in double quick time; I did by gum! Yes, Sam, always look up,—*Look up in manners, and look up in politicks.*

XVIII

THE OLD MINISTER

AS we approached Slickville, the native town of the Clockmaker, he began to manifest great impatience and an extraordinary degree of excitement. He urged on old Clay to the top of his speed, who, notwithstanding all the care bestowed upon him, and the occasional aid of a steam-boat whenever there was one running in the direction of our route, looked much thinner for this prodigious journey than when we left Halifax. Come, old Tee-total, said he, you are a-goin' home now, and no mistake. Hold up your old oatmill, and see if you can snuff the stable at minister's, if the smell of these inion fields don't pyson your nose. Show the folks you hante forgot *how* to go. The weather, squire, you see, has been considerable juicy here lately, and to judge by the mud some smart grists of rain has fell, which has made the roads soapy and violent slippery; but if he can't trot he can slide, you'll find, and if he can't slide he can skate, and if he breaks thro' he can swim, but he can go somehow or another, or somehow else. He is all sorts of a hoss, and the best live one that ever cut dirt this side of the big pond, or t'other side other, and if any man will show me a boss that can keep it up as he has done in the wild wicked trot clean away from Kent's Lodge, in Nova Scotia, to Slickville, Conne'ticut, and eend it with such a pace as that are, I'll give him old Clay for nothin', as a span for him. Go it, you old coon you—go it! and make tracks like dry dust in a thunder storm. There now, that's it, I guess! hit or miss, right or wrong, tit or no tit, that's the tatur! O squire, he *is* a hoss, is old Clay, every inch of him! Start him agin for five hundred miles, and you'll find he is jist the boy that *can* do it. He'd make as short work of it as a whole battalion does of a pint of whiskey at gineral trainin'. If you want to see another beast like him in this world, put your spectacles on, and look as sharp as you darn please, for I reckon he is too far off to see with the naked eye, at least I could never see him yet.

But old Clay was not permitted to retain this furious gate long, for recognition now became so frequent between Mr. Slick and his old friends, the people of Slickville, that the last mile, as he said, "tho' the

shortest one of the whole bilin', took the longest to do it in by a jug full."
The reception he met with on his return to his native land was a pleasing
evidence of the estimation in which he was held by those who best knew
him. Nothing could exceed the kindness with which he was greeted by his
countrymen. An invitation to a public dinner, presented by a deputation
of the select men, as a token of their approbation of his "Sayings and
Doings," was, however, so unexpected an honour on his part that his
feelings nearly overpowered him. Perhaps it was fortunate that it had that
effect, for it enabled him to make a suitable reply, which, under any other
circumstances, his exuberant spirits and extravagant phraseology would
have disqualified him from doing. He said he was aware he owed this
honour more to their personal regard for him than his own merits; but tho'
he could not flatter himself he was entitled to so gratifying a distinction,
it should certainly stimulate him to endeavour to render himself so. In our
subsequent travels he often referred to this voluntary tribute of regard and
respect of his countrymen in terms of great satisfaction and pride. He said
there were but three days in his life that he could call rael tip-top ones:
one was when he was elected into the House of Representatives, and
made sure he was to be President of the United States; the second when,
after finding his mistake, he ceased to be a member, and escaped out of the
menagerie; and the third, when he found himself thus publickly honoured
in his native land.

The reception he everywhere met with was most kind and flattering;
but Mr. Hopewell, the ex-minister of the parish, embraced him with all
the warmth and affection of a father. He pressed him most cordially and
affectionately to his bosom, called him his good friend, his kind-hearted
boy, his dear and dutiful son. They were both affected to tears. He thanked
him for having brought me to his house, to which he welcomed me in
the most hospitable manner, and did me the favour to say, that he had
looked forward with much pleasure to this opportunity of making my
acquaintance.

The appearance of this venerable old man was most striking. In stature
he exceeded the ordinary standard, and though not corpulent, he was
sufficiently stout to prevent an air of awkwardness attaching to his height.
Notwithstanding his very great age, his voice was firm, and his gait erect.
His hair was of the most snowy whiteness, and his countenance, though
furrowed with age and care, gave evidence of great intelligence and

extraordinary benevolence. His manner, though somewhat formal, like that of a gentleman of the old school, was remarkably kind and prepossessing, and the general effect of his bearing was well calculated to command respect and conciliate affection. Those persons who have described the Yankees as a cold, designing, unimpassioned people, know but little of them or their domestic circles. To form a correct opinion of a people, it is necessary to see them at home, to witness their family reunions, the social intercourse of friends, and, to use Mr. Slick's favourite phrase, "to be behind the scenes." Whoever has been so favoured as to be admitted on these intimate terms in New England, has always come away most favourably impressed with what he has seen, and has learned, that in the thousand happy homes that are there, there are many, very many, thousands of kind, and good, and affectionate hearts in them, to make them so. The temperature of Mr. Slick's mind was warm, and his spirits buoyant, and, therefore, though overcome for a time by various emotions, on the present occasion his natural gaiety soon returned, and the appearance of Mr. Hopewell's sister, a maiden lady "of a certain age," who resided with him, and superintended his household, afforded him an opportunity of indemnifying himself.

Is that aunt Hetty, sir? said he, addressing himself to "the minister" with much gravity. Why yes, Sam, to be sure it is. Is she so much altered that you do not know her? Ah, me! we are both altered—both older than we were and sadder too, Sam, since you left us.—Altered! I guess she is, said Mr. Slick; I wouldn't a-know'd her nowhere. Why, aunt Hetty! how do you do? What on airth have you done with yourself to look so young? Why, you look ten years younger?—Well, if that don't pass! Well, you ain't altered then, Sam, said she, shaking him heartily by the hand, not one mite or morsel; you are jist as full of nonsense as ever; do behave, now, that's a good feller.—Ah! he continued, I wish I could alter as you do, and that are rose-bush of yourn onder the parlour winder; both on you bloom afresh every month. Lord, if I could only manage as you do, grow younger every year, I should be as smart as a two-year-old soon: then, lowering his voice, he said, Brought you a beau, aunty,—that's the squire, there,—ain't he a beauty without paint, that? The sarvant maid stole his stays last night, but when he has 'em on, he ain't a bad figure, I tell you. The only thing against your taking such a fat figure, is, that you'd have to lace them stays every mornin' for him, and that's no joke, is it?—Now, *Sam*, said she, (colouring at the very idea of a gentleman's toilet,) do behave, that's a dear! The intire stranger will hear you, I am sure he will, and it will make me feel kinder foolish to have you runnin' on that way: ha' done, now, that's a dear!—Sit your cap for him, aunty, he said, without heeding her; he is a Blue-nose to be sure, but rub a silver-skinned inion on it, and it will draw out the colour, and make him look like a Christian. He is as soft as dough, that chap, and your eyes are so keen they will cut right into him, like a carvin'-knife into a punkin' pie. Lord, he'll never know he has lost his heart, till he puts his ear to it like a watch, and finds it's done tickin'. Give me your presarves, tho', aunty, when you marry; your quinces, and damsons, and jellies, and what not, for you won't want *them* no more. Nothin' ever tastes sweet arter lips. O, dear! one smack o' them is worth—Do get along, said Miss Hetty, extricating, at last, her hand from his, and effecting her escape to her brother. What a plague you be!

It was a happy meeting, and at dinner, Mr. Slick's sallies awakened many a long-forgotten smile on the face of his old friend, the minister. It is delightful to witness the effect of a young and joyous heart upon one that has become torpid with age, or chilled with the coldness and neglect of the world; to see it winning it back to cheerfulness, warming it again into animated existence, and beguiling it of its load of care, until it brightens into reflecting on its surface the new and gay images that are thus thrown upon it.

After the cloth was removed, the conversation accidentally took a more serious turn. So you are going to England, Sam, are you, said Mr. Hopewell? —Yes, minister, replied the Clockmaker, I am a-goin' with the squire, here. Spose you go with us. You are a gentleman at large now you got nothin' to do, and it will do you good; it will give you a new lease of life, I am a-thinkin'. The allusion to his having nothing to do was, to say the least of it, thoughtless and ill-timed.—Yes, Sam, said he, evidently much distressed, you say truly, I *have* nothin' to do; but whose fault is that? Is it mine, or my parishioners? When my flock all turned Unitarians, and put another man in my pulpit, and told me they hadn't no further occasion for me or my sarvices, was it the flock that wandered, or the shepherd that slept? It is an awful question, that, Sam, and one that must be answered some day or another, as sure as you are born. I try to make myself believe it is my fault, and I pray that it may be so considered, and that I may be accepted as a sacrifice for them; for willingly would I lay down my life for them, the poor deluded critturs. Then, sometimes I try to think it warn't the fault of either me or my flock, but the fault of them are good-for-nothin' philosophers, Jefferson, Franklin, and them new-school people, that fixed our constitution, and forgot to make Christianity the corner-stone. O, what an awful affliction it is for a country, when its rulers are not attached to the Church of God! If poor dear old Gineral Washington had a-had his way, it would have been different, and he told me so with tears in his eyes. Joshua, says he, for him and me was very intimate: Joshua, says he, the people ascribe all the praise of our glorious revolution to their own valor and tome, because I am one of themselves, and are a-going to build a great city for a capital, and call it after me, Washington; but for *Him*, Joshua, said he, a-pintin' up to the skies with one hand, and devoutly oncoverin' his head with the other, but for Him who upheld us in the hour of battle and in the day of trouble—for Him, to whom all honor, and praise, and glory is due, what have we done? why, carefully excluded the power to endow Christianity from every Constitution of every state in the Union. Our language is at once impious and blasphemous. We say the Lord is better able to take charge of his clergy than we are, and we have no doubt he will. Let him see to them, and we will see to ourselves. Them that want religion can pay for it. The state wants none, for it is an incorporeal affair, without a body to be punished or a soul to be saved. Now, Joshua, said he, you will live to see it, but I won't—for I feel as if they was a-goin' to make an idol of *me*, to worship, and it kills me—you will see the nateral consequence of all this in a few years. We shall runaway from the practice of religion into theory. We shall have more sects than the vanity of man ever yet invented, and more enthusiasm and less piety, and more pretension and less morals, than any civilised nation on the face of the airth. Instead of the well-regulated, even pulsation, that shows a healthy state of religion, it will be a feverish excitement or helpless debility. The body will sometimes appear dead, as when in a trance; a glass over the lips will hardly detect respiration; it will seem as if the vital spark was extinct. Then it will have fits of idiotcy, stupid, vacant, and drivelling; then excitement will inspire zeal, genius, and eloquence, and while you stand lost in admiration of its powers, its beauty, and sublimity, you will be startled by its wildness, its eccentric flashes, its incoherences; and before you can make up your mind that it has lost its balance, you will be shocked by its insanity, its horrible frantic raving madness.

Joshua, said he, we ought to have established a Church, fixed upon some *one,* and called it a *national* one. Not having done so, nothing short of a direct interposition of Providence, which we do not deserve and therefore cannot hope for, can save this great country from becoming a dependency of Rome. Popery, that is now only a speck in these States no bigger than a man's hand, will speedily spread into a great cloud, and cover this land so no ray of light can penetrate it: nay, it is a giant, and it will enter into a divided house and expel the unworthy occupants. We tolerate Papists, because we believe they will inherit heaven equally with us; but when their turn comes, will they tolerate us whom they hold to be Heretics? O, that we had held fast to the Church that we had!—the Church of our forefathers—the Church of England. It is a pure, noble, apostolical structure, the holiest and the best since the days of the Apostles; but we have not, and the consequence is too melancholy and too awful to contemplate. Was it for this, said he, I drew my sword in my country's cause? and he pulled the blade half out. Had I known what I now know,—and he drove it back with such force, I fairly thought it would have come out of t'other eend, —it should have rusted in its scabbard first, it should, indeed, Hopewell. Now, Joshua, said he,—and he oncovered his head agin, for he was a religious man was Washington, and never took the Lord's name in vain,—recollect these words: "visiting the sins of the fathers upon the children, unto the third and fourth generation of them that hate me, and shewing mercy unto thousands of *them that love me.*" May the promise be ours; but, oh! far, far be the denunciation from us and our posterity! Franklin, Joshua, has a great deal to answer for. Success has made him flippant and self-sufficient, and, like all self-taught men, he thinks he knows more than he does, and more than anybody else. If he had more religion and less philosophy, as he calls scepticism, it would be better for him and us too. He is always a-sayin' to me*, leave religion alone,* Gineral: leave it to *the voluntary principle*; the *supply* will always keep pace with the *demand*. It is the *maxim of a pedlar,* Joshua, and onworthy of a statesman or a Christian; for in religion, unlike other things, the demand seldom or *never precedes,* but almost *invariably follows* and increases with the supply. "An ignorant man knoweth not this, neither doth a fool understand it." I wish he could see with his own eyes the effects of his liberality, Joshua, it would sober his exultation, and teach him a sad and humiliating lesson. Let him come with me into Virginia and see the ruins of that great and good establishment that ministered to us in our youth as our nursing mother,—let him examine the ninety-five parishes of the State, and he will find twenty-three extinct, and thirty-four destitute, the pastors expelled by want, or violence, or death.

His philosophy will be gratified too, I suppose, by seeing the numerous proselytes he has made to his enlightened opinions. In breaking up the Church, these *rational religionists* have adopted his maxims of frugality, and abstained from destroying that which *might be useful*. The baptismal fonts have been preserved as convenient for watering horses, and the sacred cup has been retained as a relic of the olden time, to grace the convivial board. There is no bigotry here, Joshua, no narrow prejudice, for reformers are always men of enlarged minds. They have done their work like men. They have applied the property of the Church to secular purposes, and *covered their iniquity under the cant of educating the poor,* forgetting the while that a *knowledge of God is the foundation of all wisdom*. They have extinguished the cry of the Church being in danger by extinguishing the Church itself. *When reformers talk of religious freedom as a popular topic, depend upon it they mean to dispense with religion altogether.* What the end will be I know not, for the issues are with Him from whom all good things do come; but I do still indulge the hope all is not yet lost. Though the tree be cut down, the roots are left; and the sun by day and the dew by night may nurture them, and new shoots may spring up, and grow luxuriantly, and afford shelter in due season to them that are weary and heavy-laden: and even if the roots should be killed, the venerable parent-stock on the other side of the water, from which ours is an offset, is still in full vigour: and new layers may yet be laid by pious hands, which, under the blessing of Heaven, shall replace our loss. Yes, even I, though lately in arms against the English, may say, long may the maternal Church live and flourish! and may the axe of the spoiler never be laid upon it by sacrilegious hands; for I warred with their King, and not against their God, who is my God also.

Washington was right, Sam, continued Mr. Hopewell. We ought to have an establishment and national temples for worship; for He has said, who is truth itself, "where I record my name, I will come unto thee and bless thee." Somehow, I fear his name is not legibly recorded here; but whose fault was this desertion of my flock, mine or them philosophers that made the constitution?

I availed myself here of a slight pause in the conversation to give it another turn, for the excitement was too much for a man of his great years and sensibility. So I said that I perfectly agreed with General Washington, of whom I entertained as exalted an opinion as he did; but that the circumstances of the times were such, and the prejudices against everything English so strong, it would have been utterly impossible for the framers of the constitution to have done otherwise than they did; but, said I, with reference to your visiting England, since steam navigation has been introduced, the voyage has been stripped of all its discomforts, and half its duration; and I am confident the trip would be as beneficial to your health as your company would be instructive and agreeable to us. Have you ever been there?—Often, said he: oh, yes! I know, or rather knew dear Old England well—very well; and I had a great many friends and correspondents there, among the bishops many dear very dear and learned friends; but, alas! they are gone now,—and he took his spectacles off and wiped them with his handkerchief, for a tear had dimmed the glasses,—gone to receive the reward they have earned as good and faithful stewards. Let me see, said he, when was I there last? Oh! my memory fails me. I'll jist step into my study and get my journal; but I fear it was to give vent to feelings that were over-powering him. When he had gone, Mr. Slick said, —Ain't he a'most a-beautiful talker, that, squire, even when he is a little wanderin' in his mind, as he is now? There is nothin' he don't know. He is jist a walkin' dictionary. He not only knows how to spell every word, but he knows its meanin', and its root as he calls it, and what nation made it first. He knows Hebrew better nor any Jew you ever see, for he knows it so well he can read it backward. He says it's the right way; but that's only his modesty, for I've tried English backward and I can't make no hand of it. Oh! He'd wear a slate out in no time, he writes so much on things he thinks on. He is a peg too low now. I'll jist give him a dose of soft-sawder, for old or young, men or women, high or low, every palate likes that. I'll put him up if I can another note or so; but he is so crotchied, and flies off the handle so, you hardly know where to touch him. The most curious thing about him is the way he acts about the stars. He has gin 'em all names, and talks of 'em as if they were humans; he does, upon my soul. There is his Mars, and Venus, and Saturn, and Big Bear, and Little Bear, and the Lord knows what all. I mind once I put him into a'most an allfired passion when he was talkin' about 'em. I never see him in such a rage before or since, for he didn't speak for the matter of three minutes. When he is mad, he jist walks up and down the room and counts a hundred to himself, and that cools him, for he says it's better to have nothin' to say than sunthin' to repent of. Well, this time, I guess, he counted two hundred, for it was longer than common afore he had added it all up and sumtotalised it. I'll tell you how it was. Him and me was a-sittin' talkin' over nothin' at all, jist as we are now, when all at once he gets up and goes to the winder, and presently sings out,—"Sam, says he, put your hat on, my boy, and let's go and see Venus dip to-night;" but here he comes. I'll tell you that are story some other time, for here comes *the Old Minister.*

XIX

THE BARREL WITHOUT HOOPS

SUCH is the charm of manner, that it often happens that what we hear with pleasure we afterwards read with diminished satisfaction. I cannot now give the words of the Minister, for the memory seldom retains more than the substance, and I am quite aware how much these conversations lose in repeating. He was, as Mr. Slick observed, "the best talker I ever heard," and I regretted that my time was so limited I had it not in my power to enjoy more of his society at this place, although I am not altogether without hopes that as I have enlisted "aunt Hetty" on my side, I have succeeded in persuading him to accompany us to England. How delightful it would be to hear his observations on the aspect of affairs there, to hear him contrast the present with the past, and listen to his conjectures about the future. With such a thorough knowledge of man, and such an extensive experience as he has had of the operation of various forms of government, his predictions would appear almost prophetic. When he returned from his study Mr. Slick rose and left the room in search of amusement in the village, and I availed myself of the opportunity to ascertain his opinions respecting the adjoining colonies, for the constant interruption he received from the Clockmaker had a tendency to make his conversation too desultory for one whose object was instruction. I therefore lost no time in asking him what changes he thought would be desirable to improve the condition of the people in British America and perpetuate the connexion with England.

Ah, sir, said he, that word change is "the incantation that calls fools into a circle." It is the riddle that perplexes British statesmen, and the rock on which they are constantly making shipwreck. They are like our friend Samuel, who changes his abode so often that removal has become necessary to his very existence. A desire for political change, like a fondness for travel, grows with the indulgence. *What you want in the colonies is tranquillity, not change.—Quod petis hic est.* You may change constitutions forever, but you cannot change man. He is still unaltered under every vicissitude, the same restless, discontented, dissatisfied animal. Even in this pure unmixed democracy of ours he is as loud in his complaints as under the strictest despotism, nay, louder, for the more he is indulged the more intractable he becomes. The object of statesmen, therefore, should be, not to study what changes should be conceded, but the causes that lead men to desire change. The restlessness in the colonies proceeds not from grievances, for, with the exception of a total absence of patronage, they do not exist; but it is caused by an uneasiness of position, arising from a want of room to move in. There is no field for ambition, no room for the exercise of distinguished talent in the provinces. The colonists, when comparing their situation with that of their more fortunate brethren in England, find all honour monopolised at home, and employment, preferments, and titles liberally bestowed on men frequently inferior in intellect and ability to themselves, and this invidious distinction sinks deeper into the heart than they are willing to acknowledge themselves. Men seldom avow the real motives of their actions. A littleness of feeling is often in reality the source of conduct that claims to spring from a virtue. A slight, an insult, or a disappointment, jealousy, envy, or personal dislike, often find a convenient shelter in agitation, and a more respectable name in patriotism. A man who quits his church in temper would have you believe he has scruples of conscience, which he requires you to respect; and he who rebels in the hope of amending his fortune ascribes his conduct to an ardent love of country, and a devotion to the cause of freedom. Grievances are convenient masks under which to hide our real objects. The great question then is, what induces men in the provinces to resort to them as pretexts. The cause now, as in 1777, is the absence of all patronage, the impossibility there is for talent to rise—want of room—of that employment that is required for ability of a certain description; at least, this is the cause with those who have the power to influence,—to lead—to direct public opinion. I allude only to these men, for the leaders are the workmen and the multitude their tools. It is difficult to make an Englishman comprehend this. Our successful rebellion, one would have supposed, would not easily have been forgotten; but, unfortunately, it was a lesson not at all understood.

This was so novel a view of the subject, and the assertion that all the recent complaints were fictitious, was so different from what I had apprehended to be the case, that I could not resist asking him if there were no real grievances in 1777, when his countrymen took up arms against us?

No, sir, said he, none; none of any magnitude except the attempt to tax for the purpose of revenue, which was wrong, very wrong, indeed; *but if that which was put forth as the main one, had been the real cause, when it ceased the rebellion would have ceased also.* But there was another, a secret and unavowed, the more powerful cause, *the want of patronage.* I will explain this to you. Statesmen have always been prone to consider the colonies as a field reserved for the support of their dependants, and they are, unfortunately, so distant from the parent state that the rays of royal favour do not easily penetrate so far. Noisy applicants, mercenary voters, and importunate suitors at home, engross the attention and monopolise the favour of those in power, and provincial merit is left to languish for want of encouragement. The provincials hear of coronation honours, of flattering distinctions, and of marks of royal favour; but, alas! they participate not in them. A few of the petty local officers, which they pay themselves out of their little revenue, have long since been held their due, and, within these few years, I hear the reformers have generously promised not to deprive them of this valuable patronage in any case where it is not required for others. Beyond this honourable parish rank no man can rise, and we look in vain for the name of a colonist, whatever his loyalty, his talent, or his services may be, out of the limits of his own country. The colonial clergy are excluded from the dignities of the Church of England, the lawyers from the preferments of the bar, and the medical men from practising out of their own country, while the professions in the colonies are open to all who migrate thither. The avenues to the army and navy, and all the departments of the imperial service, are *practically* closed to them. Notwithstanding the intimate knowledge they possess on colonial subjects, who of their leading men are ever selected to govern other provinces? A captain in the navy, a colonel in the army, a London merchant, or an unprovided natural son, any person, in short, from whose previous education constitutional law has been wholly excluded, is thought better qualified, or more eligible, for these important duties than a colonist, while that department that manages and directs all these dependencies, seldom contains one individual that has ever been out of Great Britain. A peerage generally awaits a Governor General, but indifference or neglect rewards those through whose intelligence and ability he is alone enabled to discharge his duties. The same remedy for this contemptuous neglect occurs to all men, in all ages. When the delegate from the Gabii consulted Tarquin, he took him into his garden, and drawing his sword cut off the heads of the tallest poppies. The hint was not lost, and the patricians soon severally disappeared. When our agent in France mentioned the difficulties that subsisted between us and Britain, the king significantly pointed to a piece of ordnance, and observed it was an able negotiator, and the meaning was too obvious to be disregarded. When Papineau, more recently, asked advice of the reformers in England, he was told, "Keep the glorious example of the United States constantly in view;" and an insurrection soon followed, to destroy what his friend called "the baneful domination."

The consequence of this oversight or neglect, as our revolution and the late disturbances in Canada but too plainly evince, is, that ambition, disappointed of its legitimate exercise, is apt, in its despair, to attempt the enlargement of its sphere by the use of the sword. Washington, it is well known, felt the chilling influence of this policy. Having attained early in life to great influence by the favour of his countrymen, not only without the aid but against the neglect of the Commander-in-chief, he saw a regular, and sometimes not a very judicious advancement, in the military operations of America, of every man who had the good fortune not to be a colonist. He felt that his country was converted into one of the great stages at which these favoured travellers rested for a time to reap the reward of their exile, and resume their journey up the ascent of life, while all those who permanently resided here were doomed to be stationary spectators of this mortifying spectacle. Conscious of his own powers, he smarted under this treatment, and he who became too powerful for a subject, might, under a wiser and kinder policy, have been transferred to a higher and more honourable position in another colony. Progressive advancement; to which his talents, and at one time his services, gave him a far better claim than most governors can exhibit, would have deprived him of the motive, the means, and the temptation to seek in patriotism what was denied to merit and to loyalty. History affords us some recent instances, in which the administration in the parent state have relieved themselves of "an inconvenient friend," by giving him an appointment abroad. Ambitious men who attain to this in convenient eminence in the colonies, might, with equal advantage to the country and themselves, be transferred to a more extended and safer sphere of action in other parts of the empire. No man now pretends to deny, that it was the want of some such safety-valve that caused the explosion in these old colonies, that now form the United States. Patriotism then, as in all ages, covered a multitude of sins, and he who preferred, like a Washington, a Jefferson, or an Adams, the command of armies, the presidential chair of a great nation, and the patronage and other attributes of royalty, to the rank of a retired planter, a practising provincial barrister, or an humble representative in a local legislature, easily became a convert to the doctrine that a stamp act was illegal, and a tax on tea an intolerable oppression. When loyalty, like chastity, is considered, as it now is, to be its own great reward, and agitation is decorated with so many brilliant prizes, it is not to be wondered at if men constantly endeavour to persuade themselves that every refusal of a request is both an arbitrary and unjust exercise of power, that denial justifies resistance, and that resistance is a virtue. Instead of conceding to popular clamour changes that are dangerous, it is safer and wiser to give ambition a new direction, and to show that the government has the disposition to patronise, as well as the power to punish. It is unjust to the Queen, and unkind to the Colonists, to exhibit the image of their Sovereign in no other attitude than that of an avenging despot exacting obedience, and enforcing dependence. Royalty has other qualities that appeal to the hearts of subjects, but parliamentary influence is too selfish and too busy to permit statesmen to regard colonists in any other light than the humble tenantry of the distant possessions of the empire. Grievances (except the unavowed one I have just mentioned, which is the prolific parent of all that bear the name of patriots,) fortunately do not exist; but ambitious men like hypochondriacs, when real evils are wanting, often supply their place with imaginary ones. Provincialism and nationality are different degrees of the same thing, and both take their rise in the same feeling, love of country, while no colony is so poor or so small as not to engender it. The public or distinguished men of a province are public property, and the people feel an interest in them in an inverse ratio, perhaps, to their own individual want of importance. To those who have the distribution of this patronage, it must be gratifying to know, that when this is the case, *an act of justice* will always appear *an act of grace.*

Here we is agin, said Mr. Slick, who now entered the room. How am you was, squire, how is you been, as Tousand Teyvils said to the Dutch Governor. Well, minister, did you find the date? When was it you was to England last? Nothing could be more provoking than this interruption, for the subject we were talking upon was one of great interest to a colonist, and no opportunity occurred of reverting to it afterwards. The change of topic, however, was not more sudden than the change of Mr. Hopewell's manner and style of speaking, for he adopted at once the familiar and idiomatic language to which Mr. Slick was more accustomed, as one better suited to the level of his understanding.—It was in '85, said Mr. Hopewell; I havn't been to England since, and that's fifty-five years ago. It is a long time that, isn't it? How many changes have taken place since! I don't suppose I should know it agin now.—Why, minister, said Mr. Slick, you put me in mind of the Prophet.—Yes, yes, Sam, said he, I dare say I do, for you are always a-thinkin' on profit and loss. Natur' jist fitted you for a trader. Dollars and cents is always uppermost on your mind.—O dear! he replied, I didn't mean that at all, I mean him that got on Pisgah. You have attained such a height as it mought be in years, you can see a great way behind, and ever so far ahead. You have told us what's afore us in our great republic, now tell us what's afore England.—First of all, said he, I'll tell you what's afore you, my son, and that is, if you talk in that are loose way to Britain, about sacred things and persons, you won't be admitted into no decent man's house at all, and I wouldn't admit you into mine if I didn't know your tongue was the worstest part of you, and that it neither spoke for the head or the heart, but jist for itself. As for the English empire, Sam, it's the greatest the world ever seed. The sun never sets on it. The banner of England floats on every breeze and on every sea. So many parts and pieces require good management and great skill to bind together, for it tante a whole of itself, like a single stick-mast, but a spliced one, composed of numerous pieces and joints. Now, the most beautiful thing of the kind, not political, but mechanical, is a barrel. I defy anyone but a rael cooper to make one so as to hold water, indeed, it tante every cooper can do it, for there are bunglin' coopers as well as bunglin' statesmen. Now, see how many staves there are in a barrel,—(do you mean a barrel organ, said the Clockmaker, for some o' them grind some very tidy staves, of times, I tell you.—Pooh! said Mr. Hopewell)—how well they all fit, how tight they all come together, how firm and secure the hoops keep them in their places. Well, when it's right done, it don't leak one drop, and you can stand it up on eend, or lay it down on its side, or roll it over and over, and still it seems as if it was all solid wood. Not only that, but put it into a vessel and clap a thousand of them right a-top of one another, and they wont squash in, but bear any weight you choose to put on them. But, he continued, but, sir, cut the hoops and where is your barrel?—(where is the liquor? you should say, said Mr. Slick, for that is always worth a great deal more than the barrel by a long chalk, and while you are a-talkin' about cooperin', I will jist go and tap that are cask of prime old East Ingy Madeira Captain Ned Sparm gave you.—Do, said Mr. Hopewell; I am sorry I didn't think of it afore; but don't shake it Sam, or you'll ryle it.) Well, sir, where is your barrel? why, a heap of old iron hoops and wooden staves. Now, in time, the heat of the sun, and rollin' about, and what not, shrinks a cask, as a matter of course, and the hoops all loosen, and you must drive them up occasionally, to keep all tight and snug. A little attention this way, and it will last for ever a'most. Now, some how or another, the British appear to me of late years to revarse this rule, and instead of tightening the hoops of their great body politick, as they had ought to do, they loosen them, and if they continue to do so much longer, that great empire will tumble to pieces as sure as we are a-talkin'.

Now, one of the great bonds of society is religion—a national establishment of religion,—one that provides, at the expense of the State, for the religious education of the poor,—one that inculcates good morals with sound doctrines,—one that teaches folks to honour the King, at the same time that it commands them to fear God,—one that preaches humility to the rich, deference to the poor, and exacts from both an obedience to the laws,—one that seeks the light it disperses to others from that sacred source, the Bible; and so far from being ashamed of it, from excluding it from schools, says to all, "Search the Scriptures,"—one, in short, that makes people at once good men, good Christians, and good subjects. They have got this to England, and they are happy enough to have it in the Colonies. It's interwoven into the State so beautiful, and yet so skilful, that while the *Church is not political*, the *State is religious*. There is nothin' like their Liturgy in any language, nor never will be agin; and all good men may be made better for their Book of Prayer,—a book every Protestant ought to revere,—for them that compiled it laid down their lives for it. *It was written in the blood of the Martyrs,* and not like some others I could tell you of, *in the blood of its miserable victims*. Now, when I see ten protestant bishops cut off at one fell swoop from Ireland, where they are so much needed, I say *you are loosen in' the hoops*. When I see aid withdrawn from the Colonial Church, their temporalities interfered with, and an attempt made to take away the charter from its college to Windsor, Nova Scotia,—when I hear that the loyal colonists say (I hope the report ain't true) that they are discouraged, agitators boast they are patronised, and rebels runnin' about with pardons in their hands,—when I hear there ain't difference enough made between truly good conservative subjects and factious demagogues, *I say you are loosenin' the hoops*: and when I hear all talk and no cider, as the sayin' is, said Mr. Slick, who just then returned with some of the old wine from the cellar, I say it's dry work; so here's to you, minister, and let me advise you to moisten them are staves, your ribs, or *your* hoops will fall off, I tell you. Put a pint of that are good old stuff under your waistcoat every day, and see how beautiful your skin will fit at the eend of a month. You might beat a tattoo on it like a drum.—You give your tongue a little too much licence, Sam, said Mr. Hopewell; but, squire, he is a sort of privileged man here, and I don't mind him. Help yourself, if you please, sir; here is a pleasant voyage to you, sir. As I was a-sayin', when I hear it said to the bench of bishops "put your house in order, for your days are numbered," I say you are more than loosenin' the hoops, you are *stavin' in the cask.* There are some things I don't onderstand, and some things I hear I don't believe. I am no politician; but I should like to go to England, if I warn't too old, to see into the actual state of things. How is it there is *hoop loose* to Newfoundland, another to the West Ingies, and half-a-dozen to Canada, another to the East, and one in almost every colony? How is it there is chartism and socialism in England, secret associations in Ireland, rebellion in your Provinces, and agitation everywhere? *The hoops want tightenin'.* The leaders of all these teams are runnin' wild because the reins are held too loose, and because they think the state-coachmen are afeerd on 'em. I hear they now talk of *responsible government* in the Colonies; is that true, sir?—I replied it had some advocates, and it was natural it should. All men like power; and, as it would place the govern*o*rs in subjection to the govern*e*d, it was too agreeable a privilege not to be desired by popular leaders.—That, said he, (and few men livin' know more nor I do about colonies, for I was born in one, and saw it grow and ripen into an independent state,) that is the last bond of union between Great Britain and her colonies. Let her sever that bond, and she will find she resembles—*the barrel without hoops.*

XX

FACING A WOMAN

THIS was the day fixed for our departure, and I must say I never felt so much regret at leaving any family I had known for so short a time as I experienced on the present occasion. Mr. Slick, I am inclined to think, was aware of my feelings, and to prevent the formality of bidding adieu, commenced a rhodomontade conversation with aunt Hetty. As soon as we rose from the breakfast-table, he led her to one of the windows and said, with a solemnity that was quite ludicrous,—He is very ill, very ill indeed; he looks as sick as death in the primer: I guess it's gone goose with him.

Who is ill? said aunt Hetty, in great alarm.—He is up a tree; his flint is fixed, you may depend.—Who, Sam? tell me, dear, who it is.—And he so far from home; ain't it horrid? and pysoned, too, and that in minister's house.—Lord, Sam, how you frighten a body! who is pysoned?—The squire, aunty; don't you see how pale he looks.—Pysoned, O for ever! Well, I want to know! Lawful heart alive, how could he be pysoned? O Sam! I'll tell you: I've got it now. How stupid it was of me not to ask him if he could eat them; it's them presarved strawberries,—yes, yes, it's the strawberries. They do pyson some folks. There was sister Woodbridge's son's wife's youngest darter that she had by the first marriage, Prudence. Well, Prudence never could eat them: they always brought on ———. Oh! it's worse nor that, aunty; it ain't strawberries, tho' I know they ain't good eatin' for them that don't like them. It's ———. And a mustard emetic was the onliest thing in natur' to relieve her. It made her ———. Oh! it tante them, it's love: you've killed him.—Me, Sam! why how you talk! what on airth do you mean?—You've killed him as dead as a herring. I told you your eyes would cut right into him, for he was as soft as a pig fed on beech-nuts and raw potatoes; but you wouldn't believe me. Oh! You've done the job for him: he told me so hisself. Says he, Mr. Slick, (for he always calls me Mr. he is so formal,) says he, Mr. Slick, you may talk of lovely women, but I know a gall that is a heavenly splice. What eyes she has, and what feet, and what a neck, and what a ———. Why, Sam, the man is mad: he has taken leave of his senses.—Mad! I guess he is—ravin', distracted. Your eyes have pysoned him. He says of all, the affectionate sisters and charming women he ever seed, you do beat all—Oh! he means what I once was, Sam, for I was considered a likely gall in my day, that's a fact; but, dear o' me, only to think times is altered.—Yes; but you ain't altered; for, says he, —for a woman of her great age, aunt Hetty is ———. Well, he hadn't much to do, then, to talk of my advanced age, for I am not so old as all that comes to nother. He is no gentleman to talk that way, and you may tell him so. —No, I am wrong, he didn't say great age, he said great beauty: she is very unaffected.—Well, I thought he wouldn't be so rude as to remark on a lady's age.—Says he, her grey hairs suit her complexion.—Well, I don't thank him for his impedence, nor you nother for repeatin' it.—No, I mean grey eyes. He said he admired the eyes: grey was his colour.—Well, I thought he wouldn't be so vulgar, for he is a very pretty man, and a very polite man too; and I don't see the blue nose you spoke of, nother.—And says he, if I could muster courage, I would propose ———. But, Sam, it's so sudden. Oh, dear! I am in such a fluster, I shall faint.—I shall propose for her to ———. Oh! I never could on such short notice. I have no thing but black made up; and there is poor Joshua ———. I should propose for her to accompany her brother ———. Well, if Joshua would consent to go with us,—but, poor soul! he couldn't travel, I don't think.—To accompany her brother as far as New York, for his infirmities require a kind nurse.—Oh, dear! is that all? How mighty narvous he is. I guess the crittur is pysoned sure enough, but then it's with affectation.—Come, aunty, a kiss at partin'. We are off, good-by'e; but that was an awful big hole you made in his heart too. You broke the pane clean out and only left the sash. He's a caution to be hold. Good-by'e! And away we went from Slickville.

During our morning's drive the probability of a war with England was talked of, and in the course of conversation Mr. Slick said, with a grave face, —Squire, you say we Yankees boast too much; and it ain't improbable we do, seein' that we have whipped the Ingians, the French, the British, the Spaniards, the Algerines, the Malays, and every created crittur a'most that dared to stand afore us, and try his hand at it. So much success is e'en a'most enough to turn folks' heads, and make 'em a little consaited, ain't it? Now give me your candid opinion, I won't be the leastest morsel offended, if you do give it agin' us; but speak onreserved, Who do you think is the bravest people, the Yankees or the British? I should like to hear your mind upon it.—They are the same people, I said, differing as little, perhaps, from each other as the inhabitants of any two counties in England, and it is deeply to be deplored that two such gallant nations, having a common origin and a common language, and so intimately connected by the ties of consanguinity and mutual interest, should ever imbrue their hands in each other's blood. A war between people thus peculiarly related is an unnatural spectacle, that no rational man can contemplate without horror. In the event of any future contest the issue will be as heretofore, sometimes in favour of one and sometimes of the other. Superior discipline will decide some engagements and numbers others, while accidental circumstances will turn the scale in many a well-fought field. If you ask me, therefore, which I conceive to be the braver people of the two, I should unquestionably say neither can claim pre-eminence. All people of the same stock, living in a similar climate, and having nearly the same diet and habits, must, as a matter of course, possess animal courage as nearly as possible in the same degree. I say habits, because we know that in individuals habits have a great deal to do with it. For instance, a soldier will exhibit great fear if ordered to reef a topsail, and a sailor if mounted on the —— Well, well, said he, p'raps you are right; but boastin' does some good too. Only get people to think they can do a thing and they can do it. The British boasted that one Englishman could whip three Frenchmen, and it warn't without its effect in the wars, as Buonaparte know'd to his cost. Now, our folks boast, that one Yankee can walk into three Englishmen; and, some how or another, I kinder guess they will—try to do it at any rate. For my part, I am pretty much like father, and he used to say, he never was afeerd of any thing on the face of the airth but a woman. Did I ever tell you the story of father's courtship?—No, I replied, never; your stock of anecdotes is inexhaustible, and your memory so good you never fall into the common error of great talkers, of telling your stories a second time. I should like to hear it.—Well, said he, it ain't an easy story to tell, for father always told it with variations, accordin' to what he had on board at the time, for it was only on the annivarsary of his weddin' he used to tell it, and as there was considerable brag about father, he used to introduce new flourishes every time, what our singin' master in sacred melody, Doldrum Dykins, used to call grace notes. Sam, he'd say, I have been married this day,—let me see, how many years is it? Do you recollect, Polly dear?—Why, says mother, I can't say rightly, for I never kept a tally, but it's a considerable some tho', I estimate. (She never would answer that question, poor dear old soul! for women don't like to count arter that if they can help it, that's a fact.)—Well, says father, it's either eight or nine-and-twenty years ago, I forget which.—It's no such thing, says mother, quite snappishly; Sam is only twenty-one last Thanksgiving-day, and he was born jist nine months and one day arter we was married, so there now. (Father gives me a wink, as much as to say, that's woman now, Sam, all over, ain't it?)—Well, your mother was eighteen when we was married, and twenty-one years and nine months and one day added to that makes her near hand to fort. —— Never mind what it makes, says mother, but go on with your story, whatever it is, and sumtotalize it. You are like Doldrum Dykins, he sings the words of each varse over three times.—Well, said he, this I *will* say, a younger-lookin' bloominer woman of her age there ain't this day in all Slickville, no, nor in Conne'ticut nother.—Why, Mr. Slick, says mother, layin' down her knittin' and fixin' her cap—how you talk!—Fact, upon my soul, Polly! said he; but, Sam, said he, if you'd a-seed her when I first know'd her, she was a most super-superior gall and worth lookin' at, I tell you. She was a whole team and a horse to spare, a rael screamer, that's a fact. She was a-most a beautiful piece of woman-flesh, fine corn-fed, and showed her keep. Light on the foot as a fox, cheeks as fair as a peach and hard as an apple, lips like cherries—Lick! you wouldn't see such a gall if you was to sarch all the factories to Lowell, for she looked as if she could e'en a'most jump over her own shadow, she was so 'tarnal wirey. Heavins! how springy she was to a wrastle, when we was first married. She always throw'd me three or four times at first hand runnin'; in course I was stronger, and it ginerally eended in my throwin' her at last; but then that was nateral, seein' she was the weakest. Oh she was a rael doll! she was the dandy, that's a fact.—Well, I want to know, said mother, did you ever? a-tryin to look cross, but as pleased as anything, and her eyes fairly twinklin' agin to hear the old man's soft-sawder: Why the man is tipsy to talk that way afore the boy; do, for gracious sake! behave, or I'll go right out; and then turnin' to me and filin' my glass, do drink, dear, says she, you seem kinder dull.—Well, she was the only created crittur, says he, I ever seed I was darnted afore.—You got bravely over it anyhow, says mother.— Courtin' says he, Sam, is about the hardest work I know on; fightin' is nothin' to it. Facin' ball, grape, or bullet, or baganut, as we did at Bunker's Hill, is easy when a man is used to it, but face-in' a woman is—it's the devil, that's a fact. When I first seed her she filled my eye chock full; her pints were all good; short back, good rate to the shoulder, neat pastern, full about the ———. There you go agin, says mother; I don't thank you one bit for talkin' of me as if I was a filly, and I won't stay to hear it, so there now: I believe, in my soul, you are onfakilized.—Well, I reconnoitred and reconnoitred for ever so long, a-considerin' how I was to lay siege to her,—stormin' a battery or escaladin' a redoubt is nothin' to it, I have done it fifty times.—Fifty times! says mother, lookin' arch to him, for she was kinder sorted wrathy at bein' talked of as a horse. Well, says father, forty times at any rate.—Forty times! says mother; that's a powerful number.— Well, d—n it! twenty times then, and more too.—Twenty times! said she; did our folks storm twenty batteries all together? —Why, tarnation! says father, I suppose at last you'll say I warn't at Bunker's Hill at all, or Mud Creek, or the battle atween the outposts at Peach Orchard ———? Or chargin' Elder Solomon Longstaff's sheep, says mother.—Well, by the tarnal! says father, who hopped with rage like a ravin' distracted parched pea; if that bean't pitikilar I am a punkin, and the pigs may do their prettiest with me. Didn't I tell you, Sam, nothin' could come up to a woman?— Except a filly, says mother; now don't compare me to a hoss, and talk of pints that ain't to be thought of, much less talked of, and I won't jibe you about your campaigns, for one thing is sartain, no man ever doubted your courage, and Gineral Gates told me so himself. Polly, says the Gineral, if you take Sargeant Slick, you take a hero.—Well, says father, quite mollified by that are title of hero, Gates was a good judge, and a good feller too. Fill your glass, Sam, for I always calculate to be merry on this night; and, Polly dear, you must take a drop too: if we do get warm sometimes, makin' up seems all the sweeter for it.

Well, as I was a-sayin', I studied every sort of way how I should begin; so at last, thinks I, a faint heart never won a fair lady; so one Sabbath-day I brushed up my regimentals and hung old Bunker by my side, and ironed out my hat anew, and washed the feather in milk till it looked as well as one jist boughten, and off I goes to meetin'. Well, I won't say I heerd much of the sarmon, because I didn't; but I know it was a little the longest I ever sot out; and when we was dismissed, I was e'en a'most sorry it was over, I was so discomboborated, and I breathed as short as if I had a-been chasin' of the British all day; but at last I moved out with the crowd, and movin' sot me all to rights agin. So I marches up to Polly Styles,—that was your mother that is,—mornin', says I, Miss Styles, and I gave her a salute.—Why, Slick, says she, how you talk! you never did no such a thing; jist as if I would let you salute me before all the folks that way.—I did tho', upon my soul, says father. I'll take my Bible-oath, says mother, there is not a word of truth in it.—Why, Polly, says father, how can you say so? I brought both feet to the first position this way (and he got upon the floor and indicated), then I came to attention this way (and he stood up as stiff as a poker, he held his arms down by his side quite straight, and his head as erect as a flagstaff), then I brought up my right arm with a graceful sweep, and without bendin' the body or movin' the head the least mite or morsel in the world, I brought the back of my hand against the front of my regimental hat (and he indicated again).—Oh! says mother, that salute, indeed! I detract, I recollect you did.—*That* salute! says father: why what salute did *you* mean?—Why, says mother, colorin' up, I thought you meant that—that—that—never mind what I meant—Oh, ho! says father, I take, I take; talk of a salute, and a woman can't think of anything else but a kiss. It's the first thing they think of in the mornin' and the last at night.—Go on with your story, and cut it short, if you please, says mother, for it's gettin' rather tedious.—Mornin', says I, Miss Styles, how do you do?— Reasonable well, I give you thanks, says she, how be you?—Considerable, says I. When that was done, the froth was gone, and the beer flat; I couldn't think of another word to say for mindin' of her, and how beautiful she was, and I walked on as silent as if I was at the head of my guard.—At last, says your mother,—Is that splendid regimental you have on, Mr. Slick, the same you wore at Bunker's Hill?—Oh, dear! what a load that word took off my heart; it gave me somethin' to say, tho' none of the clearest.—Yes, Miss, says I, it is; and it was a glorious day for this great republic,—it was the cradle of our liberty.—Well done, Slick! says her father, as he rode by jist at that moment; you are gittin' on bravely, talkin' of cradles already.—Well, that knocked me all up of a heap, and sot your mother a-colorin' as red as anything. I hardly know what I said arter that, and used one word for another like a fool. We had twenty thousand as fine gallant young galls there, says I, that day as ever I laid eyes on.—Twenty thousand! said Polly, do tell! Why, what on airth was they a-doin' of there?—In arms, says I, a-strugglin' for their liberty.—And did they get away? said she, a-laughin'.—Poor things! said I, many of them, whose bosoms beat high with ardor, were levelled there that day, I guess.—Why, Mr. Slick, said she, how you talk!—Yes, says I, nine of them from Charlestown accompanied me there, and we spent the night afore the ingagement in the trenches without a blankit to cover us.—They had little to do to be there at such hours with you, said Polly.—Little to do! said I; you wouldn't have said so, Miss, if you had a-been there. you'd a-found that lyin' exposed—I don't want to hear no more about it, said she; let's join mother, and I'll axe her about it.— Do, said I, and she'll tell you they fell on a bed of glory. —Mother, says Polly, Sargeant Slick says there were twenty thousand galls at Bunker's Hill; did you ever heer tell of it afore?—Men, says I.—No, galls, said she.—No, men, says I.—Twenty thousand galls, they all repeated; and then they laughed ready to kill themselves, and said, what onder the sun could put such a crotchet as that are into your head?—Miss, says I, if I did say so ——. Oh! you did, said she, and you know it.—If I did say so, it was a mistake; but *that* put it into my head that put everything else out.—And what was that? said she.—Why, as pretty a gall, said I, as ——. Oh! then, said she, they was all galls in the trenches, after all? I won't hear no more about them at no rate. Good-bye!—Well, there I stood lookin' like, a fool, and feelin' a proper sight bigger fool than I looked.—Dear heart! says mother, gittin' up and goin' behind him, and pattin' him on the cheek,—did she make a fool of him then?—and she put her arm round his neck and kissed him, and then filling up his tumbler, said—go on, dear.—Well, it was some time, said father, afore I recovered that misstep; and when ever I looked at her arterwards she larfed, and that confused me more; so that I began to think at last it would be jist about as well for me to give it up as a bad bargain, when one Sabbath-day I observed all the Styles's a-comin' to meetin' except Polly, who staid to home; so I waits till they all goes in, and then cuts off hot foot for the river, and knocks at the door of the house, tho' I actilly believe my heart beat the loudest of the two. Well, when I goes in, there sot Polly Styles that was, your mother that is, by the fire a-readin' of a book. Goin' to meetin? says I.—I guess not, said she; are you?—I guess not, said I. Then there was a pause. We both looked into the fire. I don't know what she was a-thinkin' on; but I know what I was, and that was what to say next. Polly, said I.—Did you speak? said she.—I—I—I—it stuck in my throat.—Oh! said she, I thought you spoke.—Then we sot and looked into the coals agin. At last she said,—What couple was that was called last Lord's-day?— I don't mind, said I; but I know who I wish it was.—Who? said she.—Why me and somebody else. — Then why don't you and somebody else get called then? said she.—I—I—I—it stuck again in my throat. If I hadn't a-been so bothered advisin' of myself, I could have got it out, I do suppose; but jist as I was a-goin' to speak, I couldn't think of any words; but now's your time, it's a grand chance. Arter a while, says she,—Father will be to home soon, I am a-thinkin'; meetin' must be near out now.—Likes as not, says I. Presently up jumps Polly, and says,—Entertainin' this, ain't it? s'posen' you read me a sarmon, it will give us somethin' to talk about.—And afore I could say a word agin' it, she put a book into my hand, and said,—Begin, and threw herself down on the settle.—Well I hadn't read a page hardly afore she was asleep, and then I laid down the book, and says I to myself, says I, what shall I do next? and I had jist got a speech ready for her, when she woke up, and rubbin' her eyes, said,—I am 'most afeerd I gave you a chance of a forfeit by nappin' arter that fashion; but, as luck would have it, you was too busy reading. I'll take care not to do so agin. Go on, if you please, sir.—Well, I began to read a second time, and hadn't gone on above a few minutes afore a little wee snore showed me she was asleep agin. Now, says I, to myself, arter such an invitation as she gin me about the gloves, I am darned if I don't try for the forfeit while she is asleep.—I didn't give no such invitation at all about the gloves, says mother: don't believe one word of it; it's jist an invention of his own. Men like to boast, and your father is the greatest bragger livin' out of the twenty thousand galls that was at Bunker's Hill.—Polly, says father, it's nateral to deny it, but it's true for all that.— Well, says I to myself, says I, suppose it was the devil or a Britisher that was there, Sergeant Slick, what would you do? Why, says I to myself, for answer, says I, I would jist shut my eyes and rush right at it; and with that I plucked up courage and run right at the settee full split. Oh, dear! the settee warn't strong enough.—Lawful heart! says mother, what a fib! did you ever? well, I never did hear the beat of that; it's all made out of whole cloth, I declare.—The settee warn't strong enough, said father. It broke down with an awful smash, your mother, Polly Styles that was, kickin' and screamin' till all was blue agin. Her comb broke and out came her hair, and she looked as wild as a hawk.—Gloves! says I.—You shan't, says she.—I will, says I.—In arms a-strugglin' for their liberty, says her father, who jist then come in from meetin'.—Polly squeeled like a rat in a trap, and cut and run out of the room full chisel. —Dear, dear, said mother, what will he say next, I wonder. —And then the old man and me stood facein' one another like two strange cats in a garret.

An accident, says I; so I perceeve, says he.—Nothin' but lookin' for a pair of gloves, says I.—As you and the nine galls did at the trenches, at Bunker's Hill, said he, for the blankit.—Now friend Styles, said I.—Now friend Slick, said he.—It warn't my fault, says I.—Certainly not, says he; a pretty gall at home, family out; used to twenty thousand galls in war, it's nateral to make love in peace: do you take?—Well, says I, it does look awkward, I confess—Very, says he. Well, Slick, says he, the long and short of the matter is, you must either marry or fight.—Says I, friend Styles, as for fightin', Bunker's Hill, Mud Creek, and Peach Orchard are enough for any one man, in all conscience; but I'll marry as soon as you please, and the sooner the better.—So I should think, said he.—No, no, neighbour Styles, said I, you don't do me justice, you don't indeed; I never had the courage to put the question yet.—Well, if that don't cap all! says mother; that beats the bugs; it does fairly take the rag off.—A man, says Mr. Styles, that has nine ladies in the trenches with him all night, in arms a-strugglin' for liberty, without a blankit to cover them, to talk of not havin' courage to put the question, is rather too good. Will you marry?—I will, says I, and only jist too happy to——. —You shall be called then this blessed arternoon, said he, so stay dine, son Slick.—Well, to make a long story short, the thing turned out better than I expected, and we were spliced in little better than half no time. That was the first and last kiss I ever had afore we was married, Polly was so everlastin' coy; but arterwards she nev——. Not one word more, says mother, to your peril, not one word more, and she got up and shook her knittin' at him quite spunky. Most o' that are story was an invention of your own, jist a mere brag, and I won't hear no more. I don't mind a joke when we are alone, but I won't hear nothin' said afore that are boy that lessens his respect for his mother the leastest grain, so there now.—Well, well, says father, have it your own way, Polly, dear; I have had my say, and I wouldn't ryle you for the world, for this I will say, a'most an excellent wife, dependable friend, and whiskin' housekeeper you have made to me, that's sartain. No man don't want no better, that's a fact. She hadn't *no ear for musick* Sam, but she had a capital *eye for dirt,* and for poor folks that's much better. No one never seed as much dirt in my house as a fly couldn't brush off with his wings. Boston galls may boast of their spinnetts, and their *gy*tars, and their eyetalian airs, and their *ears for musick;* but give me the gall, I say, that *has an eye for dirt,* for she is the gall for my money. But to eventuate my story—when the weddin' was over,

Mr. Styles, that was your grandfather that is, come to me, and tappin' me on the shoulder, says he, Slick, says he, everybody knew you was a hero in the field, but I actilly did not think you was such a devil among the galls. Nine of them in the trenches at one time, in arms, a-strugglin' for their liberty, and so on. You must give over them pranks now you are married. This is all very well as a joke, says father; but Sam, my son, says he, them that have seed sarvice, and I flatter myself I have seed as much as most men, at Bunker's Hill, Mud Creek, and Peach Orchard, et sarterar, as the Boston marchants say;—veterans I mean,—will tell you, that to face an inimy is nothin', but it is better to face the devil than to *face—a woman*.

XXI

THE ATTACHÉ

THIS being the last day at my disposal at New York, I went on board of the Great Western and secured a passage for myself and Mr. Slick; and, as there were still several vacant berths, had the gratification to find there was room for my worthy friend Mr. Hopewell, if he should incline to accompany us, and arrive in time to embark. I then sauntered up through the Broadway to a coach-stand, and drove to the several residences of my kind and agreeable friends to bid them adieu. New York is decidedly the first city of the western world, and is alike distinguished for the beauty of its situation and the hospitality of its inhabitants. I left it not without great regret, and shall always retain the most pleasing recollection of it. In this respect, I understand, I am by no means singular, as no stranger, bringing proper introductions, is ever permitted to feel he is alone here in a foreign land. Soon after I returned to the hotel Mr. Slick entered, with a face filled with importance,—Squire, said he, I have jist received a letter that will astonish you, and if you was to guess from July to eternity you wouldn't hit on what it's about. I must say I am pleased, and that's a fact; but what puzzles me is, who sot it a-goin'. Now, tell me candid, have you been writin' to the British embassador about me since you came ?—No, I replied, I have not the honour of his acquaintance. I never saw him, and never had any communication with him on any subject whatever.— Well, it passes then, said he, that's sartin: I havn't axed no one nother, and yet folks don't often get things crammed down their throats that way without sayin' by your leave, stranger. I hante got no interest; I am like the poor crittur at the pool, I hante got no one to put me in, and another feller always steps in afore me. If Martin Van has done this hisself he must have had some mo-*tive*, for he hante got these things to throw away; he wants all the offices he has got as sops to his voters. Patriotism is infarnal hungry, and as savage as old Scratch if it tante fed. If you want to tame it, you must treat it as Van Amburg does his lions, keep its belly full. I wonder whether he is arter the vote of Slickville, or whether he is only doin' the patron to have sunthin' to brag on. I'd like to know this, for I am not in the habit of barkin' up the wrong tree if I can find the right one. Well, well, it don't matter much, arter all, what he meant, so as he does what's right and pretty. The berth is jist the dandy, that's a fact. It will jist suit me to a T. I have had my own misgivin's about goin' with you, squire, I tell you, for the British are so infarnal proud that clockmakin' sounds everlastin' nosey to them, and I don't calculate in a gineral way to let any man look scorney to me, much less talk so; now this fixes the thing jist about right, and gives it the finishin' touch. It's grand! I've got an appointment, and, I must say, I feel kinder proud of it, as I never axed for it. It's about the most honorable thing Martin Van ever did since he became public. Tit or no tit, that's the tatur! and I'll maintain it too. I'll jist read you a letter from Salter Fisher, an envoy or sunthin' or another of that kind in the Secretary of State's office. I believe he is the gentleman that carries their notes and messages.

PRIVATE.

MY DEAR SLICK,

Herewith I have the honor to enclose you your commission as an *attaché* to our legation to the Court of Saint Jimses, Buckin'ham, with an official letter announcin' the President's nomination and Senate's vote of concurrence. Martin ordered these to be put into the mail, but I have taken the chance to slip this into the paper-cover. It is the policy of our Government to encourage na*tive* authors and reward merit; and it makes me feel good to find your productions have made the name of this great and growing republic better known among Europeans, and we expect a considerable some, that this appointment will enable you to exalt it still further, and that the name of Slick will be associated with that of our sages and heroes in after ages. This commission will place you on a footin' with the princes and nobles of England, give you a free ticket of admission to the palace, and enable you to study human natur' under new phases, associations, and developements; that is, if there is any natur' left in such critturs. With such opportunities, the President expects you will not fail to sustain the honor of the nation on all occasions, demanding and enforcing your true place in society, at the top of the pot, and our exalted rank at foreign courts as the greatest, freest, and most onlightened nation now existin'. It would be advisable, if a favorable opportunity offers, to draw the attention of the Queen to the subject of her authors and travellers,

—carelessly like, as if it weren't done a purpose, for it don't comport with dignity to appear too sensi*tive*, but jist merely to regret the prac-*tice* of hirein' authors to abuse us in order to damp the admiration of Europeans of our glorious institutions.

We have every reason to believe that Captain Hall received five thousand pounds for this purpose, and Mrs. Trollope the same sum; that Miss Martineau is promised a royal garter, (it's a pity she warn't hanged with it,) and Captain Marryatt to be made a Knight of the Royal Baths. This conduct is onworthy of a great people like the English, and unjust and insultin' to us; and you might suggest to her Royal Highness that this mean, low-lived, dirty conduct will defeat itself, and that nothin' short of kickin' out her ministry will be accepted as an apology by the American people. You might say to her ladyship, that the city articles in the Times newspaper are very offensive to us, and that tho' individually we despise such low blackguardisms, yet collectively the honor of the nation demands satisfaction. That her Government pays for their insartion there can be no doubt; and the paltry trick of Mr. Melburne bribin' opposition papers to let 'em in, is an artifice that may cover the rascallity to ignorant British, but can't draw the wool over our eyes. If you have no opportunity to say this to her, tell Albert Gotha, her bridegroom, to tell her plainly, if she don't look sharp, we'll retaliate and *hunt red foxes for her* in Canada, as we did two winters ago.

Caution is necessary in conversation, in speakin' of our army, navy, and resources of war, for the ministers will pump you if they can. Boastin' without crackin' is the true course. For instance, if war is talked of, regret the smallness of our navy; for, if they had to contend with France and England at the same time, the issue would be extremely doubtful. That is a clear intimation we could lick either, and ain't afraid of both, and yet don't say so. So, in speakin' of the army, deprecate a war, and say marchin' one hundred and fifty thousand men into Canada would interfere with intarnal improvements by raising the price of labor. It is this species of delicate brag that best becomes a high functionary.

It is not to be doubted you will return as you go, a republican at heart, and that future honors await you. Your name is now well and favorably known, and, what is better, is popular, as you may infer, when I tell you that the very pen with which this is wrote is a "Sam Slick pen." The highest gift in the hands of man, the presidential chair, should now and henceforth be the object of your ambition. We look forward with much gratification to your delineation of English character, their exclusiveness, their self-sufficiency, their strong-hold of slavery—the factories, their overfed clergy, overpaid officials and antiquated institutions, their defenceless condition, half-manned navy, and radical army, their proud and dissolute aristocracy, their turbulent and factious commons, and brutally ignorant peasantry. I estimate when they hear of your appointment, they will feel considerable streaked, for they must know you won't spare them.

While you are visitin' among the gentry and nobility, you might keep a journal on the sly, and send it out by the steamers to some leadin' papers, which would be killin' two birds with one stone, livin' free of cost and makin' money out of them at the same time. Where you can, give the real names in full: where it ain't safe, for fear of a scuffle, say Duke A——, Lord B——, Lady C——, and occasionally the Q—— told me. It sounds well this, and shows your standin' is high and is peak-aunt. Anecdotes of high life sell well if they are racy. Then collect them together into a book onder some takein' onpretending title, as "Mems of a mum," or scrawlin's afore bed-time, or some such name. The proceeds will enable you to cut a better dash to court; only don't tell 'em you are a-doin' of it to England. No man entertains a spy if he can help it. "A word to the wise——will always suffice——." This will pave the way well for your progress to the presidential chair. While on this subject, it might not be amiss to hint a change of party might occasion a change of office-holders; and that tho' too strong to require any aid for ourselves, we hope for your family ticket in Slickville and its vicinity to enable us to keep you in your present honorable position. Without this berth, you would find the first circles as stiff as an ongreased mast; this appointment will ile that beautiful, and make you slide as easy as on well-slushed ways. Avail it. Sustain the honor of the nation, and pair the name of Sam Slick indelibly on the dial-plate of Fame, that the finger of Time may point it out to admirin' posterity, to all etarnity.

Yours to command,
SALTER FISHER.

P.S.—I will give you a wrinkle on your horn that's worth havin'. Should our great gun be absent and you left in London, recollect we do as the British do, give no instructions we can help; write what must be wrote so it will *read any way,* and leave subordinates to incur all responsibility of actin' and readin'. Meet 'em in their own way by referrin' all home, and puttin' the saddle on the right horse in spite of him. Let the shafter do his own work. Do you take?—S. F.

As soon as the Clockmaker had read this epistle, he observed in a half soliloquising, half conversational tone "An Attaché." Well, it's a station of great dignity too, ain't it? It makes me feel kinder narvous and whimble-cropt, for I have got to sustain a new character, and act a new part in the play of life. To dine at the palace with kings, queens, and princes; what a pretty how-d'ye-do that is, ain't it? Won't it be tall feedin' at Queen's table, that's all; and I am a rael whale at ducks and green peas. Lord, I am afeerd I shall feel plaguy awkward too, with a court dress on. I once seed a colony chap rigged out in a suit he hired of a Jew, for le*vee* day, and I am tee-totally extinctified if he didn't look for all the world like the baboon that rides the pony to the circus. He was small potatoes and few in a hill, that feller, I tell you. He looked as mean as a crittur with one eye knocked out and t'other a-squint. He seemed scared at himself, as the bull did when he got opposite the lookin' glass. Heavens and airth! if the dogs had only seed him, they'd agin' him a chase for it, I know; the way they'd a-foxed him and a-larned him fleas ain't lobsters, would have been a caution to monkeys to hold up their tails afore they shut-to the door arter them. A crittur with a good nose would put up some tarnal queer birds in the long stubble at St. Jimses, that's a fact. Yes, I am afeerd I shall feel monstrous onconvenient, and as if I warn't jist made to measure. Carryin' a sword so as to keep it from stickin' atween your legs and throwin' you down, ain't no easy matter nother, but practice makes parfect, I do suppose. Well, I vow our noble institutions do open avenues to ambition and merit to the humblest citizens too, don't they? Now, tell me candid, squire, don't it make your mouth water? How would you like Mr. Melburne to take you by the seat of your trowsers with one hand, and the scruff of your neck with the other, and give you a chuck up stairs that way, for nothin', for he is jist the boy that can do it? but catch him at it, that's all; no, indeed, not he, for breeches ain't petticoats, nor never was, except in Turkey and Egypt, and when kissin' goes by favour, who would look at a dispisable colonist. Well, Martin Van has done that to me, and he *is* a gentleman every inch of him, and eats his bread buttered on both sides.

Only to think, now, Sam Slick, the Clockmaker, should be a member of our legation to the greatest nation in the world next to us. Lord, how it would make poor dear old mother stare, if she could only lift herself up out of the grave, and open her eyes. It would make her scratch her head and snicker, *I* know; for only thinkin' of it kinder gives me the peadoddles myself. What on airth do they talk about, I wonder, when they get together to the palace, them great folks and big bugs. Clocks, I do suppose, must be sunk, and hosses and tradin' in the small way too; it wouldn't convene with dignity that sort o' gab. One good thing, I've seed a considerable of the world in my time, and don't feel overly daunted by no man. Politics I do know in a gineral way as well as most men; colonies and colony chaps, too, I know better than any crittur I'd meet, and no mistake. Pictur' likeness is a thing I won't turn my back on to no one, nor bronzin', nor gildin, nother, for that's part of the clock bisness. Agriculture I was brought up to, and gunnin' and trappin' I was used to since I was a boy. Poetry is the worst; if the galls to the palace begin in that line I'm throwd out as sure as a gun, for I shall hang fire, or only burn primin', for I hante even got two fingers of a charge in me, and that's damaged powder too: I never could bear it. I never see a poet yet that warn't as poor as Job's turkey, or a church mouse; or a she poet that her shoes didn't go down to heel, and her stockin's look as if they wanted darnin', for it's all cry and little wool with poets, as the devil said when he sheared his hogs. History I do know a little of, for I larned Woodbridge's Epitome to school, and the Bible, and the history of our revolution I know by heart, from Paradise to Lexin'ton, and from Bunker's Hill to Independence. But I do suppose I must rub up a little on the passage. Musick, I don't fear much, for I rather pride myself on my ear and my voice; and psalmody I larned to singin' schools; so operas and theatres will soon set met right on that. But dancin' is what I can take the shine off most folks in. I was reckoned the supplest boy in all Slickville. Many's the time I have danced "Possum up a gum tree" at a quiltin' frolic or huskin' party, with a tumbler full of cider on my head, and never spilt a drop;—I have upon my soul. He then got up and executed several evolutions on the floor which would have puzzled an opera-dancer to imitate, and then said with an air of great self-satisfaction,—Show me any Lord to England that could do that, and I'll give him leave to brag, that's all. Oh dear, I'll whirl them maids of honour to the palace round and round so fast in a waltz, no livin' soul can see me a-kissing of them. I've done it to Phoebe Hopewell afore her father's face and he never know'd it, tho' he was lookin' on the whole blessed time—I hope I may be shot if I hante. She actilly did love them waltzes, the wickedest I ever did see. Lick! there is some fun in that are, ain't they? It ain't often they get a smack from rael right good genuwine Yankee lips, sweet fed on corn and molasses, I know. If they only like them half as well as dear little Phoebe did, I'm a made man, that's all. The only thing in dancin', like boatin', is to keep a straight keel. That's the rael secret. P'raps the best way arter all is, I believe, at first to play mum, say little and hear everything, and then do jist like other folks. Yes, that's the plan; for liquor that's well corked is always the best up. "*An Attaché!*" well that sounds dreadful pretty, too, don't it? Then, as for dress, I guess I'll wait till I reach London, that my coat may be the rael go, and up to the notch; but the button I'll get now for't would look shockin' hansum, and more like the rael thing. Yes, I'll jist step into the chamber and slick up my hair with a taller candle, and put my bettermost coat into a silk pocket handkerchief, and take it down to Hellgo and Funk the tailors, (I knowed 'em to Boston,) and get the legation button put on, for it will command respect on board the Great Western. I larned that from brother Josiah; he always travels with several trunks; he says it brings the best rooms and best attendance at inns always, for they think that you must be somebody to have so much luggage. He told me, as a fact, they paid carriage very well. "*An Attache!!*"

Well, it's funny, too, ain't it? It sounds rael jam that. I must say I feel kinder obleeged to Mr. Van Burin for this good turn he has done me. I always thought he was very much of the gentleman in his manners, and the likeliest man in the States, and now I swear by him. Yes, loco-foco as he is, I go the whole figur' for Martin Van, that's a fact. Hit or miss, rough or tumble, claw or mudscraper, I'm his man; I'll go in for him up to the handle, and so will all us Slickville folks, for in elections we pull like inions all on one string, and stick to our man like burrs to sheep's wool. And now, squire, said he, jumping up, and taking me by the hand; and now, my friend, shake flippers along with me, and congratulate me. When I return from the tailor's I shall be a new man. You then will meet the Honourable Samuel Slick, an "*Attaché*" to our Legation to the Court of Saint Jimses, Victoria's Gotha. And him you will have as a feller passenger. You had sense enough not to be ashamed of me when I was a hoein' my way as a tradin' man, and I won't go for to cut *you* now, tho' you are nothin but a down East Provincial. All I ask of you is, keep dark about the clocks; we'll sink them, if you please; for by gum you've seen the last of Sam Slick the Clockmaker. And now, squire, I am your humble servant to command,

THE ATTACHÉ

THE END.

The Attaché; or Sam Slick in England details the adventures of the American wordsmith, as he delivers his brand of home-spun wisdom upon this green and pleasant foreign land, once again faithfully recorded by his companion the Squire.

ISBN 1 84588 049 8
Price £6.00
256 pages

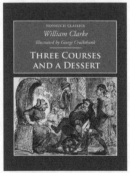

A collection of humorous and satirical short stories by William Clarke, with West country, Irish and legal settings (the 'Three Courses') together with a more miscellaneious selection (the 'Dessert'). Packed with vivid characters this book will delight the modern audience.

ISBN 1 84588 072 2
Price £6.00
448 pages, 50 illustrations by George Cruikshank

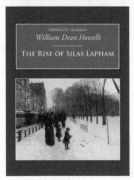

An elegant tale of Boston society and manners, regarded as a subtle classic of its time and written with humour and delicacy. After inheriting his father's business, the eponymous hero moves his family to the sophisticated city of Boston and attempts to break into a world inhabited by wealthy, 'established' families.

ISBN 1 84588 041 2
Price £6.00
384 pages